It was the mos̶̶ ̶̶̶̶̶̶̶̶̶̶̶̶̶̶̶̶̶̶̶̶̶̶̶
executed art ra̶̶ ̶̶̶̶̶̶̶̶̶̶̶̶̶̶̶̶̶̶̶—̶one
that threw the p̶̶ ̶̶̶̶̶̶̶̶ ̶̶̶̶ into turmoil as the
entire city ground to a halt at the height of the
rush hour.

The police surrounded Grand Central Station
barring it to all commuters in their desperate
search for the five perpetrators of the robbery
who had to be hidden in there somewhere. All
incoming trains were checked and all outgoing
trains boarded, every inch of them covered with
a fine-tooth comb. Even those that left the
Station during the raid were halted mid-country
and thoroughly searched. But there was no
trace of the wanted men, somehow they had found
a hole in the net and it was up to Police Chief,
Max Kauffman, to find that hole then track
his quarry down. . . .

Pandora's Box

Thomas Chastain

CORGI BOOKS
A DIVISION OF TRANSWORLD PUBLISHERS LTD

PANDORA'S BOX
A CORGI BOOK 0 552 09865 5

Originally published in Great Britain
by Cassell & Co. Ltd.

PRINTING HISTORY
Cassell edition published 1975
Corgi edition published 1975

Corgi Books are published by
Transworld Publishers Ltd.,
Cavendish House, 57–59 Uxbridge Road,
Ealing, London W.5.
Made and printed in the United States of America
by Arcata Graphics,
Buffalo, New York

PANDORA'S BOX

CHAPTER ONE

The bar, a long, narrow room, was crowded with customers. A huge air conditioner set in an opening above the street entrance dripped water down the side of the wall as it fought a losing battle against the muggy night air outside and the combined body-heat of the people jammed into the room. All the stools in front of the bar were taken, and there was another row of drinkers standing behind those seated at the bar. More customers were gathered around the small tables which occupied the rest of the room opposite the bar. At one of these tables two men sat talking. They were able to talk in relative privacy because of all the other conversations and noise taking place in the room.

"I dunno," the blond man said, shaking his head. "If this job's such a sure thing, and I've only got your word for that, how come somebody hasn't pulled it off before?"

"I explained all that to you already," the other man answered patiently. "Nobody ever put the right combination together before."

The blond man took a couple of swallows of his rye and ginger ale. " 'Course I can't judge whether it's the right combination or not," he said peevishly, "since you won't tell me any of the details."

The other man rubbed his eyes wearily. "Jesus, Griff, we've been over all that. It's not that I won't tell you the details. It's I *can't* tell you. The others would kill me. And they'd be right to. It's bad enough I had to tell you we're going to pull the job. They'd kill me even for that, if they knew, much less I gave you any details."

"Then I don't know," the man named Griff said again. "The prisons are full of guys who were sure they had a sure thing. You're talking to an expert on the subject."

"Let me put it to you this way, Griff," the other man said, hunching forward so their heads were only inches apart. "It ought to be enough I told you the others and I are going to knock the whole city on its ass and walk away with four million dollars. All you got to worry about is keeping out of sight, seeing you don't get picked up meantime. Soon as I get my share, I'll take care of you."

J. T. Spanner got to the Criminal Court Building at 100 Centre Street in lower Manhattan a few minutes after 10 A.M. It was a hot day, a Tuesday in mid-August, the morning full of oppressive, bearing-down heat that you could feel through your clothes and the soles of your shoes. The heat had already begun to wilt his freshly pressed suit. The suit was a sand-colored gabardine, the jacket fitted loose to conceal the bulge of the S&W .357 Magnum in the clip-on holster resting against his right hip.

Spanner paused at the entrance to the building. He had walked only a couple of blocks from the parking lot where he'd left his car, west of Lafayette Street, but it had been enough to start him sweating lightly. He wiped his face with his handkerchief and lit a cigarette. He was a reasonably trim man at five feet, ten inches, and a weight he managed to keep at around one hundred and seventy pounds. His hair was black and cropped close to the skull. He had brown eyes, now hidden behind horn-rimmed sunglasses, and a face which thirty-seven years of life had imprinted with enough lines and creases around the corners of the eyes and mouth and across the lower part of the forehead to give his otherwise bland features a definition of firmness.

Although most people said, as soon as they first discovered he was a private investigator, that he *looked* like a cop, he knew that was a lot of crap. There had been too many times, when he was still a plainclothesman on the force, that he had stood in a line-up with nine or ten other guys and had some witness pick him out as a murderer or rapist or bad-check passer.

The cigarette he had just lit tasted bitter, and he flipped it away after a couple of drags. Then he realized it wasn't the cigarette that was bad but the stink of the city. The moist still heat of the morning was intensified by that kind of godawful smothering smell—he thought of it as the intermingled odor of rank river water, residue from the city's incinerators, and the accumulated stench of butyric acid expelled through the pores of eight million human bodies—which always seemed to hang over sections of Manhattan Island in the dead of summer. Even the air appeared to have a metallic sheen.

The sour, acrid texture of the day matched Spanner's mood. He had no stomach for the job he was about to undertake. A strictly nickel-and-dime assignment to try to track down some cretin who'd jumped bail on a robbery charge. He'd have liked to have said no when Hymie Rosen, one of the city's biggest bail bondsmen, had called him an hour earlier and asked if he'd take the assignment. He'd worked for Hymie Rosen a couple of times before, but only when he was strapped for dough. He wasn't bothered by the fact that the work was a form of modern-day bounty-hunting. What he didn't like was that there'd just never been any money in it for him, and probably wouldn't be this time. Perdiem expenses—Hymie Rosen would pay him twenty-five dollars a day while he looked for the jumper—was all he could definitely count on.

Of course, there was always the chance he'd get lucky and find his man, in which case he stood to collect a percentage of the bail money. He knew there were some private investigators who made a full-time living out of hunting down bail-jumpers. The money was there to be had; Hymie Rosen had once explained to him that bail bondsmen in the United States write close to four million dollars in bonds each year and that one out of every five persons on bail disappears before trial. When that happens, bail bondsmen, like Hymie Rosen, either have to pay off the bond in full or find a way—usually through the services of a private investigator—to bring the fugitive back to court.

Still Spanner would have turned the job down that morning if business hadn't been so slow.

For the past couple of years he'd done all right in his business, by hustling, averaging around thirty grand per year. But now four weeks had gone by since he'd collected his last fee, a modest sum from an insurance company for recovering a stolen Mercedes-Benz.

Meanwhile, his office and living expenses, rent for his apartment, and alimony payments continued to eat up most of his money. So, reasoning that twenty-five dollars per day was better than nothing per day, he'd agreed to meet Hymie Rosen at the Criminal Court Building and get the run-down on the bail-jumper. He wiped his face again with his handkerchief and went into the building.

Anyone who'd ever dealt with Hymie Rosen knew that although the bail bondsman had an office over on Nassau Street, a few blocks away, he conducted most of his business between the hours of 10 A.M. and 4 P.M. weekdays out of one of a row of five public telephone booths in the rear of the Criminal Court Building. Spanner found him there now, talking on the phone, with the booth door closed. Two men were pacing the corridor outside the phone booth. Spanner figured them for lawyers waiting to discuss bail for their clients with the bondsman.

It was gloomy inside the building after the harsh glare of the sun, and several degrees cooler, but still hot. Spanner took off his sunglasses and leaned against a wall opposite the phone booth. From that spot he had a clear view of Hymie Rosen inside the lighted glass cubicle.

The bail bondsman was a short, fat man with dark, curly hair, a swarthy complexion, and a thick neck which sagged in rolls of flesh over the top of his shirt collar. At the moment he was a pantomime figure; lips moving rapidly as he talked on the phone, scribbled hastily on a piece of paper, mopped his perspiring face with a large white handkerchief. Now and then as he gestured with his hands, Spanner could see the dark sweat stains under the armpits of his blue silk suit. On the little finger of his right hand Hymie Rosen wore a diamond pinky ring with a stone so large it looked as though it had to be fake. Spanner knew the stone was a certified multicarat blue-white gem.

The bail bondsman finally finished with his phone conversation, conferred briefly, one after another, with the two men waiting to see him and, tapping on the glass window on the phone booth with his ring, waved Spanner over.

"How's the boy, J. T.?"

"I'm okay, Hy. And you?"

"*Tsuriss,*" Hymie Rosen said. "A nice Jewish boy like you, you know what the word means: troubles. *Tsuriss* is what I got." He ran his soggy handkerchief over his face and looked sideways at Spanner, half-grinning. "You sure you're not Jewish, J. T.?"

"No more'n I'm sure a pig's ass is pork," Spanner said. Both men laughed.

"Anybody tell you you're a character, J. T."

"Yeah," Spanner said. "Both my ex-wives have been known to mention it. What've you got for me, Hy?"

The fat bail bondsman sighed mournfully, hoisted himself a couple of inches up from his seat, and slid out from under him a manila envelope he had been sitting on. "A run-out son-of-a-bitch, J. T. Could cost me twenty-five Gs. Practically put me out of business."

"Yeah, sure, Hy," Spanner said. "Like it could practically put the U.S. mint out of business. Let's hear it."

Hymie Rosen passed over the manila envelope. It was sticky with the fat man's sweat and stank of the pungent cologne he had doused over himself that morning. Spanner took the envelope gingerly between two fingers.

"It's all in there," Hymie Rosen said. "His name's Warren Griffith. Griff, they call him. He's got a prior record, four arrests, all robbery, one conviction, served time in Sing Sing."

"Uh-huh," Spanner said. "What charge was he bailed on?"

Hymie Rosen shook his head sadly. "Same old thing. Two guys stuck up a check-cashing office over on the West Side a month back. One guy got caught, the other one got away. The guy they nabbed later fingered Griffith as his partner and the police picked him up. Three witnesses who were in the office that day identified him as the second holdup man. Griffith drew a soft-hearted judge and a soft-headed bondsman, me, and was released pending a preliminary hearing. The hearing was set for five days ago. Need I tell you he didn't show? The judge gave me thirty-one days to produce him. Otherwise, I can kiss twenty-five Gs goodbye."

Spanner had withdrawn a photograph of the fugitive from the envelope. Before he looked at it, he glanced at Hymie Rosen. "How about security for the bond? Where'd that come from?"

"Griffith put up the deed on a house he owns in Elmhurst, Queens. His mother died a couple of years ago, while he was still in prison, and left the house to him. He's never stayed there. He rents it out and lives in a room in Flushing. The addresses of both places are in the envelope."

Spanner nodded. He was studying the photograph of Warren Griffith. The bail-jumper looked to be in his late twenties, early thirties. He was a fair-skinned man with dirty-looking blond hair that hung down in lanky strands over his forehead, and dark, half-hooded eyes. It was the eyes and slack-jawed mouth which overlaid his face with an expression of sullen weariness. Spanner shoved the photograph back into the envelope.

"I want you to nail this goniff for me, J. T.," Hymie Rosen said, swabbing his face with his handkerchief.

"Yeah, Hy. Well, we'll give it the old try."

Hymie Rosen nodded toward the envelope. "Your notarized copy of the bond's in there, too."

"Good," Spanner said. The copy of the bond would make his pickup of Griffith, if and when he found him, legal. "What kind of money are we talking about on this, Hy? Assuming I bring him in?"

"Since the bail's twenty-five Gs," Hymie Rosen said quickly, "how about we say ten per cent?"

"Fifteen."

"Twelve." The bail bondsman was frantically mopping his face.

"Twelve per cent would be two thousand, seven hundred and fifty dollars," Spanner said. "Suppose we make it an even three grand?"

The two men looked at each other steadily for a moment. Hymie Rosen nodded. "Three grand. It's a deal." He lightly patted his sweating face with his handkerchief.

"Plus expenses, of course," Spanner said.

"Uh—yeah." Hymie Rosen dug a thick wad of bills out of his pants pocket, extracted three tens and held them out to Spanner. "You got a five?"

Spanner gave him a five-dollar bill and put the three tens in his wallet. He and Hymie Rosen shook hands.

"Good luck, J. T." The bail bondsman turned back to the phone, dropping a dime into the slot.

"I'll be talking to you, Hy."

On his way out of the Criminal Court Building, Spanner passed several men he had known when he worked in the Homicide Bureau, a judge, two plainclothesmen, a man from the DA's office, and they exchanged nods. Outside, he trudged back through the heat to the parking lot beyond Lafayette Street, got

his car, and headed up the FDR Drive, alongside the
East River, toward the Queensboro Bridge. In the near
distance, waves of shimmering heat drifted ghost-like
above the asphalt pavement, watery mirages that
steadily receded before he reached them.

Traffic was light, flowing uptown, and kept moving
even though there were cars stalled from overheated
engines at regular intervals along both sides of the
Drive. In the inbound lanes, where the morning traffic
was still heavy there were some tie-ups created by the
stalled cars. Spanner was grateful he could proceed at a
steady forty-five to fifty and for the comfortable air
conditioning inside his car. The car was a two-door,
dark blue T-Bird, the previous year's model, and was
equipped with a telephone. For the past several years
he had driven a Thunderbird, trading it in toward the
end of each year—not on a new model but on the cur-
rent year's model—so his cars were always unused but
one year behind in styling.

When he reached the approach to the bridge, and
the line of cars ahead slowed, he used the car telephone
to call his office.

A female voice answered, brisk and all businesslike:
"J. T. Spanner's office. May I help you?"

"This is J. T., Ellie, honey. Any messages?"

"Oh hi, J. T.," she said. "John Macauley's secretary
called about fifteen minutes ago. She said he said to
tell you he'd probably have a job for you in two or
three days, and he hoped you'd be available."

"Fine," Spanner said. "Call her back and tell her as
far as I know now I'll be free. But ask her to please
let us know as soon as possible that the job is definite."

The law firm of Hogarth, Whittaker, Macauley was
one of Spanner's regular clients. They paid him an
annual retainer plus additional fees for services he
performed for them during the year. In return, he tried
to give them priority over his other accounts. He
figured that one way or the other the job he was on
now, for Hymie Rosen, would be finished within a
couple of days. The pattern was almost always the

same with bail-jumpers. If the jumper was still around somewhere, he'd be with a person he knew well enough to hide him. That's the person Spanner would really be looking for. If he didn't find such a person in Warren Griffith's life—or if he did and Griffith wasn't there—then the odds were Griffith was long gone. In that case, he and Hymie Rosen and the court could forget all about the jumper until or unless he was picked up again on another charge.

"Anything else?" Spanner asked.

"Well—yes," Ellie said hesitantly. "Lee called."

"Yeah?"

"Now don't be like that, J. T. You always get that tone in your voice when you're annoyed," Ellie said and, in a rush, she added: "She was very sweet when she called. She said she didn't want to bother you again but that if you could let her have anything at all on her August alimony she'd love you for it. Be reasonable, J. T., you know she wouldn't call unless she needed the money."

"I *am* being reasonable," Spanner said, and even he could hear the impatience in his voice, "but for God's sakes, I just had a long talk with her about the same subject two nights ago. She said then she understood the situation and that she'd manage to get by until I had some money to give her."

"I suppose something must have come up," Ellie said. "She's meeting me for lunch, then she's going to take over the office this afternoon. Can I tell her you'll call her?"

"Look, Ellie, I don't know whether I can call her. I took the job from Hymie Rosen. I'm on my way to Queens now. I don't know what I'll be doing today or tonight. It's going to be a long stretch. Just tell Lee I'll talk to her when I can."

"All right, J. T. Now don't forget, I'll turn the phones over to the answering service while we're out to lunch. Otherwise, Lee'll be here or I will. 'Bye now, darling."

Spanner hung up the phone and shook his head in exasperation. He supposed he ought to be amused by the solicitude his two ex-wives, Eleanor Stanton Spanner, his first wife, and Lee Coates Spanner, his second, showed for each other and, equally, for him. He knew that their friends, people who knew all three of them, thought the relationship was amusing, if unorthodox; Eleanor and Lee were best friends, both worked part-time in Spanner's office, neither had remarried or apparently planned to, and Spanner still dated and (although this fact couldn't have been known but was probably suspected) slept with both of them, separately of course, while still having other girlfriends as well.

A male chauvinist prick was how the women's libbers would regard him, Spanner had thought more than once. But the thought had never bothered him. He shook his head again, ruefully, and turned his mind to Warren "Griff" Griffith.

CHAPTER TWO

The first stop Spanner made in Queens was at the house Warren Griffith had inherited from his mother in Elmhurst. The house was in a run-down, lower-middle-class residential block with the tracks of the Long Island Railroad practically running through its back yard. Even though he knew Griffith didn't live there, there was always the chance he'd be able to pick up a line on him from the people who rented the house.

It wasn't much of a place, a faded brown, shingled structure, two stories high, with a garage and sunken driveway taking up half of the front of the house. Next to the garage were six stone steps leading up to a small stoop and the front door. The woman who answered the door had her hair up in curlers and was wearing a thin, soiled, sleeveless cotton dress. She was a plump young woman with a pale, drawn face and she was obviously irritated when Spanner identified himself and told her he was trying to locate Warren Griffith. She didn't invite him in and he had to stand on the stoop and talk to her through the latched screen door. Spanner could hear the sound of children, they sounded young, crying somewhere in the house.

"I got nothing to tell you, mister," the woman said, "Just like I told the police when they came here asking about him a few days ago. I only saw this fellow once in my life when I and my husband signed the lease to rent from him a year and a half ago. We always mail

11

rent to him the first of the month at One-One-Six
Dover Street in Flushing. You knew he lives in Flushing?"

"Yes," Spanner said. "I have the address. Did you
mail him the rent for this month?"

"On the first, like always," she said. She brushed a
moist strand of hair back from her face and frowned.
"Jesus, Mary and Joseph, we never thought we were
getting into anything like this, the police coming around
and all, when we rented the house. We're decent
people."

"Sorry I had to bother you," Spanner said, turning
away. "Thanks for talking with me."

He hadn't really expected to find out anything at the
house which would help him find Griffith—and he
hadn't—but routine backing-and-filling was a dull and
boring, yet necessary, part of the job at the beginning
of almost every investigative case. He went back to his
car and drove on out to Flushing.

116 Dover Street, Warren Griffith's last-known
address, was just around the corner from Flushing's
main shopping thoroughfare. Spanner had to drive
past the house and on for two blocks before he could
find a spot to park, and then walk back. It was a
shabby neighborhood. Many of the buildings on the
street had their doors and windows boarded over and
here and there were vacant lots littered with broken
bottles, tin cans, discarded automobiles tires and other
assorted refuse. It was hotter out here than it had
been in Manhattan. Or maybe it was just because the
unfamiliar streets seemed to him to be narrower and
created the illusion of trapping and containing all the
heat at ground level.

As he approached the doorway at 116, a tall, wiry,
white-haired man came out, carrying a garbage can
which he placed at the edge of the sidewalk. The man
was dressed in dark work pants and a white shirt with
long sleeves buttoned at the wrists. His shirt collar was
buttoned, too, although he wore no tie.

Spanner nodded to him and said, "Wonder if you could help me? I'm trying to find a Warren Griffith. I understand he lives here."

The man fixed sharp, blue eyes on Spanner and said, "Yep. He rents a room here. But he hasn't been around for a while. I'm the manager. Michael Finney's the name." He stuck out his hand.

"J. T. Spanner." Spanner shook hands with the man. "I'm a private investigator. I'm trying to find Griffith for a client."

"I guessed it was something like that," Finney said. "You look like a cop. The police have been here trying to locate him, too. But I expect you know that."

Despite the old man's age, which Spanner judged to be around seventy, his handshake was firm and his manner spry. "Come on in out of the heat," Finney said. "Don't know as there's anything I can tell you. I'll be glad to help, though, if I can. Besides, you'll probably want to take a look at his room. The police did."

He led the way into a dark, airless hall and closed the front door behind them. Spanner could see the hall ran straight through to the back of the house, a long, narrow building which reminded him of the old railroad flats that once stood on the East Side of Manhattan. All the doors to the rooms off the hall were closed and there was a staircase leading to the upper floors. The house smelled musty and the air was heavy with dust.

"I suppose I shouldn't rightly be showing off his room to people," Finney said, starting up the stairs, with Spanner following. "I wouldn't, either, except for him being a fugitive and me being a believer in Law and Order."

The room was on the second floor, in the front of the house and overlooked Dover Street. There was threadbare carpeting on the floor and the furnishings consisted of a double bed, a chest of drawers and two wooden, straight-backed chairs. The windows had shades but no curtains and over against one wall was a sink with a mirror above it.

"His rent's paid through the end of the month," Finney said, "so everything's just the way he left it. He hasn't been here since last Tuesday, a week ago tomorrow."

Spanner poked around the room and saw that some of Warren Griffith's clothes were still there, a few shirts in the drawers of the chest, along with socks and underwear, four suits hanging in the closet, a couple of pairs of shoes on the floor. A pile of soiled clothing was wadded up in the back of the closet. Two empty suitcases were shoved under the bed. On top of the chest were July and August issues of *Playboy,* one lying opened to the nude centerfold of Miss July who was blonde on top, a little darker below. There was also a copy of *Racing Form* lying on top of the chest. The racing sheet was folded back to the selections at Roosevelt Raceway for August 6. In a corner of the room next to the chest was a bowling bag with a ball inside it. All the evidence in the room seemed to indicate that Warren Griffith had left on the spur of the moment, or wanted it to appear that way.

"Anything you can tell me about Griffith," Spanner said, "his habits, friends, that kind of stuff, I'd appreciate, Mr. Finney."

"He had a room here for the last eight months," the old man said. "Stayed pretty much to himself. I got six other roomers, some of them been here only half the time he has, and I know them better'n I know him. I knew he didn't work regular, but he always seemed to have a little bit of money, and he always paid his rent on time. He said he owned some property, and I knew he got a letter with a check the first of every month."

"How about friends—did anybody ever come to visit him?"

Finney shook his head. "Not friends, exactly. There was a girl, a woman, he used to take up to his room.

That was a while back, though. And he had a brother, used to call on the phone sometimes, but he never came to the house."

"This woman," Spanner said, "can you tell me anything about her?"

"Well, as I mentioned, that was a while back. I told the police about her. Warren Griffith, he introduced me to her once. Her name was Alma something or other, I can't remember the last name. I always thought she was maybe a waitress."

Spanner, curious, asked: "What made you think that?"

Finney grinned slightly. "The times he took her to his room, they always got here late, one, two A.M. Other nights I'd hear him talking to her on the phone, it's a pay phone in the downstairs hall, and then later, one, two A.M. he'd go out. To meet her, I figured. So I always thought she was working, and I guessed she was a waitress because he used to spend a lot of time drinking in the bars around, and it was likely that's how he met her."

The old boy had a sharp eye, all right, Spanner thought. "But you can't remember her last name, Mr. Finney?"

"Nope. The police asked me the same thing. And I've given it a lot of thought, too."

"Could you describe her then?"

"Let's see now," Finney said. "She wasn't too young, forty or thereabout, I'd say. Brown hair, a little heavy, not too pretty, came up to about my chin." He paused, then added, "I can't think of anything else about her. She wasn't, well, you know, special to look at." He glanced down at the *Playboy* nude on the top of the chest and winked at Spanner. "Not like *her*," he said and gave a snorting laugh.

Spanner laughed and then said, "Anything else you can tell me about Griffith, Mr. Finney?"

"The trotters," Finney said. "He played the trotters. At Roosevelt Raceway and Yonkers. Used to go a lot.

In fact, the trotters was about the only subject he ever did talk to me about. Once he hit a Superfecta, won over a thousand dollars. He talked about that a lot."

"Anything else?" Spanner asked. He pointed to the bowling bag in the corner. "Was that his?"

Finney nodded. "He went out bowling at one time. But that was a long while back, too. Even before he started bringing his woman friend to the house."

"This brother of his—did you ever catch his name? You have any idea where he lives?"

"No. Griffith never talked about him at all. The only way I knew it was his brother was the fellow called once and said Warren Griffith was his brother. I'd recognize his voice times he called afterwards."

Spanner stuck out his hand. "Mr. Finney, I thank you for your time. I'd like to leave my phone number with you. If you think of anything else, or Griffith shows up, I'd sure like to know about it."

Finney took the card, glanced at it, and put it in his pants pocket. "You just can't tell about people, can you, Mr. Spanner? That Warren Griffith, I knew he was a hard one but I'd never thought he was mixed up with the law. Even served a prison term, the police said. You just can't tell."

The old man walked him down to the door and they shook hands again. Spanner returned to his car and rode around until he found a drive-in where he ordered two hamburgers and an iced coffee. While he ate, he looked at the material in the envelope Hymie Rosen had given him. Warren Griffith's arrest record was there, all typed up neatly in chronological order, like the carefully prepared resume of an experienced applicant seeking a criminal position:

SIX YEARS EARLIER: ARREST—SUSPICION OF ROB-BERY OF HAMBELL'S DRUGSTORE—BELLEROSE, QUEENS—CASE DISMISSED; ONE YEAR LATER: AR-REST—SUSPICION OF THE ROBBERY OF THE G&G SUPERMARKET, BRONXVILLE, N.Y.—CASE DIS-MISSED; ONE YEAR LATER: SUSPICION OF ROBBERY

OF AN APARTMENT ON GARTH ROAD, SCARSDALE,
N.Y.—CASE DISMISSED; ONE YEAR LATER: ARREST
—SUSPICION OF ROBBERY OF THE CASHIER OF
THE TRANS-LUX MOVIE THEATRE—MANHATTAN—
CONVICTED, SERVED TWO YEARS IN SING SING,
PAROLED; SEVEN MONTHS LATER: ARREST—
SUSPICION OF ROBBERY OF THE OFFICE OF THE
ACE CHECK-CASHING CORPORATION, MANHATTAN
—RELEASED ON $25,000 BAIL, PENDING TRIAL.

Spanner stuffed the sheet of paper back into the envelope and shoved the envelope under the car seat. Then he lit a cigarette to get rid of the odor of Hymie Rosen's cologne, which still came wafting up from the envelope when he handled it.

He didn't think much of his chances for collecting the three-grand fee from the bail bondsman. The only lead he had to Warren Griffith—if it was a lead—was some woman named Alma who might or might not be a waitress in a bar. And if she was a waitress in a bar, she probably wouldn't be going to work until evening. Since he was damned if he was going to make a round-trip to Manhattan, he decided he might as well use the afternoon to check out some of the Griffiths in the Queens telephone directory and see if he could find Griffith's brother, as well as pay a visit to the local police to inquire whether they had a record on Warren Griffith.

The sultry heat held throughout the afternoon. The sun, blurred by layers of smog, cast a curious, copper-hued glaze over the streets and buildings and faces of people. Spanner drew a blank on the Griffiths he contacted, by phone or in person. None admitted ever having heard of a Warren Griffith. At the police station, he talked to a detective named Ed Gowley, a chunky, red-faced man in a sweat-soaked sport shirt who kept complaining of the heat but who was co-operative and showed Spanner the only file the Queens police had on Warren Griffith. All the file contained was a warrant from the NYPD, dated five days previously, citing Warren Griffith as a fugitive, and a follow-up report from two patrolmen who had visited the house in Elmhurst and the building where Griffith had roomed in Flushing. There was nothing there that Spanner didn't already know.

"You get a lead on this guy," Gowley said, as Spanner pushed the file back to him, "anything we can do to help, you let us know."

Spanner nodded and left. He finished the afternoon in Flushing with a dinner of steak and salad in an air-conditioned restaurant.

It was close to 9 P.M., although there was still light in the sky, when he began his rounds of the local bars to look for Alma the waitress. The places he visited had different names, usually spelled out in neon signs out front, AL'S, GIMPY'S, PETE'S, THE GREEN SHAMROCK, THE OAKS, SAILOR'S, and sometimes simply BAR or TAVERN or COCKTAILS or BEER, but almost all were basically the same inside. The bar itself was usually the focal point, and the most crowded area, in every place, although there were always some customers drinking at the tables. Invariably there was a television set or a jukebox playing and sometimes both, and frequently the smell of the places was the same: a moist, not unpleasant, malt smell that was probably ingrained in the wood from countless spilled drinks and drippings.

Spanner sized the places up, for the most part, as regular neighborhood hangouts where the customers, the bartenders and the waitresses were known to each other. In each that he visited, he followed the same routine of standing at the bar and ordering one beer while he looked the place over. He wanted no trouble and to attract as little attention as possible, so he was careful to keep an area of space between him and the person closest to him.

Now and then he was conscious of the eyes of some of the customers upon him and once in a while he was aware that one of the loners drinking at the bar almost imperceptibly sidled away when he entered. He observed waitresses of all shapes and types and names, but none was Alma. By midnight he had a headache, his eyes burned, and he had lost track of the number of places he had visited.

He was back in his car and driving on the opposite side of town from where Warren Griffith had lived, still looking for new drinking places, when he saw a sign up ahead: BOWLING—20 ALLEYS—BOWLING and, underneath, a second sign: BEER COCKTAILS—THE BOWLING BAR. He parked the car and crossed the street to the bar which had a separate street entrance from the bowling alley, although the two were connected. The first person he saw as he entered was a waitress with brown hair, who was a little heavy in the hips, was around forty years old, and had a plain face. Before he had even had a chance to order a beer, a customer at one of the tables called out to the waitress, "Hey, Alma, how about another round?"

CHAPTER THREE

The neon lights in front of the building went dark a few seconds before 2 A.M. Across the street, Spanner watched the darkened doorways of the bowling alley and bar from his parked car. The street was silent and deserted. Soon a couple of men came out of the bowling alley and headed up the street. Several minutes passed and the waitress, Alma, and another woman appeared. They stopped just outside the doorway and Alma tied a bright-colored scarf over her head. The sound of the voices of the two women drifted back as, still on the opposite side of the street, they walked past Spanner's car without glancing in his direction, and continued toward the corner.

He let them get a half block ahead and then followed in the car, at a discreet distance, the headlights off. He followed them for six blocks until they stopped in front of a building near the corner a half a block away. He let the T-Bird's motor idle, and waited. Neither of the women had glanced back. They stood talking briefly and then the other woman walked on, more hurriedly now, while Alma—he could identify her because of the scarf she wore over her head—turned into the building.

When the other woman was out of sight, Spanner drove on and found a place to park a few yards beyond the door of the building Alma had entered, on the opposite side of the street. The building was four stories high, with a sandstone facade, and all the windows were dark.

Spanner studied the building briefly before he reached into the back of the car and opened a Louis Vuitton case resting on the back seat. The luggage had been a present from Ellie, when they were still married. Now it contained some of the equipment he had brought along for the job, including extra clips for his gun and several pairs of handcuffs. He took from the case an instrument that resembled a standard-model spyglass.

The spyglass was actually a powerful nocturnal snooperscope. For years the instruments had been the exclusive property of the United States Government, which had used them for military purposes. Recently the snooperscopes had become available on the general market where they sold for several thousand dollars apiece. Spanner had paid considerably less for the model he held in his hands, having bought it from another private investigator who had been convicted of illegal wiretapping, had lost his license, and gone out of business.

Spanner lifted the snooperscope to his eye and scanned the building. The 135mm f/2.8 objective lens permitted him to see with low-light-level clarity into the darkened rooms where the shades weren't drawn. He caught a movement inside a darkened window on the third floor, focused on the spot, and adjusted the lens until he had a clear picture of the room: Alma was there. She had removed the scarf from her head and was unbuttoning her blouse as she walked toward the window. Viewing her through the snooperscope was like looking at a lighted television set in a darkened room.

When Alma reached the window, she discarded her blouse. She stood there, looking out, as she unfastened her bra, let it drop, and with her hands scooped up her large breasts which had big, dark nipples. Watching her, Spanner felt his pulse quicken when she turned her head as if she were speaking to someone out of sight behind her in the room. When she turned back to the window, she pulled the shades down and a light went on in the room, showing around the edges of the shades. The light stayed on for close to half an hour and then the window, like the others in the building, went dark.

Spanner put the snooperscope back into the case. Now that he knew where Alma lived, and that there was a chance Warren Griffith might be there with her, he had to keep the place under surveillance overnight. If Griffith didn't show, he'd have to wait until Alma left the apartment the next day and try to flush him out.

The night was still stifling hot even though the sky was overcast and heat lightning flickered across the horizon to the south. With the air conditioning turned off, the interior of the car was like an oven with the temperature set at a low, steady broil. Three times, during the long wait, Spanner had to get out and— committing a misdemeanor in violation of the City and Borough Sanitation Code—relieve himself in the street between his car and the car parked behind. It was all that beer he had drunk. Twice a prowl car rolled slowly past and he ducked down in the seat of the T-Bird so he wouldn't be seen. God, all he needed was to be picked up by the police as a peeping-tom suspect.

At 3:15 his car phone buzzed and he snatched up the receiver. It was Lee, his second wife, calling. Her voice was soft and husky as she whispered: "I was thinking about you and I got lonesome. Ellie told me you were going to be on a case tonight. I thought you might be in the car and that maybe you were lonesome, too. What are you doing?"

"I'm on a stake-out," he said. "And it's hot and I'm tired."

"J. T.?" she whispered.

"Yeah?"

"I wish you were here with me right now. I just took

a bubble-bath and I'm lying here in my pink shorty nightgown, the one you like, and nothing else. You know what we'd do if you were here?"

"Lee—" he said. She got like this sometimes and called him, whether he was at home or in the office or in the car. And she knew it drove him up the wall when she made calls like this to him on the car phone because there was always the possibility that some ham-radio operator had tuned in on the same wavelength and was listening.

"We'd do all the things you like," she went on, her voice a silken whisper. *"M'mmmm."* The sound was her code phrase for lovemaking.

In spite of himself her words were, as always, arousing him. "Tomorrow, Lee," he said, "tomorrow when I get home. Now go to sleep."

"M'mmmm," she whispered again and laughed softly. "Nighty-night, darling."

He hung up the phone and lit a cigarette, shielding the glow with the palms of his hands. It seemed more lonesome than ever on the silent, deserted street after he had talked to her. But he was glad she had called. He propped his back against the door on the passenger side of the car and stretched out across the seat. In that position he could keep his eye on the front of the building across the street. For the next several hours he smoked cigarettes, and waited, until at last dawn lighted the sky to the east. It was going to be another scorcher.

Soon after sunrise the street began to come slowly to life. Delivery trucks began to appear in the block and so did a few people, those coming home from a night shift and those leaving early for work. An elderly man carrying a lunch pail entered the building where Alma lived. And not long afterwards three children came out and ran up the block and out of sight. The shades in Alma's apartment stayed down.

Spanner felt tired and grimy. When he decided he wouldn't look conspicuous on the street, with other people about, he got out and stretched his legs. Before he did, however, he took the precaution of removing two pairs of handcuffs from the case in the back seat. He hooked one pair on his belt and put the other pair in the car's glove compartment.

Several people entered and left the apartment building he had under observation but none of them matched Griffith's description. Spanner had been walking back and forth near the building for three-quarters of an hour when at a few minutes past 8 A.M. a man came out of the door, paused on the sidewalk, head down, and lit a cigarette. Spanner couldn't see the man's face and he hesitated. The man looked up, glanced both ways along the street, then turned and began to walk in the opposite direction. It was Warren Griffith.

Spanner followed as Griffith crossed the street at the corner. When Griffith reached the opposite curb, his head turned and for a moment he and Spanner looked at each other.

"Griffith," Spanner called, "Warren Griffith! I have a warrant for your arrest."

Griffith turned and ran. Spanner could see his hand fumbling under his coat. They were several yards apart when Spanner went after him, drawing his gun.

From a legal standpoint this was the trickiest part of the pickup. Spanner knew the law and was aware that he had to be careful of the way he conducted himself during the capture.

All such bounty-hunting was governed by a Supreme Court ruling, dating back to 1872, which stated that anyone released from custody on bail was still in custody, the custody of the bondsman, and if the bonded person didn't appear for trial, the bondsman or his hired agent—in this case Spanner—could seize the fugitive and bring him back to court. A certified copy of the bond and the power of a citizen's arrest made such a seizure legal. Spanner was safe in using so-called reasonable force and handcuffs to capture the fugitive. However, he knew, the law did not permit him to fire his gun except to protect himself. There were too many people out on the street, anyway, for

him to risk firing a shot. Also, those same people who
had stopped to watch the drama being played out by
the two men, could serve as witnesses to his excessive
use of force.

Spanner was gaining on Griffith but hadn't caught up
to him until Griffith paused and half-turned, a gun in
his right hand. Before he could raise the gun to fire,
Spanner lunged at him and clubbed him repeatedly
across the right shoulder with the barrel of his S&W
Magnum. Griffith's gun fell, clattering, to the sidewalk
and he grunted and cursed, then twisted away to run
again. Spanner grabbed him by the back of the coat
collar and jammed a knee in his spine. Griffith still
tried to pull away but Spanner hung on. Griffith's coat
ripped and he lost his balance and fell to his hands and
knees, pulling Spanner down on one knee. The sweat
was pouring from both men and both were breathing
in ragged gasps. Griffith tried to scramble away on all
fours, dragging Spanner with him. Spanner's left knee
was scraped raw on the concrete sidewalk before he
finally managed to stagger to his feet.

Still clutching Griffith by the back of the collar,
Spanner stood and, chest heaving, yanked the fugitive
upright. He spun Griffith around and shoved him up
against the front of the nearest building.

"Get those hands up, flat against the building,"
Spanner said, and at the same time kicked Griffith's
legs apart so the fugitive stood spread-eagled facing
the building. Griffith hung there, head down, while
Spanner quickly frisked him. He was clean. Spanner
handcuffed him, then reached down and picked up the
gun Griffith had dropped. It was a nickel-plated .38
revolver. Spanner put the gun in his coat pocket and,
grabbing Griffith by the back of the belt under his
coat, force-marched him across the street, and shoved
him into the T-Bird. He took the second pair of handcuffs from the glove compartment and snapped them
around Griffith's ankles.

A small crowd had collected on the sidewalk across
the street and as Spanner walked around the front of

the car and got in behind the steering wheel, he nodded
to the crowd and said, "Police business. It's all right."
He didn't want carloads of Queens cops swarming over
him before he got back to Manhattan with his prisoner.

Spanner made good time driving back from Flushing until he reached the Queensboro Bridge. Across
the river, the city's skyline danced and shimmered in
the still heat as if the earth below were undergoing a
minor tremor. From there on, the traffic was bumper-
to-bumper across the bridge, into Manhattan and down
to the Drive. It would be another forty-five minutes to
an hour before he'd reach the Criminal Court Building
in Lower Manhattan. Normally, the delay would have
bothered him. Not this morning, though. He felt too
good. He'd actually brought the damn thing off in less
than twenty-four hours, captured Warren Griffith and
stood to collect three thousand dollars. He could afford
to feel pleased. He was tempted to call his office with
the good news and to call Hymie Rosen, too, but he
decided to wait.

Warren Griffith hadn't spoken a word since his capture. He had sat slouched down in the seat, manacled
hands in his lap, eyes closed, for most of the time.
Finally, however, he roused himself and looked at Spanner. "You got a spare cigarette?" he asked.

Spanner stuck a cigarette in Griffith's mouth and lit
it for him. Griffith smoked silently for several seconds,
holding the cigarette between his lips, eyes squinted
against the smoke. He raised both hands to his face
and removed the cigarette. "You're not a cop," he said.
"Right?"

"Private investigator," Spanner said, looking at him
out of the corner of his eye.

Griffith nodded, took a couple more drags from the
cigarette and said, "Listen, I got to talk to you. It's
important." He pushed himself up straighter in the seat.
"I got some information the police'll want to know
about. A tip. You know anybody in the police? High
up, I mean, I can talk to?"

"You can talk to the judge," Spanner said.

Griffith shook his head. "That's no good. I want a deal. This information I'm talking about it's plenty big. Only I got to get to somebody up high enough. You know anybody like that? You'll come out looking good yourself."

"I already look good," Spanner said. "I caught you."

"Man, you're not listening," Griffith said disgustedly. He stubbed his cigarette out in the ash tray. "Me, I'm peanuts alongside the information I'm talking about. Listen, it's going to rock the whole fucking city." His head jerked up and down. "A heist. A big job."

Spanner kept his eyes on the road ahead. "When the judge asks you if you have anything to say before he sentences you, you tell him about this big heist."

The sweat popped out on Griffith's face and he hunched his shoulder up and tried to wipe it away. "You turn me over to that judge, I'm finished. But put me next to the right party in the cops, he hears something he wants to hear and I got a deal."

Spanner shook his head. "The police aren't going to make a deal with you. All that'll happen is I'll wind up looking like a horse's ass for listening to you."

Griffith became agitated, the muscles in his face twisted as he said hoarsely, "Listen, I'm going to tell you. I met this guy in a bar in Queens one night last week. I know him from around. He's got a load on, he starts yakking. He's in on a job, he tells me, a heist, could run three, maybe four million dollars. That's big, right? And it's going to come off here in Manhattan, this week, maybe next. No later. He was bragging it was guaranteed to bust the city wide open. He didn't tell me what the job was, but you can't con me the police wouldn't like to hear about it."

The sweat was running down Griffith's face, soaking through his shirt and coat despite the car's air conditioning. Spanner studied him briefly. In spite of himself, he was interested. "This guy got a name?"

"Happy, they call him," Griffith said eagerly. "His name's, I think, Hap. I told you, I know him from around. And I know he's got the connections for a job like this." He paused and said in a rush of words: "Look, why you think I was crazy enough to hang around Queens there where you picked me up? You think I didn't know the risk I was running? I was hanging around till the job was pulled and I could put the bite on this guy so I'd have enough to run."

Spanner grinned wolfishly. "It's a cute story, Griffith. But there's nothing in it that would prove you're not trying to palm off a big con on me."

"I'm telling you the truth," Griffith said desperately. "This guys exact words to me were: 'the others and I are going to knock the whole city on its ass and walk away with four million dollars.' Look, what would it get me to make up a story like that if it wasn't true?"

Spanner shrugged. "I don't know. But it sure as hell sounds to me like you made it up. And it'll sound that way to the police, too."

"No, it won't," Griffith said, shaking his head. "You haven't heard the rest of my proposition. I got the whole thing worked out so it'll be fair for them, fair for me." He paused and then said, "Can you spare me another cigarette?"

After Spanner had given him another cigarette and lighted it for him, Griffith said, "What I'll tell them, the police, is to lock me up for a few days, a week, until the job comes off. That way they'll see I'm telling them the truth. Big as this heist's going to be, once it happens I'm not worried they won't fix me up with a deal if I lead them to a guy who's in on it. How about it?"

Spanner was still skeptical. But, Goddamn it, he thought, it was just possible there was a grain of truth in Griffith's story. The story would explain why Griffith had cleared out of his room in such a hurry but hadn't gone far. And what Griffith probably really planned of course, and wasn't saying, was he meant to shake the guy down, blackmail him, once the job was done. Now that Griffith had been caught he wanted to try to barter what he knew for a chance to save his own skin. Also, it occurred to Spanner, why would Griffith offer to let himself be locked up until after the robbery—to prove he was telling the truth—if he'd made the whole thing up? True, he was going to be locked up anyway on the fugitive charge, but why go through all these extra complications unless events would prove the truth of his words?

"How about it?" Griffith asked again, "are you going to take me to talk to somebody? It seems to me if I can make a positive ID on this guy, it ought to be worth plenty to the police. After all we're talking about a four-million-dollar heist. The guy says to me it's a sure thing. His exact words were: 'nobody ever put the right combination together before.' And I can put the finger on him for the cops."

Spanner himself had been a cop long enough to know that many a big case had been cracked on just such dumb luck information as Griffith seemed to possess. The ex-con's story was still pretty flimsy, and Spanner wasn't sure he was telling the whole truth. Nevertheless, he decided reluctantly, the fugitive probably did know something the police would want to hear.

"How about you take me to the Commissioner himself and let me talk?" Griffith urged.

Spanner didn't answer him. The hell of it was, Spanner realized, if the police did buy Griffith's story he wouldn't be able to collect his fee from Hymie Rosen until the whole thing was over. He was tempted to ignore his prisoner and drive straight on to the Criminal Court Building. Instead, silently cursing himself for a fool, he made his decision.

"I can't get you to the Commissioner," he said to Griffith, "but I can get you to somebody high enough up to give you a yes or no."

Griffith nodded, satisfied, and slumped back on the seat.

Spanner used the car phone to call Deputy Chief Inspector Max Kauffman at the 16th Precinct, Patrol Boro Manhattan Central. After the call had gone through the precinct switchboard, he was surprised

when a woman's voice answered: "Inspector Kauffman's office, Sergeant O'Dell speaking."

Christ, Spanner thought, things had changed since
the days he worked out of the 16th.

"This is J. T. Spanner calling," he said. "Inspector
Kauffman knows me. I don't want to talk to him now.
I just want to know if he's going to be in his office for
the next hour or so."

"Yes," the Sergeant said, after a slight hesitation.
"He'll be here all morning."

"Tell him I called, please," Spanner said. "And tell
him I'm coming in on urgent business. I should be
there in half an hour, forty-five minutes. Tell him it's
very important and I'd like to see him."

CHAPTER FOUR

Deputy Chief Inspector Max Kauffman did not nod or speak when Sergeant Margaret O'Dell showed J. T. Spanner and Spanner's handcuffed prisoner into the office. The inspector's manner was, as always, distant, remote, intimidating. Sergeant O'Dell watched closely to see how it affected the two men. Spanner covered the interval of awkward silence by lighting a cigarette and opening the manila envelope he held in his hand. The reaction of the blond prisoner was, as she had guessed it would be, more visible; he appeared to literally shrink in size. She felt a passing twinge of sympathy for the man, recalling her own first meeting with the Inspector, only four months earlier.

She hadn't known what to expect, that day in April, when she reported for the first time to the 16th, a weathered, dirty brick building, in the West Forties. The first surprise had come after she had ridden the creaky elevator up to the third floor and found the plainclothesman on temporary duty at the desk she was to occupy, just outside the closed door of the Inspector's office. The plainclothesman told her Max Kauffman wasn't there, mumbled something about a meeting, and motioned her to a chair in the outer office.

As she waited, she could see there was nothing about the surroundings where she'd be working to cheer her up. The decor was what she thought of as the usual precinct-drab; the walls grimy and cracked, the floor, under the worn linoleum covering, slightly buckled, the furniture, desk, chairs and filing cabinets, scarred and chipped and worn with age. And, over all, was the distinctive station house smell; a blend of dust, mold, and disinfectant.

A short while later Max Kauffman appeared, strode swiftly past her, and beckoned her to follow him into his office. He had already crossed to his desk and was talking on the phone when she came into the room. She immediately collapsed into a chair. She had never seen an office like Max Kauffman's in any police precinct in Manhattan. The room was enormous, the walls paneled in oak, with exposed oak beams across the ceiling, and the floor was carpeted with a dark blue, deep pile, wall-to-wall rug. The windows were hung with rich, blue drapes that lay in folds against the matching carpet. Behind the drapes dark, wooden, louvered shutters covered the windows, and the indirect lighting came from behind fixtures recessed in the ceiling and the tops of the windows. In one wall was a huge stone fireplace (she had no doubt it worked in cold weather), and in another wall a vent let in fresh, cooling air from what she guessed, was a special air-conditioning unit on the outside of the building.

At one end of the room, where she sat, was a massive mahogany desk polished to a gleaming shine. A swivel armchair, covered in leather, sat behind the desk and there were two leather-covered armchairs in front of the desk. At the opposite end of the room was a long, leather-covered sofa and several more chairs arranged around a mahogany coffee table on which sat a silver coffee service and a crystal vase filled with fresh-cut chrysanthemums. There were a dozen abstract oil paintings on the walls and several pieces of sculpture standing on low pedestals around the room, paintings and sculpture alike placed so they would be illuminated by the soft lighting. The room had a clean smell of rich leathers and oil polish, and reminded her of what she imagined a study in some fine English manor house

might look like. She wondered how Max Kauffman
rated such an office.

Her second surprise came when Deputy Chief Inspector Max Kauffman finished his phone call, settled
back in the chair across the desk from her, and she gave
him her full attention. She had, somehow, expected
an older man. At fifty-two, Max Kauffman's wavy black
hair was barely tinged by a few streaks of gray at the
temples. He was a powerful-looking man, broad-
shouldered and barrel-chested, and his stocky build
made him appear shorter than his five-foot, eleven-inch
height. She couldn't help noticing that his hair looked
styled, his dark-skinned face well-massaged, and his
fingernails manicured, although he wore no polish on
them. Also, unless she was mistaken, his summer-
weight pencil-striped blue suit bore the classic lines of
Savile Row tailoring. At first impression, she found his
sleek, well-groomed appearance too fastidious, almost
prissy.

Then he looked up from the desk. For the first time
his piercing blue eyes bore into her. She felt a shock
run through her body. She could feel the—she didn't
quite know how to describe it—virility, *maleness,* exud-
ing from him. Her face flushed. She was visible to him
only from the waist up, but she felt a hot, itchy sen-
sation between her thighs beneath the desk. He apparently noticed nothing, and, after glancing at her
coolly for a moment, looked back down at her personnel file lying open on the desk in front of him.

"Radcliffe?" he said.

"Yes, sir." Did he think that was good or bad?

"How long have you been attending John Jay College at night?"

"Three—three years," she said. "Ever since I joined
the Department. I would like—hope—to get my law
degree."

He nodded. "I see you were out on the street, as a
decoy, for a year. Two citations. Why did you request
inside duty?"

She had regained some of her composure. "I wanted

to learn as much as I could about the overall workings of the Department. I hope to practice criminal law one day. I feel the more I know about the actual day-to-day machinery of justice the better attorney I would be."

He looked at her sharply. "You don't plan to make a career in the Department, then, Sergeant O'Dell?"

She knew, somehow, he meant his question as a rebuke. Choosing her words carefully, she answered, "Sir, I said I *hope* to practice one day. But who knows? It may be that I'll stay on the force."

He had dismissed her then, telling her that Sergeant Linquist, on temporary assignment at the desk outside the office, would brief her on her duties. There had been no welcoming speech, no particular friendliness, no expression of personal interest at all except for the probing of those chilling, blue eyes which had made her so uncomfortable.

A cold fish, she thought and then, with crude Irish wit, amended the thought to: a cold gefilte fish.

During the first few days she worked at the 16th, she began to speculate that perhaps the Inspector resented being assigned a female sergeant. A week later she had to revise that theory when she came across an earlier letter in the files from him to Headquarters specifically requesting a woman officer to work as his administrative assistant, ánd adding his opinion that women should play a larger role in police work.

Meanwhile, day by day, she was learning other facts about him. He was a hard worker and frequently put in fourteen to sixteen hours a day on the job. It was not unusual for her to come in in the morning and find him still at his desk from the day before, red-eyed and haggard. Later, he would disappear for a few hours and return clean-shaven, looking rested, and wearing a change of clothes. He led most of the raiding parties from the 16th and was almost always on the scene when major arrests were made. He had a total of eleven commendations for bravery to his credit. Sergeant O'Dell had found that virtually all the men under the Inspector's command had respect for him although they referred to him, behind his back, as "his lordship."

As far as Max Kauffman's personal life was concerned, she was able to discover that he was independently wealthy and, with special permission from the Commissioner had had his office decorated to his personal taste and paid for it with his own money. He was married, as she had guessed, and had two children, a boy at Harvard, nineteen years old, and a girl at Dalton, thirteen. Sergeant O'Dell was right about his clothes, too; twice a year, she learned, Max Kauffman and his wife vacationed in Europe, where he replenished his wardrobe. He had also graduated from Harvard Law School magna cum laude, and had been a Rhodes scholar. And she had once harbored a suspicion that he might hold it against her that she had finished Radcliffe! None of the information she uncovered about the Inspector came from him. He remained as uncommunicative, on matters other than police business, as he had on the day she had met him.

By the end of the first month, she started to imagine that perhaps he found her unattractive even though she had always had admirers and boyfriends and, at twenty-six, her pretty face and shapely figure got low, appreciative wolf-whistles from all the other men at the station house whenever she walked through the halls. She couldn't even reasonably explain to herself why the Inspector's icy impassiveness became a challenge to her very femininity. But it did and she was determined to find a way, whatever it took, to make him respond to her.

Soon after that she began to daub on a light perfume each time just before she went into his office, something she had never done before, while she was on duty, since she'd joined the Department. He took no notice of her perfume and in fact she wasn't even sure he could smell it since they were seldom that close to one another.

Usually they were only alone together for a brief period each day, when he dictated to her. At those times he sat on the leather sofa on one side of the coffee table and she in a chair on the other side so there was still a distance between them. However, their proximity when he was dictating had given her an idea. Regulations required her to wear her standard policewoman's uniform while on duty, so there had been nothing she could do about her outer garments to attract his attention. She did, however, begin wearing bright-colored Pucci underwear and occasionally sat with her legs rather carelessly apart. Frequently, after that, she was able to catch him stealing glances at her thighs. She considered it to be a victory of sort, despite the fact that his manner toward her continued to be stern and aloof.

One day, during this period, he asked her to stay late, and afterwards offered her a ride home in his limousine, chauffered by the plainclothesman who was the regular driver. When they got to her apartment she invited the Inspector in for a cup of coffee and he accepted. They hadn't been busy at the office that night, and as far as she could see there had been no reason for him to ask her to work overtime, so she assumed he'd planned the whole business as a pretext to taking her home. Once the two of them were alone in her apartment, she braced herself for the pass she expected him to make. Instead he drank his coffee, asked if he could use her phone, made one call, and left. So much for her perfume and Pucci underwear, she had thought wryly.

Her brief reverie, while she still stood in the doorway to Max Kauffman's office, ended when the Inspector said sharply, "That will be all, Sergeant O'Dell." She withdrew hastily, closing the door on the three men inside.

Max Kauffman leaned back in his chair and said, "What's this all about, Spanner?"

Spanner laid the certified copy of the bail bond and the copy of Warren Griffith's arrest record on the desk. He nodded toward his handcuffed prisoner. "This man's Warren Griffith, Inspector. He's a bail-jumper. A bondsman named Hymie Rosen hired me to look for him. I picked him up a couple of hours ago out in Queens. He claims to have some information which, if it's true, I think you might want to hear."

"Sir, I—" Griffith started to say and Max Kauffman, glancing up from the papers Spanner had put on his desk, stopped him.

"I don't know what it is you're going to tell me," the Inspector said in a flat voice, "but I have to warn you: you have the right to a lawyer before you make any statement. If you don't have a lawyer, we'll provide you with one. And you understand that anything you tell me can also be used against you in court."

"Yes, sir," Griffith said quickly. "I already know about that Miranda business."

Spanner was amused by Warren Griffith's respectful manner since being confronted with Max Kauffman. The Inspector was a formidable figure, especially here in his office. There was an undeniable aura of power and authority surrounding him.

"Go ahead then," Max Kauffman said impatiently.

Griffith fidgeted in his chair, wet his lips with his tongue, and began to repeat the story he had told Spanner. His words were halting, although the story was essentially the same.

Max Kauffman listened impassively, his eyes narrowing only when Griffith came to the part of the story where he offered to let himself be locked up until after the heist.

When Griffith had finished his account, the Inspector questioned him sharply. The man's last name? Griffith said again he didn't know. Just that he was called Hap or Happy. Griffith also said in reply to further questioning that he didn't know where the man lived and that, anyhow, he'd gotten the impression the man was going to be in hiding until the job was pulled. Again and again, between questions, Griffith assured the Inspector that he would be able to lead the police to the man once the robbery was over. "I think you're going to thank me, sir, after you see how big this job is."

It was chilly in the room, with the air conditioner turned up full, but Spanner, watching silently, could see the sheen of sweat on Griffith's face and neck.

Max Kauffman looked steadily at Warren Griffith for a moment and leaned forward in his chair.

"What night did you talk to this man?"

"It was—uh—Monday. Last week."

"Where did you talk to him? The name of the place. A bar, I think you said."

"It was different places. We went from one to the other."

"They had names, didn't they? Don't you remember any of them?"

Griffith squinted his eyes. "I was drinking pretty good myself, you understand. But let's see, there was a place called Sailor's we was in. Paddy's too, I think. And some others."

"Was this man, Hap or Happy, known to the people in these places?

"It could be."

"And you're sure you don't know where he lives?"

Griffith shook his head. "But I positively guarantee you I can find him for you. Later."

Max Kauffman studied Griffith in silence for a moment before he said, "You know what I think, Griffith? I think you're a worm-eaten, lying, thieving, miserable Mother who dreamed this whole cock-eyed business up out of your own pin-headed brain."

Griffith squirmed in his chair and then, in a cracking voice, said, "What—what would it get me if I was to do that?" He shook his head. "I'm leveling, Inspector. This guy, he told me, 'the others and I are going to knock the city on its ass and walk away with four million dollars.' I didn't make that up. No way. When I came in here, I came in figuring that information's important. Say they get away with it, it ought to be worth something I can make a positive ID on the guy and you can grab him and the others."

"Let's get a couple of things straight." Max Kauff-

man said flatly. "First, I want a full, signed statement
from you, including everything you know, especially
about this man you allege you talked to, and with a full
description of him. Second, I guarantee you nothing in
return."

Griffith's face glistened with sweat, sweat had soaked
through his clothes, and the clothes had turned dark
and stuck to his body. But he nodded eagerly. He knew
he had his deal.

"And Griffith," Max Kauffman said softly, "I warn
you, if you're bullshitting me, I'll see to it you're
slapped with additional charges of conspiracy and
perjury." The Inspector pressed the intercom on his
desk. "Sergeant, I want Detectives Bucher and Rojas,
on the double. Buzz me when they get here."

A couple of minutes later the intercom buzzed. Max
Kauffman went out of the office briefly and came back
with the two detectives. Both men were in their shirt-
sleeves and wore holsters, empty, under their armpits.
They gave Spanner a brief nod and Max Kauffman said
to Griffith, "These men will take your statement. You
go with them."

Griffith's wrists were still handcuffed. Spanner had
removed the manacles from the ex-con's ankles before
he had brought him in from the car. When Spanner
handed Rojas the keys, the police officer removed the
handcuffs and gave them and the keys back to Spanner.
Then the three men, Bucher and Rojas walking on
either side of Griffith but not touching him, left the
room. Rojas was already loosening his tie.

Max Kauffman swung around in his chair and gave
Spanner a hard look. When the two men had worked
together, at the time Spanner was a Detective First
Grade in the 16th Homicide Bureau and Max Kauffman was a Captain in charge of the Bureau, they had
never had any disagreements but they had never been
comfortable with one another. This was the first time
they'd met since Spanner had left the force.

"You believe his story?" Max Kauffman asked.

Spanner shrugged.

"You never know what a sneak son-of-a-bith like that has in mind," Max Kauffman said sourly.

"True," Spanner agreed. "But I think he probably knows something all right. And it's obvious he's anxious to save his own skin. I'm not sure he's telling the whole truth, though."

Max Kauffman grunted. "Look, I'll let the judge who issued the warrant on Griffith know we're holding him. Meanwhile, I expect you to keep quiet about all this with that bondsman who hired you. Let's see where this thing's going. You understand that?"

"I understand," Spanner said. He stood up. He felt tired, soiled, almost out on his feet. He remembered the .38 revolver he had taken off Griffith. He gave it to the Inspector who stuck it in a desk drawer for later routine testing by ballistics.

"Inspector," Spanner said, "take good care of that punk. I got a lot invested in him, comes to three grand." He started toward the door, then stopped. "And you know, Inspector, you could say thanks. I didn't have to bring Griffith to you."

"Thanks for what?" Max Kauffman asked. "As far as I'm concerned, all we've got here is a possible psychopathic liar."

Up yours, too, Deputy Chief Inspector Max Kauffman, Spanner thought. But he only nodded and continued toward the door.

As soon as Spanner left, Max Kauffman called Detective Captain Ben Sybert to his office. Sybert headed up the 16th Intelligence Unit. He was a thin, furtive-looking individual, red-haired and freckled, who could never stop moving, standing or sitting. He kept rocking back and forth on his feet in front of the desk until Max Kauffman waved him to a chair. Sybert nervously crossed and uncrossed his legs while the Inspector tersely briefed him on the interview with Warren Griffith and Spanner.

"Bucher and Rojas are interrogating Griffith," Max Kauffman concluded. "You'll get a transcript of the statement as soon as it's completed. Meanwhile, I want you to get moving on the case, Ben. What I want you to do is contact the DA and start proceedings for a court order to tap Spanner's office and home phones. The DA can draw up his affidavits based on Griffith's statement, something like suspicion of conspiracy to commit robbery, maybe suspicion of conspiracy to obstruct justice. You know. Whatever, I want a tap on him and surveillance until we see what this is all about. Spanner may be clean, but I want it verified."

Sybert was already up and out the door.

Alone again, Max Kauffman tilted back in his chair and gazed reflectively at the paintings and sculpture on the opposite side of the room. Christ, he didn't want a possible hot potato like Warren Griffith dropped in his lap at this particular time. He had some personal business to take care of in the next few days. His wife was leaving that afternoon for a ten-day visit at Elizabeth Arden's Maine Chance resort in Arizona, and for weeks he'd been looking forward to the period when she'd be gone and he'd have some time to himself. Now this had to come up. God only knew what kind of complications would result from Griffith's story. The Commissioner would have to be informed, probably this afternoon, as soon as Bucher and Rojas finished their interrogation.

He glanced to see that his office door was closed, then opened his desk drawer and took out his private phone. While he was dialing the number, he swiveled around in his chair so his back was to the door. When Catherine Devereux answered, he said softly, "Good morning, Kit."

"Good morning, darling," she said. "I was just thinking about you."

"It looks like it's going to be a busy day. I thought I'd call you early in case you wanted to go out later and couldn't reach me. We're all set for this evening?"

"Oh, yes," she said. "I've been thinking about it all morning."

"I may not get a chance to call you again today, so I'll see you about eight. All right?"

"I'll be waiting for you." Her voice dropped low. "I love you."

"I love you," he said, in whisper.

He left his office and went downstairs to look in on the interrogation of Griffith by Bucher and Rojas. He stood in an area next to the interrogation room and observed them through a one-way window. The ex-con, flanked at a table by the two detectives, was flipping through the mug-shot files, in the hope that the man he claimed he'd talked to in the bar had a record and his photo would be somewhere in the records.

Inside the office, although the Inspector had no way of knowing it, Warren Griffith had just received one hell of a jolt: he'd actually spotted a mug shot of the man he'd been with in the Queens bar. With great effort he concealed his shock and surprise, and went on examining the photographs in the files, without giving anything away to the two detectives. *Jesus,* Griffith thought, *I never even knew he had a record.*

Max Kauffman watched the scene in the room for a few moments more, unaware of the discovery Griffith had made. Then the Inspector turned away. Maybe, he told himself hopefully, the two third-degree experts would succeed in making Griffith confess that his story was a pack of lies. Or, just as satisfactory to him, maybe the Commissioner would take the whole thing out of his hands and turn it over to the Central Intelligence Bureau for investigation.

CHAPTER FIVE

The city simmered in early afternoon heat outside the
window of the Police Commissioner's office at 240
Centre Street. Max Kauffman stood at the window
staring out as he waited for the Commissioner to complete a phone call. The day was still full of hard, brassy
light, although the sun was hidden by the staggered
heights of the buildings stretching westward from Police
Headquarters across the city.

The Deputy Chief Inspector was morose. Earlier,
both his third-degree experts had believed, when they
completed their interrogation of Warren Griffith, that
the ex-con was telling the truth, or at least part of it,
when he said he had been told there would be a big
robbery some time in Manhattan. But neither Bucher
or Rojas had been able to pry any additional information out of Griffith, if indeed he had any. Later, Max
Kauffman had called the judge who had issued the
warrant for Griffith's arrest on the bail-jumping charge,
but hadn't been able to reach him until the noon recess
of the court where the magistrate was presiding. After
talking with the judge, the Inspector had sat thought-
fully at his desk for a long time before directing that
Warren Griffith be booked and held as a material witness. Griffith had been locked away in the 16th's
"Honeymoon Suite," an isolation cell separate from the
station-house holding tank where the other prisoners
were kept. Soon after noon, when Max Kauffman had

completed his report on the case and Warren Griffith's statement had been typed, he had brought the papers downtown to Headquarters for a meeting with the Police Commissioner.

Commissioner John Kenyon Hilliard had read the papers through twice, now and then making a comment or asking a question. He was a tall man with a craggy face and a bald head which he kept shaved as clean as his cheekbones. He sat hunched over his desk and when he looked up to speak, his head emerged from the cavity between his shoulders like a turtle's from its shell.

He remarked on the delicate legal point regarding the witness, saying. "There may be repercussions later on but I think you've probably anticipated them by booking Griffith as a material witness on his own freely offered testimony." He asked about the wiretap and surveillance on J. T. Spanner and seemed satisfied when Max Kauffman explained, "I have no particular reason to suspect Spanner, but because of the unusual circumstances of this case, it occurred to me that he and Griffith could have cooked something up between them and I ordered the wiretap and surveillance simply as precautionary measures. Spanner was always straight when he worked on the force, a little too independent, maybe, but he had a good record, and as far as I know he's still straight."

"A most curious case," the Commissioner commented.

That was when Max Kauffman had said hastily, "Yes, sir, it is. I thought perhaps you might want to turn it over to the CIB—"

At that point the Commissioner had interrupted him with an emphatic shake of the head. Placing the papers to one side, John Hilliard began to speak forcefully. He was putting Max Kauffman in charge of the investigation into the possible robbery and the robbery itself if it actually occurred. The Inspector would be responsible only to the Commissioner, would have the full cooperation of the Commissioner's office, and would be free to draw upon manpower and equipment city-wide. The Commissioner realized that Warren Griffith's information might turn out to be wholly fabricated. He felt, nevertheless, that the police had to proceed on the assumption it was true. Consequently, some kind of preparatory action had to be taken. If they could get no more information from Warren Griffith and the man, Hap or Happy, couldn't be located, then it was probably impossible to prevent the robbery. In that case, the Commissioner stressed, he wanted a special police unit, operating under Max Kauffman's direction, to be prepared to move fast enough to capture the perpetrators as soon as the robbery took place. "Inspector," the Commissioner had said, "I want a detailed contingency plan from you on my desk as early as possible tomorrow." Before the Commissioner could add to his remarks, he had received a phone call and Max Kauffman had wandered over to the window to brood over his assignment.

The Inspector's first reaction was one of anger. He felt he had been shafted and the whole damn thing unfairly dumped back into his lap. His anger passed swiftly, as it always did, and he viewed the Commissioner's decision more philosophically. Of course he was the logical person to be assigned to the case. He had taken the initial action on Griffith and was already involved with him. There was, after all, an element of security to be observed here, both because of the informant's legal position and because of a possible leak from the Department. The fewer the people who knew the basic facts of the case, the better. Besides which, he respected the Commissioner. He could guess what a ball-breaking job it must be to hold the office of PC and have responsibility for over 30,000 policemen.

Still, it did seem like an impossible assignment. How could he prepare to deal with a crime which was yet to be committed, and which could take place at any time, anywhere, within the 365.4 square miles of the city? Of course he'd assign men to look for this fellow who was alleged to have talked to Griffith. The police would

keep Griffith going through the mug shot files and, of
course, the ex-con would continue to be grilled—not
that he expected to get anything from him. If Griffith
knew more, he'd keep his mouth shut since he'd be a
stronger bargaining position after the robbery was committed, so Kauffman couldn't count on having much
more to go on than he had now.

There was, also, the matter of preparing a contingency plan to have ready for the Commissioner tomorrow. He had hoped to be able to go straight from
Headquarters to his apartment and accompany his wife
to JFK Airport, as he'd promised he would. Now he'd
have to stop by the 16th Precinct and remove from the
files all past departmental contingency plans. He knew
that most of the material in the files had been prepared
to deal with riots, sabotage, earthquakes, fire storms
and other such major catastrophes which might at some
future date threaten Manhattan. There wouldn't be
much there he could see, but he wanted the material to
help guide him in drawing up his plan.

The Commissioner completed his phone call and
joined Max Kauffman at the window.

"Max, I want you to know that I appreciate the
odds you're up against," John Hilliard said sympathe-
tically. He stared somberly out the window.

"If we just had something more concrete to go on,"
Max Kauffman mused aloud. "All we know from
Griffith is that it's going to be big. So I guess we're
talking about a bank, maybe, a jewelry store, some
place in the diamond exchange. Hell, I guess it's use-
less to speculate. It could be anywhere. East Side, West
Side, Uptown, Downtown, take your pick."

At that same moment, a hundred or so blocks uptown from Police Headquarters, Joe Conant was standing in the Metropolitan Museum of Art, on Fifth
Avenue, contemplating Rembrandt's masterpiece, *Aristotle Contemplating the Bust of Homer.*

Priceless, Conant thought, the thing was priceless.
He meant the word two ways: to describe the painting

itself and to describe the heist of the Museum, which
he and the other four men had so painstakingly planned over the past several weeks. He still hadn't decided whether the Rembrandt was to be part of the
haul. He remembered, from the research he had done
on the Museum's art treasures, that the Metropolitan
had purchased the painting in 1961 for $2.3 million
dollars. He knew that in the year since then art authorities had stated that it was virtually impossible to fix
the value of the Rembrandt if it were offered for sale
today. Except that no *single* museum would have the
money to buy it. Priceless.

Still, Conant hadn't made up his mind yet about
stealing the Aristole. He knew it was one of the world's
most widely known and best-loved paintings. Snatching it might bring down too much heat on them. No use
pushing their luck. There was another reason, too, for
not taking the Rembrandt work, although he'd never
let the other four who were in on the robbery plan
know it. He had too much love for this particular work
of art to risk having it damaged in the robbery. That
was the beauty of their plan. They could pick and
choose what they wanted to take—the Metropolitan was
a storehouse of riches—as long as the total value of the
paintings came to the three million, seven hundred fifty
thousand dollar-payoff he'd fixed as the figure for their
labors. He liked the sound of the figure: three million,
seven hundred fifty thousand dollars—which would
average out to three-quarters of a million dollars for
each of the five of them who pulled off the robbery. He
looked at the painting again.

Conant stood there, a lean, fit man in his late
twenties, neatly dressed in a white button-down shirt,
rep tie, madras jacket, gray slacks and black loafers
shined to a high gloss. His features were regular, his
hair straight and cut close, which might have indicated
white genes somewhere in his bloodlines, except that
his skin was as shiny black as his loafers.

Turning away from the Rembrandt, Conant strolled
leisurely through the cavernous corridors of the Metro-

politan. Conant was very much a connoisseur, appraising first one, then another, of the monumental works of art that hung on the walls from Cezanne through Degas, Eakins, El Greco, Halbern, Homer, Michelangelo, Picasso, Velazquez, Van Dyck to van Gogh.

For six weeks now, since they'd first begun planning the job, he had visited the Museum two or three times a week. Today, as on previous visits, the place was crowded with visitors, local sightseers and tourists, school-aged children, couples walking hand-in-hand, and the inevitable would-be artists and art students arranged in front of many of the paintings, busily making copy-sketches of the masters' works. Hot as it was outside, there was a dank, not-quite comfortable, coolness along the length of the high-ceilinged hallways, and a slightly stale smell to the air.

On the second floor, at the top of the wide, balustraded marble stairs, Conant moved more purposefully. Now he was on his way to check out the part of the Museum which figured most prominently in the robbery plans.

He went along the corridor until he reached a section of the building where construction renovation had just been completed on the south wing of the Metropolitan. The refurbished gallery was empty, and there was a velvet rope stretched across its entrance-way. It was silent and deserted over in this corner of the Museum and hotter, from the sun which poured in through the undraped windows. The walls of the closed-off wing were in paneled sections, freshly painted white. There was nothing to see in the gallery, but Conant stood at the entrance, in front of the rope, his eyes fixed on a section of panel near the back of the reconstructed gallery. The panel appeared to be untouched, and he was satisfied that the materials hidden behind it remained in place.

He suddenly became aware that he was being watched. He turned slowly and saw a uniformed Museum guard standing a few feet behind him For a moment Conant felt his gut tighten with fear. What if they'd discovered the stuff behind the wall and were just waiting to see who came to check on it? Conant forced himself to stay calm as the guard advanced toward him.

"It's a funny thing," the guard said, "with all the things there are to see in this place, you'd be surprised how many people stop and stare at that empty room. I get a kick out of watching it happen."

"Just plain old curiosity, I suppose," Conant answered, breathing easier. Nobody knew yet that just a few feet away from where he and the guard stood was a stash of materials which was going to blow a three million, seven hundred fifty thousand-dollar hole in the Museum.

"Yeah, I guess that's it, all right," the guard said. He nodded and walked on. Conant glanced at his watch. It was almost three-thirty. Holly would be waiting for him. Which was all right, because his business at the Museum was finished. He headed for the first floor.

When he came out of the Museum and started down the massive stone steps that fronted on Fifth Avenue, Conant blinked his eyes against the almost-blinding hot light of the day. From the steps he could see the candy-striped awning of the outdoor cafe at the Stanhope Hotel, across Fifth Avenue, at 81st Street. Traffic was heavy on the avenue, with the flow of cars, taxis, buses, even a couple of horse-drawn hansom cabs, streaming downtown. More buses were parked along the curbs, at the edge of Central Park, for several blocks on either side of the Museum, and the sidewalks were crowded with people.

He crossed the street and as he approached the hotel, he spotted Holly sitting at one of the tables under the striped awning. Her back was turned to him as he made his way around the other tables to reach her. She looked lovely. Her dress was a white shark-skin with a V-neck and cap sleeves. Around her waist was a red and white polka-dot sash. Her dress was just tight enough and short enough to show off the shapely curve of her body and the good legs. She wore high-heeled pumps the color of the red in the polka dots of the sash, and her hair was pulled back, under a matching turban scarf, to accentuate her high cheekbones. The white sharkskin was in dramatic contrast to her skin, which was just a shade lighter than Conant's. Style was what she had, he thought, as he slipped into the chair beside her.

She turned her head and said, "Hey!" smiling, and offered her lips which he kissed lightly. She took his hand and intertwined her fingers with his. He was conscious that people at the other tables were watching them, and he was sure some of the men were envious of his good luck.

"I didn't keep you waiting too long, did I?" Conant asked.

Holly shook her head. "It's nice here. I like to watch the people."

He'd discovered the Stanhope Hotel and its outdoor cafe by accident on one of his first visits to the Museum and had immediately known she'd like it. This was the sixth or seventh time they'd had drinks there in the afternoon before going to his apartment.

They sipped their daiquiris and she talked about her day. She did fashion modeling, and he had known she had an appointment that morning to audition for a magazine advertisement. She told him she had canceled the appointment because she was afraid it would make her late for her meeting with him. She said she'd been looking forward to being with him from the moment she woke up. Instead of going to the appointment, she'd browsed through Saks, I. Miller's, and Bonwit's with stops at Harry Winston's and Tiffany's. "Slumming on Fifth Avenue," she called it.

He listened to her, nodding his head from time to time, but his mind was really on the robbery. He wondered idly what her reaction would be if he told her he was getting ready to try to pull off a multimillion-dollar heist.

She paused in the middle of a story about a bracelet she'd seen in Tiffany's, and said, "What's wrong,

Conant?" Her large brown eyes were studying him solemnly.

"Nothing," he said, smiling at her. "I'm listening."

She didn't believe him. She tightened her grip on his hand and leaned close, whispering into his ear.

He was still always surprised, but liked it, that when she was ready to make love, she said so. She had repeated the words "yoni" and "lingam" in her whisper. They had begun to use the Hindu sexual expressions as a joke after she brought a copy of the *Kama Sutra* for them to read together one day. In time, however, they had made the words a part of their own private language of love.

Conant paid the bill, and the hotel doorman got them a taxi. As they headed toward Conant's apartment on East 88th Street, east of Park Avenue, Holly pulled him to her, her hand insistently rubbing the inside of his thigh. Once again he was amazed at the sensual hold she had over him, had had over him since the first time he'd seen her.

The first time had been on a night three months earlier at the singles bar on First Avenue in the Sixties, called The Knickerbocker Pub, where Conant worked as bartender. A group of eight people, four men and four women, had come into the bar at about 12:45 A.M., and she was among them. He had noticed her right away, not because she was the only black in the group but because she was the most strikingly beautiful woman he had ever seen, of any color.

The eight of them had taken a table in front of the bar and ordered drinks. Since business was slow at the time, Conant came from behind the bar and helped the waitress serve the drinks. It was obvious that the group had been drinking before they arrived at The Knickerbocker, and the men especially showed it in loud talk and boisterous laughter. Conant hardly glanced at the others at the table, except for the man who was with her. The man was young, white, stocky, light-haired, and well-dressed. He was also quite drunk, his eyes bloodshot, his hands unsteady. A couple of times Conant heard her ask the man if they could leave but he kept shaking his head.

After half an hour and a couple of rounds of drinks, the party broke up, and Conant thought she would leave and he'd never see her again. Instead, when the other three couples started out the door, the stocky man with the light hair took her by the arm and pulled her, protesting, over to the bar, announcing that he wanted a nightcap. Conant could see her embarrassment as they sat on the bar stools and he served them more drinks, Scotch for the man, a Tom Collins for her. She barely sipped her drink while the man quickly downed his Scotch, ordered another, and then slid off the stool and staggered to the men's room at the back of the bar.

By then it was almost closing time, the lights had already been turned off out in front, and the waitresses were changing their clothes to leave. There were no other customers in the place. When the man didn't return after fifteen minutes, Holly—Conant didn't know her name then of course—looked up at him and said, "Please, could I ask you to go see if my husband's all right?"

Conant nodded, and went to the men's room where he found the man passed out on the tile floor, his back propped up against the wall. His clothing was soiled from the dirt and grime on the floor. Conant managed to get him to his feet and half-carried him back to the bar. The man was still only semiconscious and Conant said to her, "You'd better let me give you a hand in getting him home. It's closing time anyway, so it's all right if I leave."

"I would be very grateful," she said.

Conant left the man sprawled in a chair and went out and got a taxi. She helped Conant drag her husband out to the taxi and gave the driver an address on East 62nd Street, between Park and Lexington Avenues. When they got there, Conant saw it was a small, three-story town house. She paid the taxi driver and she and Conant carried her husband into the house and into a first-floor bedroom in the back. Conant took the man's coat and shirt off and left her to do the rest.

He waited in the living room for her to come out. It was a beautiful room, with a cool, elegant look, the walls and rugs stark white, the furniture modern and expensive. Huge pots of ferns stood at scattered points against the walls and more ferns spilled out of holders on the sides of the floor-to-ceiling windows, giving the room an air of serenity. Everywhere he looked he saw blown-up photographs of her in various poses. He was standing in front of one of the photographs—a portrait of her in a diaphanous Grecian gown—when she came into the room and thanked him for helping her. She offered him a drink or coffee, but he declined. Much as he'd have liked to stay, he could see how exhausted she appeared. As he was leaving, she asked his name and introduced herself as Holly Broome. Then Conant left, believing once more he'd never see her again.

It was several days after that night when she came back to the bar. Conant worked five seven-hour shifts a week at The Knickerbocker Pub, 12 noon to 7 P.M. on Tuesday, Wednesday, and Thursday; 7 P.M. to 2 A.M. Friday and Saturday, with Sunday and Monday his days off. She came in on a Wednesday, late in the afternoon, and sat at the bar drinking a Tom Collins until he was ready to leave.

When they were out on First Aveune, she surprised him by suddenly rising up on her tiptoes and kissing him.

"Take me home with you, Conant," she whispered. "Take me to your bed."

They made love that evening and almost every day after for the next month. He discovered that she had been born and raised in Southern California, in and around Hollywood. She was an only child. Both her parents were musicians. Her mother, Nola Jones, had been an almost-successful singer and had worked at various times with some of the big-name bands. Her father, Ernest Sandrin, played the clarinet, had been a member of two California symphony orchestras, and now was lead clarinet with one of the television network bands.

When Holly reached her teens she started modeling for fashion photographers. All of the early photographs of her had appeared only in black publications. Gary Broome, who was then working in Hollywood, was the first photographer to get her pictures in *Vogue, Harper's Bazaar* and other top fashion publications.

She had married Gary Broome when she was seventeen years old, and they had moved to New York, where both had continued to have successful careers. They had been married for five years which meant, Conant was surprised to learn, she was only twenty-two years old. She had all the poise, presence, and sophistication of a woman several years older.

She never spoke of her husband and Conant never asked. But sometimes when they were lying together after they had made love, she would murmur, "I feel it all with you, Conant. You make me feel it all."

He would caress her silently. He had no answer for her because by that time he was deeply involved in plans to rob the Museum, he didn't know what might happen after that, and life had taught him you can't have everything you want.

CHAPTER SIX

Conant's apartment always reminded Holly of a
dark, cool cave once the drapes were drawn blocking
out the sun—and the city—and the window air conditioner turned on. The apartment was on the first floor
of a well-preserved brownstone building on East
Eighty-First Street. The quarters were spacious, a large
living room with a big bay window across the front of
it, a dining area, kitchen, and bath. The furniture was
Mediterranean modern, the chairs and sofa of chrome
covered with vivid-colored velvet fabric, the coffee
table chrome, the dining table chrome and glass. There
was a huge fireplace set in one wall and surrounding it
were floor-to-ceiling bookcases filled mostly with art
books. On the walls were a collection of modern art
prints, a delicate Matisse watercolor, a bold Picasso, a
somber Buffet, among others. Oriental rugs, laid over
the waxed hardwood floors, led like a series of bridges
from the front of the apartment to the rear.

Now, on the August day after they had come from
the Stanhope Hotel, Conant sat on the side of the bed,
fully clothed, while she began to undress. There was
a ritual they followed preparatory to making love. As
he watched, she unzipped her sharkskin dress and
stripped down to her bra and panties. She carefully
folded the dress and frilly slip and placed them on the
chest of drawers, then stepped out of her high-heeled
shoes and peeled off her stockings. She turned to face

him as she unsnapped her bra and it fell away to reveal her high, thrusting breasts with the pink-tipped nipples erect. Her body was firm and a smooth satin black, except for the pink buds of her breasts and the matching pink polish on her toenails.

Still wearing her sheer white panties, she came and stood between his legs. He pressed his face into her flesh, running his lips across her stomach. She bent forward and cupped the back of his head with her hand, guiding his mouth to one, then the other, of her breasts. He continued until he could feel her body begin to quiver under his tongue. Then she pushed him gently away and began to undress him slowly, coat, tie, shirt, T-shirt, shoes, socks and finally, trousers. Kneeling, she carefully worked his shorts down over his hips and legs, and began to stroke him. He stopped her, after a time, reaching out a hand and pulling her to her feet. Her eyes were on his when she stood in front of him. She hooked her fingers in the elastic of her panties and wiggled out of them, letting them flutter from her fingers to the bed. He encircled her naked thighs with his arms and buried his face in her body as they fell together across the bed.

Afterwards, she lay with her head against his chest and he held her close to him with one arm around her waist. She felt peaceful and secure, as she always did when they'd made love and he held her like this. She listened to his heart beat and reflected again upon the vagaries of the human psyche. How was it possible for her to feel so close to this man, so much a part of her—as no other man had ever been—when they'd only known each other for such a short time? How was it possible she had felt the stirrings of this same emotion about him on the very first night they met?

Even before she had told him all about herself, she had sensed he already knew her, as she knew him. All the facts they'd exchanged about themselves were just words. She knew him instinctively, even before he told her the details of his life; that he had been born and raised in Baltimore, where his father had been em-

ployed as a porter at the May Company department
store and his mother had been a domestic worker. He
did not find it easy to talk, not because he was ashamed
of his parents' background—as contrasted with her
parents, for example—but because, she sensed, he did
not feel comfortable talking about himself. And, as a
matter of fact, he had had a reasonably happy upbring-
ing, full of love. Both his parents were now dead but
she could hear the love he had had for them in his
voice when, on infrequent occasions, she could get him
to talk about himself.

He also, sometimes, had talked of his grandparents,
his father's parents, who had lived with them in Baltimore and who had, too, since died. The Conant family
had originally come from Louisiana where Conant's
great-great-grandmother had been a slave. "I reckon,"
he had once said to Holly, in one of the few references
he had ever made to the color of his skin, "there must
have been one of those Frenchmen in the woodpile
with my great-great1grandma and that's where the
family got the fancy name." They had laughed together.

Even though he had been willing to tell her that
much about himself, all the really important things
about him she had to find out for herself by rummaging
through his apartment. He never objected and seemed
amused when she dug out his scholastic records and
found he had been a straight-A student all through
high school, had received a partial scholarship to
Columbia University, and had graduated with a B.A.,
with a major in Psychology, a minor in Fine Arts. He
had also spent an additional year on a second scholarship at Yale University. He had wanted to get his
Master's in Psychology but found he couldn't afford to
continue his studies. As it was, to get his B.A. while
attending Yale, he had had to work nights as a waiter
and sometimes filled in as bartender, first in Harlem
and later in New Haven. His parents had also helped
him. His mother had died when he was in his last year
at Columbia, and the following year, while he was

attending Yale, his father died. Meanwhile, there was a war in Vietnam—sooner or later he'd probably have been drafted—so he enlisted in the Air Force.

Holly had uncovered all his military papers, too, the orders sending him, because of his high IQ, to the Air Force Navigation School in San Antonio, Texas, his commission as a lieutenant when he completed his officer's training, his assignment as a navigator to Southeast Asia.

Once, when she asked him why, after all he had proved he could accomplish in his life, he was willing to settle for a job as a bartender, he had looked at her quizzically for a long time before he answered, "Holly, I've never been uptight about being black, like some of the—ah—brothers, as they say. It's never been a big thing with me. Oh, sure, when somebody puts me down simply because of the color of my skin, I burn. It's unjust. But I've always tried to be philosophical about it. A long time ago I observed, hell, the world is full of other people, some of them with white skins, who suffer some of the same kind of injustice, if you stop to think about it. People whose physical appearances work against them because they were born with mean, pinched faces, or ungainly bodies or just plain ugly as sin on a broad daylight Sunday morning. They're not liked on sight, either, and more often than not they got the short end of the stick whatever they try to do. Still, some of them do well in life, and others fail. You understand?"

Holly smiled. "I guess so."

"What I'm trying to say," Conant went on earnestly, "is I thought it was up to me to overcome the handicap of color on my own if I wanted to live well in this life. So, I tried to do it by the rules as I saw them—I worked damn hard to get through school and college and to get that Air Force Commission. And then you know what?"

He paused and smiled crookedly. "When I came back from the service and tried to get a job, it appeared that all I qualified for was the position of glorified office boy or clerk or some such meaningless and miserable occupation. Good joke, huh? The rules didn't work for me. My B.A., my training and background as an Air Force officer, counted for nothing."

"And that made you angry?" Holly asked.

Conant shook his head. "Oh, not happy, but amused, too. The whole thing is so ironic. Here I am with all this valuable education and experience to offer, and the only really decent-paying job I can get is a bartender."

"But you have a comfortable place here," Holly said, indicating the apartment.

"Comfortable, yeah," he answered. "But this is a long way from what I want out of life. I want to enjoy the luxuries of life, not just the comforts. I'm going to, too," he added vehemently. "You see, I've learned that if you're black, like me, and want what I want, you've always got to have an edge working for you. I've got an edge going for me now and one of these days soon—"

He paused and she felt an involuntary shiver run through her. She knew then he was going to do something, something she didn't want to know. Something she was afraid to know, afraid for him, afraid of losing him. She asked no more, saying only, "I don't care what you do, Conant. I think you can do anything you want. Only remember, whatever you do, wherever you go, I want you if you want me."

He had kissed her and laughed. "Oh, Holly," he had said, "you're beautiful. Can't you tell when I'm just dreaming out loud?"

She had looked at his eyes, seen that they were veiled, and wasn't fooled. But she knew that she mustn't press him, mustn't cling to him, or she'd lose him.

Now, lying with her body pleasurably draped over his, she once again felt a shiver run through her; she had sensed a difference in him this day as soon as she had met him. Whatever it was he was going to do, it was going to be soon.

She raised herself and took him by the shoulder to pull him over on top of her again. He had just started to turn his body when they heard a hammering on the front door of the apartment. He swung up and away from her, his feet on the floor, and standing in one swift, fluid motion. The hammering continued and now they could hear a muffled voice shouting outside the door!"

"Oh, my God!" she said. "It's Gary. That's Gary out there. My husband. Oh, Conant, I'm sorry. I'm so sorry. I didn't want it to be like this."

Conant nodded his head. "It's all right," he said quietly. "Get your things together and go into the bathroom. I'll have to open the door before he breaks it down." He pulled on his shorts and trousers and walked barefooted to the front room. He stood at the door, waiting until she darted into the bath, her clothes in her arms. The pounding and shouting continued. Conant unlocked the door and pulled it open. Broome hurled himself into the room. He shoved the door back savagely into Conant's left shoulder, numbing it.

Broome's face was contorted with anger. "Where is she? Where's Holly?" he raged. He tried to push past into the apartment and Conant grabbed him by the arm, pushing him into the front of the living room.

"Take it easy," Conant said. "Who are you? What do you want?" He was still holding Broome by the arm with both hands.

"You—ba—bastard!" Broome yelled, the words exploding out of him. "You know what I want! Holly, *my wife!*" He wrestled free from Conant's grasp, and took a couple of steps toward the back of the apartment, lurching as he went from the intensity of his emotion.

Conant sprang after him, flung his arms around Broome's waist, and swung him around toward the living room. "Cool it, man," Conant said, his voice steady. He still thought he could reason with Broome. "Just for Christ's sake, take it easy. There's nobody here but me."

Instead of answering, Broome drove an elbow into Conant's ribs, breaking Conant's hold.

Conant shook his head disgustedly. "Oh, God, man. Knock it off. This is stupid."

For a moment Broome stood still and Conant could see the embarrassment on his face. Conant thought that, finally, he had gotten through to the other man and Broome had begun to recognize how ridiculous the situation was. Then, suddenly, Broome turned and took two quick steps forward. Conant's hands were down at his side when Broome threw two hard punches, catching Conant high on the cheekbones and snapping his head back. Conant, momentarily dazed, raised his hands to protect his face. Broome rushed at him, legs working like pistons, trying to knee Conant in the groin.

Conant swung away and turned. He had been trying to hold himself in check. Now, with a hoarse roar, he let himself go, seized by a murderous fury. Head down, he flung himself at Broome, butting him backwards. Broome stumbled against the coffee table, overturned it, and landed sprawled on the floor. Broome was afraid now, the fear was there in his face. Conant could see the fear, but that didn't stop him. As Broome got to his feet, Conant circled around the table, fists upraised.

Broome tried to retreat. Conant, roaring again, hit him hard with a left, then a right, and another left. Broome was cursing, his head bobbing from side to side, as he threw wild punches at Conant. Conant hit him again before Broome managed to grab him in a bear hug and both fell, grappling, to the floor. Broome began screaming curses in a high-pitched, hysterical voice when Conant managed to pin him to the floor, his legs straddling Broome's chest. Conant dodged the fingers jabbing at his eyes while his own hands probed for the fleshy white throat beneath him. All he wanted to do was lock his hands around that neck and squeeze and squeeze until the screams stopped.

Conant was so intent upon his murderous business that he saw nothing, heard nothing, in the room until a blow struck him hard across the top of his bare back.

"What the fu—?" he started to snarl, turned and

saw the two uniformed policemen standing behind him.
They had come in through the open door and stood,
eyes narrowed, billy clubs in their hands. Both policemen were young, and, Conant could see, edgy.

Conant released Broome and stood on shaking legs
even before one of the cops ordered, "Break it up!"

Broome, still full of anger, came up from the floor
and tried to rush at Conant. One of the cops stepped
between them, restraining Broome.

"What's going on here?" the other policeman demanded of Conant.

Conant shook his head. "It's a mistake," he said.
"It's nothing."

The cop took a step toward him. "What do you
mean, it's nothing? We got a call from the other
tenants in this building. They thought there was a
murder taking place in here. Whose apartment is this,
anyway?"

"It's mine," Conant said. He nodded toward Broome.
"This gentleman came here by mistake. He must have
thought I was someone else."

The cop swung around to Broome. "That right?"

Broome's face was still flushed and he was breathing
rapidly. "I was told my wife was here," he said. "I'm
still not sure she isn't."

What the hell, Conant thought, he was *told* Holly
was here? That meant he must have had somebody
tailing her.

The cop who was doing all the questioning gave
Conant a hard look. "Anybody else here?" Conant
shook his head.

"You mind if we take a look around?"

Conant shook his head again.

The one cop went toward the back of the apartment. When Broome tried to follow him, the other
cop stopped him. Conant saw the first policeman go
into the bedroom and then come out and open the bathroom door and look inside. After a moment, he came
back to the living room, shaking his head. "There's
nobody else here," he said.

"I don't believe it," Broome said, still flushed. I want to see for myself."

The policeman looked at Conant. "Any objections?"

"Let him look," Conant said.

Broome searched the back of the apartment, the bedroom and bath, and returned, still looking angry but saying nothing. The bathroom door was now wide open, and Conant could see the window in the bathroom raised a few inches from the sill. Good girl, he thought, knowing that Holly must have dressed, climbed out the window into the alleyway behind, and fled.

The officer who had done all the talking since the two policemen had arrived at the apartment took a summons book from his hip pocket. He looked from Conant to Broome. "Either of you gentlemen want to prefer charges against the other?"

Conant spoke quickly, "It was all just a mistake, officer. No harm done. Why don't we just forget the whole thing?"

"How about you?" the policeman asked Broome.

"No, no," Broome said. "It's all right. Forget it." He was dabbing at his bleeding lip with a handkerchief.

The policeman took down both their names and the two cops left, trailed by Gary Broome who threw one final scowl at Conant on his way out.

Conant slammed and locked the door, stepped back and, in a futile gesture, gave all three of them the finger. His groin hurt like hell, and his legs were still trembling when he straightened the coffee table and the rugs in the living room and then went into the bedroom. He kept shaking his head mechanically. Goddamn, he could easily have killed Broome if the police hadn't arrived when they did. That crazy bastard, Broome. He started to make the rumpled bed and found Holly's panties still lying under the top sheet. Great, he thought, just great. If the cop or Broome had spotted them, his ass would really have been in a sling. He tossed the panties on the top of the bookcase. He took a shower and dressed. Then he dragged his suitcase out of the closet.

As he headed out the door to go catch a train at Grand Central Station, he was disgusted with himself. Here he was, with everything set to pull off a multi-million-dollar heist which would set him up for life, and he'd been careless enough to blow the whole thing. Christ, he'd come close to being run in by the cops, and why hadn't it ever occurred to him that Broome might have had somebody following Holly? That scared him; the thought that somebody could have been secretly observing him while he was making preparations for the robbery. Son-of-a-bitch, he was supposed to be so smart, and here he'd almost blown a four-million-dollar deal over a piece of tail!

CHAPTER SEVEN

When Joe Conant arrived at the house in Bronxville, a couple of hours later, carrying his suitcase and two shopping bags, he found the four men in the living room. They had been holed up in the house for the past five days. Outside, there was still light in the late afternoon sky but the room was in shadows, it was hot, and the air was hazy with cigarette, cigar, and pipe smoke. A television set over in a corner was on but the sound was turned down and nobody was watching it. The men were gathered around a table playing poker, as they had been for most of their waking hours during the past five days and nights.

There was Vince De Angelo, who was sitting with his shirt unbuttoned down to his waist and his sleeves rolled up over the hard, bulging muscles of his olive-skinned arms. He had a strong face with big bones, framed by a great shaggy mop of very black hair. Although he was a burly man, with a chest that puffed out like the breast of a pouter pigeon, his movements were quick with little waste motion, giving evidence of a body which was disciplined and physically well-coordinated. Next was Eddie Chilton, tall, slim, and wearing an undershirt, with a towel draped around his neck. Chilton's face was long and narrow, all planes and hollows, and he had pale blue eyes which blinked constantly, as if he was surprised by all he saw and heard. The third man was George "Red" Hager. He

was sitting at the table bare-chested, a big, rangy man
with red hair worn long and curling up the back of his
neck in the mod style. Scraggly red bristles showed
around his unshaved jaw. Next to Hager was Augie
Kroger. Despite Kroger's square, stocky frame which
was ample enough to accommodate plenty of flesh, he
still had the beginnings of a potbelly beneath the T-shirt
which was stuck to his body with sweat, and his cheeks
had begun to balloon out under his bushy thatch of
straw-colored hair.

Conant, looking around at the four men for a moment, was struck by the fact that they were an unlikely
crew to be planning the robbery of the Metropolitan
Museum of Art.

De Angelo, Hager, Chilton, and Kroger had been
friends for most of their lives. They had grown up
together in Bronxville and had had in common a lower-
middle-class background in a predominantly upper-mid-
dle-class suburb of New York City. They hadn't been
really underprivileged as children—Vince De Angelo's
father owned a one-man barbershop, Red Hager's parents ran a bakery, Eddie Chilton's father was a steam-
fitter and all of Augie Kroger's male relatives worked
for the railroad—but, nevertheless, they had been
aware that they did not possess the material resources
of their more affluent classmates and acquaintances in
the town.

It was this knowledge which bound them together in
friendship and led them into their few rebellious acts as
juveniles, for truancy, once for stealing a car for joy-
riding, and several narrow escapes when shoplifting
fruit and candy from the corner grocery store or items
from the hardware store and five-and-dime. When they
were older, they had always gone on dates together
while in high school and after they graduated. None
of them went to college, and all of them went to work
as soon as they finished high school. De Angelo and
Red Hager got a job working together for a construction company in New York City, Eddie Chilton, who

had always been a car nut—he was the one who had egged them on to steal a car to joyride when they were youngsters—was employed at a local garage, and Augie Kroger had gone to work as a maintenance man in a Manhattan luxury apartment building.

Once grown, the seeds of discontent planted in them in their childhoods, of somehow having been short-changed, remained just below the surface of their lives. They still talked from time to time of striking it rich one day and sometimes in bull sessions fantasized about executing some enormous and daring caper which would set them up in great wealth. But it was all just talk and they all knew it.

Vince De Angelo was the only one of the four who married. The girl had been his high-school sweetheart, a shapely blonde named Betty Folger who, as it turned out, had been everybody's high-school sweetheart, and who hadn't been able to change her ways even though she and Vince were married. After the divorce, he had joined the Air Force and was sent to Southeast Asia. When he returned, he had gone back to his job with the construction company, and had resumed his friend-ship with the other three.

Standing in the living room, still holding the shopping bags and his suitcase, Joe Conant was delighted when he learned that the poker game the four were playing had turned crazy a couple of days ago after starting out at the usual, modest, nickel, dime and quarter stakes. By common agreement, two days earlier, the players had upped the stakes to one hundred, five hundred, and a thousand dollars, using IOUs—against the money each of them expected to collect from the robbery—to cover their bets. Frequently after that, a single pot would total more than fifty thousand dollars, all in IOUs. Conant wanted them in precisely that psychological frame of mind, thinking big, for the robbery.

Conant placed the two shopping bags on the table and said, "Come on, you guys, clear all that crap out of

the way. I want you to start learning to live with a little
class." He took from the bags several bottles of chilled
champagne, jars of caviar, and a couple of loaves of
black bread, and spread them out on the table.

There were cheers and whistles of appreciation from
the other four men. They put the cards and their IOUs
away, and Vince De Angelo went out and got a table-
cloth, a knife, and some glasses. Champagne corks
popped and all five of them began to eat and drink.

"You check the Museum today, Joe?" De Angelo
asked.

Conant made a circle with his thumb and forefinger.
"Everything's A-OK. We go as planned."

Conant and De Angelo had met in the service, at a
U.S. air base on the Gulf of Thailand. Conant was a
lieutenant and navigator aboard a B-52, De Angelo
was a master sergeant in charge of the ground crew
servicing the base's big bombers. It was the winter of
1972–73, an unreal period at the air base. There were
rumors that a peace treaty was about to be signed and
most of the men at the base believed the war was almost over. All everybody wanted to do was get the hell
home. At the same time, the B-52s were flying around-
the-clock bombing missions over Hanoi which, rumor
had it, was the most heavily fortified city in the history
of warfare.

Many of the planes were being shot down, and there
were few which returned to the base unmarked. There
was a lot of goofing off around the base since most of
the men thought a peace treaty would soon be signed,
but De Angelo worked his crew hard, sometimes two
and three days and nights without sleep.

Conant, unlike the other officers, frequently spent a
couple of hours after each flight going over his plane
with the ground crew. Soon he and De Angelo fell into
the habit of having a beer together in the base PX, or
a drink in Conant's quarters after they'd finished checking out the B-52.

De Angelo was pleased but puzzled that Conant

sought him out for a companion. De Angelo had never had a black man for a friend and, especially, had never had for a friend a man like Conant. On the base, the lieutenant had a reputation for knowing his way around and being in on things, a very cool guy. There was a lot of illegal action going on at that period, drug dealing and black-market activities, and for a time De Angelo thought Conant might be involved. Later Conant was to tell him he had had plenty of opportunities to get in on the drug- and black-market traffic, but that he considered it "sucker stuff." What the lieutenant was doing, De Angelo discovered, was considerably less unsavory. Conant ran the base gambling pool, making book on the sports events, football and hockey, back in the States which were televised via satellite to the base. He also handled a numbers game. The tonnage amount of bombs dropped by B-52s over the North was posted at the base each day. In Conant's pool, the winning numbers had to coincide with the last three digits of the daily posted tonnage figure.

At one point, when the raids were temporarily suspended, Conant arranged with the base C.O. for a couple of passes for him and De Angelo for a weekend leave in Saigon. Conant had explained: "When it's your ass up there in the stratosphere, depending on a lot of gadgets to get you down safely, it's comforting to know, sergeant, that they're all in good working order. You're a dependable man. You haven't let me down yet. I owe you."

On that weekend, after a tour of the bars and cafes along Saigon's Tu Do Street where they picked up a couple of Vietnamese girls and spent the night with them, De Angelo discovered Conant had a proposition for him. Over breakfast the next morning, in the roof-top restaurant of the Caravelle Hotel, Conant told De Angelo that one of the enlisted men, a corporal who had helped him run the gambling pool, was being shipped home. He asked De Angelo if he'd replace the corporal and offered him a quarter of the total take, which usually averaged out to somewhere around a thousand dollars a week, a part of which Conant explained he had to pay off to officers above him for permission to run the pool.

De Angelo accepted, and their friendship began. They were only in Southeast Asia for another couple of months, but it was enough for De Angelo to sock away a few thousand dollars for which he was grateful to Conant. By that time they had exchanged some information about their backgrounds and Conant had heard all about De Angelo's three friends back in Bronxville.

Sixty days later when the two of them got out of the service, De Angelo went back to the construction company where he'd worked before he'd joined the Air Force and Conant settled in New York City, made the rounds looking for a decent job, and finally went to work as a bartender at The Knickerbocker Pub. During the next several months Conant and De Angelo talked a couple of times over the phone but they saw each other only once when, one night, De Angelo stopped in the bar for a drink and to say hello to Conant.

The Knickerbocker Pub was a popular place, and Conant enjoyed working there. As was the case in most of the other singles bars on First Avenue in the Sixties, the bar was usually filled from late afternoon to the 2 A.M. closing with unattached men and women looking for a companion to share a drink or an evening or a bed. Conant himself had a variety of girls, of almost every description, shade, and nationality, to choose from on any given night. Frequently, he left the bar with a different girl for every night of the week for long periods at a time.

In addition, his earnings averaged between five and six hundred dollars a week—a portion of it in tips which he didn't intend to report on his income tax— so he was able to rent and furnish a nice apartment and live reasonably comfortably. Hell, he chided himself from time to time, he had a pretty good life even if somewhere in the back of his mind he was rankled by the knowledge that he'd tried to play fair by the rules of success and had failed and that the color of his skin was a factor in that failure. He had no intention, he had determined long since, of settling for a job as bartender, and he knew that sooner or later he had to find another way to get what he wanted, and that it was probably going to have to be something which was illegal.

One big score was what he wanted. A chance to get his hands on enough money so he could hightail it to some place—like the Costa del Sol, for example—and spend the rest of his life thumbing his nose at the world. All it took, he knew, was putting together the right combination and a willingness to run a certain amount of risk. It was a matter of taking advantage of the right opportunity.

Still, despite his fantasy of pulling off some far-out caper one day, Conant would never in a million years have thought of trying to rob the Metropolitan Museum of Art if he hadn't spotted an item in *The New York Times* a few months later. The news story stated that construction would begin soon in the Metropolitan to renovate a wing of the museum. The reconstructed wing would, when completed, house a recently acquired collection of Mexican art.

The news item intrigued Conant. Christ, he knew at first hand from his visits there dating back to the days when he was a student at Columbia that the Museum was filled with art treasures worth millions of dollars. Now suppose, he thought, you were able to place a man—Vince De Angelo, for instance—inside as one of the construction workers. That would give you that all-important edge you always had to have. The problem then would be: how do you use him to help you heist some of the art?

As familiar as Conant was with the interior of the Museum, he returned there frequently during the following several days to study the interior, now with a different motive in mind. What he was seeking was a way to pull off the caper, using Vince De Angelo inside, without risking damage to the paintings—which he loved—and without employing weapons so there'd be no violence or bloodshed; in brief, what he wanted was a plan to commit a crime in which, as he conceived it, there would be no real victim. It was a challenge he considered to be as much a test of his brain and wits as a method of getting even for all the opportunities he felt he'd been denied.

It took him another week to put the plan together, slowly and painstakingly, until he felt all the elements were in place. At the end of the week he phoned Vince De Angelo and told him he wanted to talk to him. That Sunday they met in Central Park and took a stroll.

Conant showed De Angelo the *Times* clipping and then asked quietly, "Vince, is there any way you could arrange things so you can get in on this construction work, get inside the Museum?"

De Angelo looked at him curiously and then answered slowly, "Yeah, sure, I guess so, Joe. There are a couple of paisans in the union could swing it for me easy. What'd you have in mind?"

Conant gave him a broad wink. "I figure maybe we can get us a deal going, like we had in the service. Only this time maybe we'll strike it rich. Very rich."

They were standing high on a slope in Central Park overlooking Belvedere Lake where, below, groups of children sailed their toy boats in the water.

De Angelo looked around them carefully to see no one was near before he asked, "You talking about trying to knock over the Museum, Joe?"

"Would that scare you, Vince?" Conant asked carefully.

"It depends upon the risk," De Angelo answered, "and the stakes. You got a plan?"

"I don't know yet," Conant said. "First, I have to know if you'll be able to do what I want done once you're working inside." Before De Angelo could speak again, Conant added, "What I'm talking about is a hiding place in there nobody'd know about, where we could stash some stuff, and large enough to conceal one or two men for a short time. I was thinking with

all the renovation that'll be going on in there, maybe
you could find a way to put up a false wall, or section
of wall, which would serve our purpose. You know
what I mean?"

De Angelo nodded. "It could probably be done. Of
course I'd have to see what the situation was in there."
He paused, and then asked, "You don't want to tell
me any more of it, Joe?"

"There's not much point in discussing the rest of it,"
Conant said, "until we get this settled first. The whole
plan rests upon knowing whether or not we can bring
off this part of it. If we can, then the risk should be
minimal and the stakes high."

"I don't know what you got in mind," De Angelo
said, "but, what the hell, I'm willing to see what I can
do. Let me try to work it out, get inside on the job,
and then report back to you. Okay?"

Conant nodded. "Okay."

"There's one other thing, Joe," De Angelo added.
"My friend, Red Hager, and I always work together.
Is it all right if he goes to work in there with me? He's
absolutely trustworthy."

"Yeah, that's all right," Conant agreed. "As a matter of fact if the plan works out, we're going to need
some other guys in on it. We'll talk about that later."

It was toward the end of the following week before
De Angelo phoned Conant and said he and Red Hager
had gotten hired to work on the renovation of the
Museum. At the beginning of the next week Conant
received an excited phone call from De Angelo saying
he had something important to tell him.

The two men met that evening in Conant's apartment. Conant could tell De Angelo was all charged up.

"I think I've gone you one better on what you were
looking for inside the Museum, Joe," De Angelo said,
pacing. "Look, what we're doing up there is knocking
down some of the walls and ceilings over in a wing
of the building and putting up new ones. So Red Hager
and I have been poking around, trying to figure out how
we'd put up this false wall of yours." He paused and

shook his head. "While hanging around in there, we discovered the damnedest thing. We found that a panel in a section of back wall in the alcove where we're working slides back and forth if you push it just the right way. Behind the panel is a hollow space that probably used to be part of an air shaft. What do you think of that?"

"Yeah," Conant said, "I like it. Go on."

"The space behind the panel is, I'd say, oh, seven feet high, a half dozen feet long, and four, five feet deep. It looks like it's been covered over for a hundred years and been forgotten. When the panel section's in place, you'd never know there was a hollow area behind it."

Conant grinned. "Sounds good, Vince. Plenty good. I think we're in business."

De Angelo sat down abruptly, a worried look on his face. "I still can't figure how you think we can get anything out of the Museum, Joe. You do know, don't you, they're got so many guards up there around the clock that they're practically falling over each other."

"I'm not worried about that," Conant said. "But what I do want to know is do they search you when you go in and out?"

"They look us over pretty good when we leave," De Angelo said. "Not so much when we arrive, though. Sometimes we have to bring in materials for the job. They don't pay any attention then."

"So you could smuggle some stuff in without any trouble and hide it behind this panel, and a couple of guys could hide in there briefly, right?"

"Right," De Angelo nodded. "No problem there."

Conant sat thinking for a moment. De Angelo watched him, then rose and began pacing again and finally, "Listen, Joe, to pull a job like this, won't we have to know an awful lot of stuff about what goes on inside there, with the guards and all, I mean?"

"No, I don't think so," Conant said. "Not the way I figure things. Not if you can get what I want in there and hide it."

De Angelo walked away for a few paces, turned and came back. He was still worried.

"Stop sweating it, Vince," Conant said. "We're not going to pull the job today."

"But I thought about something else, Joe," De Angelo said nervously. "I mean, they're probably bound to have some kind of electronic security system up there we don't know about. Some kind of business where if any of the paintings are moved, an alarm goes off."

"The way I've planned this thing," Conant said, "that's not going to make any difference."

"Then for God's sakes, Joe, come on, tell me what we're going to do!"

"What we're going to do," Conant answered, obviously enjoying himself, "is grab ourselves about three or four million dollars' worth of paintings and ransom them back to the Museum. We're going to need help on this—there's another small job has to be pulled before we knock over the Museum—and I think your friends, Hager, Chilton, and Kroger, might work out just fine. If you think they'd be interested. Incidentally, I calculate we'll get a cut of three-quarters of a million each."

De Angelo blinked rapidly before he managed to say hoarsely, "I think they'd be interested."

"Good." Conant leaned forward. "Now here's what we're going to do—"

He spoke rapidly, telling De Angelo the plan in detail. He'd worked out every step of the robbery, from the snatching of the paintings, through their getaway, to the method they'd use to collect the ransom money, and he even explained how they'd do it all without ever being seen close enough by anyone to be identified.

When he had finished, he looked at De Angelo's stunned face.

De Angelo just nodded his head in speechless admiration. Son-of-a-bitch, he thought, Conant had really done it, had put together a brilliant plan which seemed foolproof.

During the next four weeks the men were busy. As part of the plan, they rented a small house in Bronx-

ville. They'd need it as a hideout later and, meanwhile,
it was here that De Angelo, Hager, Chilton, and Kroger
worked on some of the materials which De Angelo and
Hager smuggled into the Museum and hid behind the
hollow panel. Conant and De Angelo bankrolled their
expenses from the money they'd brought back with
them from the service.

At the beginning of their discussion of the robbery,
Conant and De Angelo had agreed that in order to cut
down the possibility of surveillance by anyone who
might accidentally stumble onto their activities, the
two of them would continue to meet alone. Conant
planned and acted as overseer of the operation while
De Angelo served as go-between with the other three,
passing on orders and instructions.

All five men met only once, just after De Angelo,
Hager, Chilton, and Kroger successfully pulled off the
one small job that had to be done before the Museum
caper, and De Angelo sensed his three friends were
cool toward taking direct orders from Conant. To them,
Conant was just another black man; they of course had
never known him as an officer in the service as De
Angelo had. De Angelo decided it had been a wise
decision for him to act as go-between and felt certain
he could keep the other three men in line despite their
reservations about Conant.

They'd set the robbery for the week after De Angelo
and Hager finished working at the Museum. Conant
anticipated that the materials hidden behind the panel
might be uncovered once De Angelo and Hager were
gone from there. If that happened, the police would
probably begin to put the pieces of the plot together
and, sooner or later come looking for the two men.

For that reason, De Angelo and Hager quit their
jobs with the construction company on the last day
they worked at the Museum, a Friday. Since it was
known around Bronxville that Chilton and Kroger were
such good friends of the other two—and would almost
certainly be questioned if the police began an investigation—they also gave up their jobs on the same day.

The four went into hiding in the small house they'd rented and were holed up there when Conant arrived on that late afternoon in August.

"Okay," Conant said briskly now, as they finished up their champagne and caviar, "since we've all gorged ourselves, there's work to be done."

He reached again into one of the shopping bags and pulled out a thick booklet titled, *Guide to the Metropolitan Museum of Art*. "What we're going to do now is decide exactly which paintings we're going to steal. And then we're going to figure out just how big a bundle three million, seven hundred and fifty thousand dollars makes in fifty- and hundred-dollar bills."

CHAPTER EIGHT

At a few minutes before 11 P.M. that evening, Deputy Chief Inspector Max Kauffman let himself in the door of his apartment. He was home considerably earlier than he had anticipated. The apartment was on the sixteenth floor of a building at 31 Sutton Place South overlooking the East River. Since his wife had left for Arizona that afternoon, both children were away for the summer, and the servants, a Swedish couple who had worked for them for ten years, were taking their vacation at the same time his wife would be gone, the apartment was silent and deserted.

Once inside he loosened his tie but kept his coat on. The apartment was cool, from the building's central air-conditioning system, in contrast to the hot, muggy city streets below. He couldn't remember the last time he had been completely alone in the apartment, and tonight it somehow seemed slightly ghostly and unfamiliar with most of the furnishings draped in slipcovers. He was still carrying his attaché case containing the file he had picked up at his office that afternoon as he went through the rooms turning on the lights. There were fourteen rooms in all, including the servants' quarters, and all the windows faced south or east so there was a sweeping view of the river from every room.

After he had completed his inspection, he got out a bottle of Chivas Regal, a glass, and a bucket of ice from the pantry bar in the hall, and took them to his den. He put the attaché case on his desk and made himself a drink.

As he stood, taking a sip of his drink, he could hear the wail of a siren and, soon, another somewhere in the distance outside the closed windows of the apartment. Sirens were a familiar sound day and night in this section of the city, in the East Fifties. First and Second Avenues to the west and FDR Drive to the east, just below the building, were main arteries for emergency vehicles moving uptown or down. He remembered that when he was a small boy living with his parents on Park Avenue, his mother always got nervous and upset at the sound of sirens, since to her they meant someone was in distress. He himself had always thought of them as signaling that there was help on the way. From the pitch and direction of the sounds he heard now, Max Kauffman determined they were fire engines—he couldn't decide whether there were two or three—speeding up First Avenue.

He sat at his desk, opened his attaché case, and took out the file, but didn't open it. He should begin working on his contingency report for the Commissioner but instead he finished his drink and made himself another. He knew what was troubling him. In addition to the unwanted assignment handed to him by the Commissioner, not much else had gone right for him that day.

After leaving Police Headquarters that afternoon and returning to the 16th Precinct to pick up the contingency plan file, he had been quite late meeting his wife. When his official limousine pulled in front of their apartment building, the hired Cadillac from the Carey Limousine Service which had been ordered to take him and wife to JFK was already parked in front of the building and the doormen were loading his wife's bags into the trunk of the car. Max Kauffman never used his police limousine for personal business if it involved other members of his family.

After Max Kauffman dismissed his driver, Detective
Henry Lukin, for the night, he could see his wife, Belle,
waiting anxiously under the canopy at the entrance to
the building. She smiled and waved when she spotted
him. He hurried across the sidewalk and kissed her.

"I was so afraid you wouldn't get here on time," his
wife murmured. "I don't think I could have gone if you
hadn't."

"You should have known I'd be here," he said,
helping her into the car. He would have liked to have
taken his attaché case up to the apartment, but he
didn't want to delay her any longer so he slid into the
seat beside her and nodded to the chauffeur.

Belle Kauffman was wearing a powder-blue Chanel
suit which the Inspector noticed was very becoming on
her. She had had her hair done earlier in the day in a
semi-bouffant. Her hair was still mostly black and was
expertly frosted so the blonde streaks blended with and
concealed the strands of gray. Looking at her face he
could see traces of the dark, luminous beauty she had
had at twenty, when they'd married. Her once-willowy
form had disappeared into the flesh she'd put on in the
twenty-seven years since then but she remained a hand-
some figure of a woman. Her legs, especially, in sheer
pantyhose, were still shapely, and her hips rounded,
rather than heavy.

As they headed out toward the airport, she talked
of the children and his family and her family. Their son,
Lawrence, was taking summer courses at Berkeley, and
the daughter, Deborah, was at a girls' camp in the
Berkshires. Belle reminded him he was supposed to
have dinner with his parents on Friday night—as if he
could forget after twenty-seven years of Friday-night
dinners with them—and she asked him to phone her
mother and father at least a few times while she was
away.

He let her talk on. He could see she was nervous,
and he kept smiling at her reassuringly. He knew she
was upset both because she would be gone from home

for ten days and because of the plane trip. Even though
they made twice-a-year flights to Europe, she had
never lost her fear of flying.

"You look tired, Max dear," she said at one point.
"I wish you'd try to get more rest." She reached for
his hand and accidentally touched his lap. She quickly
snatched her hand away and turned to stare out the car
window. There had been a time when her reaction
would have angered or hurt him. At that moment, however, it seemed only natural. After all, it had been ten
years or more since they'd been physically intimate.
Not that they had ever been close, physically, even
from the beginning of their marriage.

The trouble had started, in fact, on their wedding
night. They had been married at her parents' house in
Great Neck, Long Island, in the afternoon. They
planned to leave the next day on a two-week honeymoon cruise to Bermuda and had spent that night in
New York City in a room at the Sherry-Netherland
Hotel. Belle had been a virgin, as he had known, but
he hadn't been prepared for the experience of that
night. He was not as knowledgeable about female
anatomy as he became later in life, but he had been
gentle, patient, understanding with her for hours that
night, and still she had remained closed to him sensually, sexually, in a way that alternately frustrated and
enraged him. She, too, was distressed and in tears.

The problem was that her flesh had shriveled when
she looked at him as he knelt above her on the side of
the bed and discarded his silk robe. Stripped, he was
transformed into a total stranger in front of her eyes.
His body, which she had never seen before, was completely covered by a mass of—to her eyes—bestial-
looking black hair. She had never thought so much
hair ever grew on a human body. His chest was matted
with it and it was thick on his arms, and under them,
and on his legs and there was a dense, dark tangle of it
solidly covering his groin. She was repelled by the sight
and bewildered by the knowledge that it was possible

to have affection, and even love, for a person and at the same time hate his body.

In the years of their marriage which followed, passion and sex receded from their relationship. Both he and Belle had their inheritances—she from her father who had run a multimillion-dollar toy business and had sold out before he died, he from his grandfather who had started the family-owned garment business—and they lived well. Their home, the children, his work, her charities; these formed the familial band which held them together.

Despite their sexual incompatibility, the bond was strong enough so that on this day when they reached the airport and she left him to board her plane, there were tears in her eyes and he felt a stab of loneliness as he watched her go. His emotion was genuine even though when he returned to the car, he gave the chauffeur instructions to take him directly to Catherine Devereux's apartment.

She lived on Beekman Place, only a few blocks from his own apartment. He had a key to her apartment, but she had met him at the door that evening and as soon as he saw her face he had known something was wrong.

She had kissed him hard on the lips before she had drawn her head back and whispered, "I'm afraid I have bad news for us, dearest. And I couldn't reach you to tell you. My sister, Anne, came up from Washington unannounced this afternoon to spend two days with me." She had kissed him again and whispered, "Please don't be angry. She'll be gone after tomorrow, and we'll have the rest of the time to ourselves. I'm as disappointed as you are."

She had never been more desirable to him than at that moment, looking sleek and cool in a lime-green linen dress with an ankle-length skirt which fell just to the top of her evening sandals. He thought the dress was probably a Pauline Trigère design. She had her ash-blonde hair pulled back and caught in a chignon and her skin was a smooth buttery brown from the sun. He could smell the scent of the Madame Rochas perfume he always bought for her and she always wore. She was tall, her body lean and supple, and although she was in her mid-forties now, he thought her a more beautiful woman than she had been in photographs he had seen of her when she was in her twenties.

He had tried that evening, as graciously as possible, to conceal his disappointment and had taken both women to dinner at La Côte Basque on East Fifty-Fifth Street. It was only a short cab ride from the apartment, but they were uncomfortable from the heat which had turned, in the darkness, into a stagnant, humid mist that hung cloyingly in the still air.

At the restaurant, they had cocktails and then wine with dinner and cordials with their coffee. The meal was, as always, excellent. But Max Kauffman knew he wouldn't have chosen this particular restaurant if he hadn't wanted to impress Kit's sister, and the phoniness of his gesture made him irritable with himself.

Anne Millgrim, Kit's sister, did most of the talking through dinner, directing virtually all her conversation to Kit, gossip about their family and mutual friends, few of whom were known to Max Kauffman. Kit tried to include him in the conversation as much as possible but he was content to sit and listen and observe the two women.

Anne Devereux Millgrim was several years younger than her sister, but plump with—so Max Kauffman thought—the tightly corseted, matronly look of middle age. She had three children, lived in Washington, D.C., and was married to a man who was some minor functionary in the State Department. She and Max Kauffman had met on previous occasions when she'd visited Kit in New York, but he could not recollect her ever addressing him by any name; not Max, not Mr. Kauffman, nor Inspector, nor even Kauffman, although he had always called her Anne. He supposed it was as good a way as any to try to put him down.

Over coffee, Anne Millgrim had turned her head

toward him—which was the only way he knew she was speaking to him—and said, "We hear such terrible stories about the crime in New York. I was saying to Kit, this afternoon, I wonder if it's safe for her to live here?"

He recognized the thrust of her remark, the accusation, really, that Kit was in danger because she lived in New York and it was his fault that she lived in New York, and was in danger. There were a dozen answers he could have given her, citing chapter and verse about crime, from his own experience, from statistics, and about the relative safety of New York City as compared to other cities in the United States, in the world. But he wasn't about to fall into that semantic trap.

He had answered mildly, "I think we all have to be more watchful these days than we did in the past. But actually, the area where Kit lives is one of the safest in the city."

"Perhaps," Anne Millgrim had said stiffly, "but I'd rest a lot easier in my mind if her building at least had a doorman."

Another whammy, Max Kauffman thought. She had to know that the reason why he and Kit had chosen that particular apartment, in one of the two or three smaller buildings on Beekman Place, was precisely because there'd be no doorman to observe his comings and goings. But he had been concerned about Kit's safety and they had hired an Irish housekeeper who lived there with her in separate quarters on the second floor.

Anne Millgrim had let the subject drop then, and Kit had given him a sly wink and smile, concealed from her sister. What it all proved was that Kit's sister had made it clear once more that she disapproved of him—a married man, a policeman, and a Jew—three strikes against him there. He had to give her credit, however, for being the only member of the Devereux family of Delaware who hadn't disowned Kit when she and Max Kauffman had first begun their affair eight years earlier.

So, for all her genteel digs at him, he had decided he could live with it if Kit could.

Nevertheless, he was relieved when they had finished dinner and he had taken them back to the apartment. Kit had stood with him in the darkened doorway after her sister had bid him good night and gone on inside.

"Please don't be unhappy, Max," Kit had whispered, pressing herself against him. "She just doesn't understand how it is with us. And I wanted tonight as much as you did. I'll make it up to you, I promise."

He and Kit had drifted into their intimacy, neither quite realizing it was happening until the night their affair actually began. From the start of their affair, she had engulfed him with her passion; in this one woman nature compensated him for all the years he had suffered sexual deprivation. There was nothing he wouldn't have done for her, but there was nothing she wanted from him, except to be made love to by him. They loved each other, he knew that, but she didn't want to be married, didn't want him to get a divorce, wanted only for them to go on as they were. She was proud of her body, took joy in being made love to, and in loving him and his body. In a curious way, he had often reflected, he and Kit were more truly married than he and Belle had ever been.

"I'll miss you tonight. Miss me," she had whispered before she left him at the door and slipped into the house.

And that was exactly the trouble, Max Kauffman thought, as he finished his second drink in his den. He did miss her, specifically, and a woman, generally. He thought of Sergeant Margaret O'Dell. He'd known from the first day she walked into his office he could have had her. A sexy little minx, he thought. He shook his head, Christ, wouldn't she be surprised if she knew that in his wall safe, just a few feet from where she sat when she was taking dictation, were tapes of almost every word and sound that had gone on in her apartment for two weeks before she had come to work for him and several weeks afterwards. Including the eve-

nings she had spent making love with her boyfriend,
a police lieutenant at one of the other precincts. He
even knew the exact sound of the cry she made when
she was at the peak of ecstasy.

Ben Sybert had planted the bug in her apartment,
on the ground that she was going to be dealing with
confidential matters while working for Max Kauffman,
and they needed what Sybert called a "security profile"
on her. The Inspector hadn't known about the bug until
Sybert had had to come to tell him that he'd managed
to install the electronic device in Sergeant O'Dell's
apartment, but now couldn't get it out, and was afraid
it would be detected. What had happened was that
Sybert had found a cooperative Intelligence Officer at
the precinct where Sergeant O'Dell had previously
worked who had agreed to date her and plant the bug.
The trouble came when the officer couldn't get a second
date with her to retrieve the eavesdropping instrument.
Max Kauffman had chewed Sybert out for the whole
asinine business and then the Inspector himself had to
get her to invite him into her house for a cup of coffee
one night, during which he had removed the listening
device, a simple bug of the type known as a *harmonica*
which had been attached to her telephone. It had all
been stupid, incredibly stupid.

He thought of calling her now and immediately dismissed the thought. Too many complications. Maybe
some day he'd get around to her, but it wouldn't be
until just before he was ready to transfer her out of the
precinct. Besides, he liked her. She was a hard worker
and a good kid. Which reminded him that he would
have to double-check one of these days and make sure
Ben Sybert hadn't made a copy of the O'Dell tapes.
It had crossed his mind more than once that Ben Sybert
got his kicks out of listening to the intimate stuff he
picked up from his various electronic surveillances. In
his own case, just to be on the safe side, Max Kauffman made periodic checks of Catherine Devereux's
apartment for bugs. He wouldn't put anything past a
kinky creep like Sybert.

Max Kauffman got up from his desk with a sigh, picked up his empty glass, the bottle of Scotch, and the ice bucket, and carried them back to the pantry bar. He took a bottle of club soda out of the refrigerator and returned to the den. Sitting at the desk, he started leafing through the file he'd brought from his office.

Most of the contingency plans he now read were familiar to him; plans to deal with the taking of hostages, of the dispersal of departmental equipment in the event of a jet-plane crash in midtown, of the containment of a revolutionary outbreak, as well as a contingency plan for the evacuation of Manhattan in the event of an A-bomb attack (dated May 1950).

He read through these and similar plans, taking sips from the bottle of club soda from time to time, before he reached for his pen and a yellow legal pad and began to compose his plan for the Commissioner. He hadn't worked it all out yet, but he knew that at least one piece of equipment he was going to request was a command helicopter for himself.

Across the top of the pad he scribbled:

CONFIDENTIAL
From: Dept. Ch. Ins. Max Kauffman
To: The Commissioner

He paused. The operation had to have a name and he thought for a moment. From outside his apartment came the sound of a siren and soon, in the distance, there was the wail of another siren. This time he was able to fix them as squad cars heading downtown on FDR Drive. The sounds of the sirens continued in the distance as he wrote:

Subj: Operation Code-Name "Pandora's Box"

He leaned back in his chair and nodded, pleased with the name he had chosen. Recalling the Pandora legend from mythology, he remembered that the ancient Greeks believed that the first woman was Pandora who

had been created by the god Jupiter, and given to
Prometheus and his brother, Epimetheus. According
to the legend, Epimetheus had among his possessions
a closed box which he warned Pandora never to touch.
But one day Pandora, seized by curiosity, opened the
box and so let loose all the evils of the world. Pandora,
the story went, quickly replaced the lid and thus managed to capture the one good thing the box contained—
Hope. The moral of the legend, the Greeks believed,
was that despite all the evils loose in the world, hope
always remained, and while man had hope, no amount
of other ills could make him completely wretched.

Max Kauffman wondered briefly if the code name
might be a trifle ostentatious. And then he thought,
fuck it, the name fits, he was going to use it.

CHAPTER NINE

Thursday morning the sky was overcast, and a few scattered drops of warm rain fell just after dawn. The rain wasn't enough to dampen the dry, dusty streets of Manhattan, and fifteen minutes later the temperature had risen to 81 degrees. By 7 A.M. Max Kauffman was in his office where he spent the next two hours putting the finishing touches to his plan for the Commissioner. When Sergeant O'Dell arrived at nine, the plan was complete and she began typing copies. Shortly after 10 A.M. the Inspector dispatched two patrolmen in a squad car to hand-deliver an envelope, containing the plan, to the Commissioner at Police Headquarters. Less than an hour later, Max Kauffman received a phone call from the Commissioner, approving the plan, and before 11 A.M. teletypes went out from Headquarters to all precinct commanders activating Operation Pandora's Box.

Simultaneous with the sending of the teletypes, the plan for the operation was programmed into the central computer at Police Headquarters. From that point on, the computer would deliver whenever necessary and in a matter of seconds a complete read-out to the operators manning the radio room.

The plan was coded PB-Zero-Zero and PB-One-One, One-One. PB-0-0 would signal a possible alert, to which two squad cars in each precinct in the borough would respond, along with a police van, carrying weapons, rescue gear and emergency equipment. PB-0-0 would also call into action a police helicopter, on constant standby around-the-clock at the heliport on East Sixtieth Street. The helicopter, when signaled, would immediately proceed to the designated site and set down for use by Max Kauffman.

PB-11-11 would signal a positive alert to which all the foregoing units would respond plus other available patrol cars from every precinct, as well as squads of Tactical Police if needed. Max Kauffman, in overall command of the operation, would be informed by the radio room at Headquarters of reports of all unusual emergencies throughout the city. It would then be his responsibility to order a PB-0-0 or PB-11-11 alert. In addition, the Inspector had been supplied with a powerful signal beeper to be carried in his pocket, which would keep him in contact with Headquarters at all times. When he was beyond the reach of a radio or phone a signal from the pocket beeper would alert him to immediately contact the radio room at Headquarters. Meanwhile, as they waited, there were other matters to be handled.

Max Kauffman, after talking with the police in Queens, picked four of his best detectives and ordered them out to Flushing to assist in the search for the man Warren Griffith claimed had told him of the robbery plans. Although they had only a part of a name and a vague description to go on, it was, nevertheless, a lead which had to be followed up.

At the same time, in the interrogation room, Warren Griffith continued to undergo intensive questioning at the hands of Bucher and Rojas, who also kept him busy hour after hour, day after day, searching the mug-shot files. Late in the morning the Inspector stuck his head in the door of the room. The three men inside looked pale and tired. Bucher was questioning Griffith at the moment, the tape recorder running. Max Kauffman silently beckoned Rojas from the room. The two of them stood in the hall a few feet from the closed door of the interrogation room.

"Well?" Max Kauffman asked. "Has he added anything new to his story?"

Rojas shook his head. "He is one stubborn son-of-a-bitch. We tripped him up a couple of times on small points but," he shook his head again, "there is nothing new to report." Rojas, who had grown up in Spanish Harlem, still had a slight trace of accent in his voice.

"Is it still your opinion and Bucher's that he's telling the truth?"

"I think so, yes. Bucher, too. We are both convinced now though that he definitely knows more than he is telling. For one thing, he is deathly afraid of a polygraph test."

Rojas leaned against the wall and lit a small, thin cigar. "Inspector," he said slowly, "a man like this, there is a way to get him to talk."

Max Kauffman made no reply.

Rojas formed a fist with his right hand and socked it into the palm of his left hand.

Max Kauffman shook his head and put a hand on Rojas's shoulder. "Just continue the questioning as you have been," he said. "Maybe later—" he left the words hanging.

Rojas nodded. "Yes, sir," he said.

When Max Kauffman returned to his office, Ben Sybert was waiting for him. Max Kauffman motioned him to a chair and shut the door.

"I haven't had the results typed up yet," Sybert said, "but I thought I'd report to you that we've had J. T. Spanner under surveillance since last evening. We've got his phones tapped and there's a man watching him. We haven't picked up much yet, except that it appears he stays busy—with the ladies. You know what I mean?"

"Never mind that," Max Kauffman said impatiently. "Did you pick up anything pertinent to the investigation?"

"Nothing yet," Sybert admitted. "But did you know about his ex-wifes? He's got two of them, and—"

"Listen, Sybert," Max Kauffman cut in sharply, "I

don't want to hear all that crap. Only information essential to the case. Understand? And, Sybert, I want all copies of the tapes you make on Spanner. All of them."

"Yes, sir." Sybert rose from his chair hastily. His face was flushed.

Max Kauffman dismissed him curtly. More and more these days Ben Sybert put him in a foul mood. He was going to have to do some serious thinking about Sybert once this case was out of the way.

The Inspector made his usual morning phone call to Catherine Devereux. He could tell from the tone of her voice that her sister was somewhere within hearing distance and she couldn't talk freely. She told him she and her sister were going shopping that afternoon and she said she'd gotten tickets for the two of them for a concert at Lincoln Center for that evening. She asked him if he wanted to meet them for a drink afterwards but he said no, it was going to be a busy day and evening, and he'd call her tomorrow.

The phone call only increased his irritation. He decided he'd have lunch at his desk and try to clear away some of the paperwork which had piled up from the day before and he phoned Reuben's, from which he often ordered lunch, and had a deli spread sent over.

At 2:15, as he was finishing the last of his lunch, his phone rang. As it did, the beeper in his coat pocket began to buzz. He snatched up the phone.

"Inspector Kauffman."

"Inspector, Officer George McCandriss, Headquarters. A report just came in of an explosion of undetermined origin at Liberty Street and Maiden Lane."

Max Kauffman swore inaudibly. Liberty Street and Maiden Lane was where the Federal Reserve Bank was located. There was, the Inspector well knew, more money in the dungeons of the Federal Reserve Bank than there was in Fort Knox. The Federal Reserve was a bank for banks, where, in rooms in five levels below the street, various nations stored their gold and moved it, in the balance of trade, from nation to nation without the gold ever leaving the building. A robbery there wouldn't just shake the city, it would shake the world.

"Put out a PB-Zero-Zero," the Inspector ordered, hung up the phone, and hurried out of the office.

Max Kauffman, in the rear of his limousine, could see the black pall of smoke rising into the air while the car was still a block away. His driver used the siren to clear a path through the narrow streets of the Financial District which were already jammed with other police cars, fire-fighting apparatus, and spectators. Foot patrolmen were busy trying to keep the crowd in check and to unclog the streets. His driver finally had to stop the car half a block from the smoke and Max Kauffman, taking a walkie-talkie with him, continued on foot.

It had been twenty-eight minutes since the Inspector had left the 16th Precinct and, overhead, he could see a helicopter circling, awaiting instructions. Police cars lined both sides of the street and more were arriving every few minutes. Police had formed a circular barricade around the perimeter of the smoking mass in the center of the street directly in front of the Federal Reserve Bank. Max Kauffman could see members of the NYPD Special Operations Division, armed with submachine guns and high-powered rifles mounted with sniper-scopes, moving into position to form a solid phalanx across the entrance to the weathered neo-Renaissance building which housed the Federal Reserve Bank.

There was the charred body of a man lying in the center of the street near where firemen sprayed water and chemicals into the clouds of smoke. The Inspector had to identify himself several times as he made his way through the police lines until he found a fire chief he knew named Sullivan. Now Max Kauffman was close enough to see that some of the smoke was coming from a burning automobile which lay on its side in the street and that the rest of the smoke was boiling up out of a manhole which had blown its cover.

"Max Kauffman, Sully," the Inspector said, identifying himself to the fire chief. "What the hell's going on?"

Sullivan shook his head grimly. "Another one of those freaky things. Looks like one of the Con Ed steam pipes exploded and must have caught the car just as it was passing on the street. The force of the explosion overturned the car and the engine caught fire. Witnesses say the poor son-of-a-bitch driving the car looked like a human torch by the time he managed to crawl out of the flames. Before he'd gone a dozen steps he was burned to a cinder."

The fire chief wiped his sweating face on his sleeve of his rubber raincoat. "Jesus," he said, "with all those old steam pipes lying just under the surface of the streets, sometimes I get the feeling it's like the whole city's just sitting on top of a giant mine field that's ready to go up at any moment."

Max Kauffman knew that such sewer explosions occurred from time to time in Manhattan but he still had to ask, "Nothing suspicious about this business, Sully?"

"No," Chief Sullivan replied. "Strictly routine, far as it looks. Why?" He glanced at Max Kauffman and saw that the Inspector was looking at the bank building. "Oh," Sullivan added, "you mean because of its proximity to the Federal Reserve? No, I don't think there's any connection, Max. Say, is that why we got this big turnout of cops? I wondered why half the police department of New York City was here."

"Yeah, that's it,' the Inspector said, moving away.

Max Kauffman stayed on at the scene for a while longer until the firemen put out the blaze and Con Edison emergency crews were able to move in and descend into the still-smoking manhole in their asbestos suits and oxygen masks. Soon after that, the steam began to diminish and more crews began to move in and rip up the pavement to repair the ruptured pipe. By then the body of the dead man had been removed

by an ambulance from Beekman-Downtown Hospital
and a police tow truck was hauling away the scorched
wreckage of the automobile. Meanwhile, the Federal
Reserve Bank stood intact.

Max Kauffman went back to his limousine and called
the headquarters dispatcher to rescind PB-0-0. If nothing else, the Inspector reflected, driving back uptown,
the fire had given them an opportunity to try out the
contingency plan, and it seemed to be functioning well.

At 4:41 P.M. Max Kauffman's pocket beeper buzzed
for the second time that day. He was out of his office,
down on the first floor at the booking center, talking to
the desk sergeant. He used the desk phone to call the
precinct switchboard and get the call transferred from
his office.

A Headquarters dispatcher, Officer Jack Geary, was
on the line.

"Sir, we have a report of an attempted holdup of a
store on West Forty-Eighth Street, in the jewelry district. The perpetrators are still inside, and there's a
shoot-out in progress."

"Right," Max Kauffman said. He gave the order to
transmit a PB-0-0, then jotted down the address, and
quickly left for the scene in his limousine.

Exactly fifteen minutes later, the Inspector's car
skidded to a stop two doors away from the store on
West Forty-Eighth Street. The street was blocked off
at both corners by police lines. Once more the area was
jammed with police cars and, this time, ambulances.
Also, Max Kauffman spotted the helicopter overhead.

The Inspector shouldered his way through the inevitable crowd of curious onlookers, flashed his shield
at the police who stepped forward to bar his way, and
reached the entrance to the store. He identified himself
to a lieutenant standing in the doorway.

"Situation's under control, sir," the lieutenant said.
"Both holdup men have been shot on the premises."

The Inspector went on into the store which was filled
with police and ambulance attendants. Some of the

police were wearing bulletproof vests and carried shotguns. There was blood all over the floor in the front section of the store, and the walls and ceilings were scarred with bullet holes. There was more blood splattered against a far wall, and one of the glass display cases had been shattered and there were pieces of jewelry lying on the floor. A woman employee of the store was having hysterics over in a corner, and the manager, mopping his face with his handkerchief, was talking to a black police captain who was writing a report.

Max Kauffman walked over to another captain he knew and asked, "Did you get them all?"

The captain flipped his thumb over his shoulder. "There were two of them," he said. "They're still there."

The Inspector saw the two big canvas bags then, lying in the back of the store. The bodies had already been strapped into the bags which covered them except for the feet. Max Kauffman turned away. In his years on the force he had seen perhaps a hundred such corpses in the canvas bags, but the sight never failed to turn his stomach. There was always something obscene-looking about the way the feet of the dead men stuck out from the bottoms of the bags, always at grotesque angles, frequently twisted almost backwards from the pressure of the leather straps drawn tight around the outsides of the bags.

Max Kauffman made his way back out the door and through the crowd to his car. There, he called the dispatcher at Headquarters and cancelled the alert. Christ, he thought, the whole operation was turning into another case of the boy who cried wolf.

There were no more alarms for the rest of the day. Max Kauffman decided to stay on at the office that evening and finish up the paperwork he had been trying to clear away earlier in the afternoon. Sergeant O'Dell buzzed him before she left and asked if he wanted her to stay and work. He told her no, and a short while later she knocked on his door and came in with a fresh-brewed pot of coffee.

"Drink a cup of this now, while it's good and hot," she said, putting the silver pot on the coffee table.

"Thank you, Sergeant," he said when she poured him a cup and brought it over to his desk.

"You sure you don't need me to stick around?" she asked.

"No, no thank you," he said distractedly. Whatever passing carnal thoughts he might have had about her the night before were now gone from his mind. He glanced up and nodded without really seeing her when she paused at the door, and said good night before she went out.

An hour later he had finished his work and his driver took him home. It wasn't until he was inside his apartment that he remembered he hadn't eaten dinner. It was too much trouble, and too hot, to go back out again. Nor did he feel like making himself a snack from the refrigerator. He fixed a strong drink of Scotch, took a lukewarm shower, and went to bed, the beeper lying on the night table next to his head. He lay in the darkness, bone-tired, and watched the heat lightning flickering outside the windows of his room until he fell asleep.

CHAPTER TEN

Early in the afternoon of the following day, Friday, Joe Conant, Vince De Angelo and Red Hager left the house in Bronxville and took the train into the city. All three men were neatly dressed in suits and ties. De Angelo had shaved the great mop of black hair from his head and now appeared completely bald. He also wore a pair of steel-rimmed spectacles and leaned on a cane as he walked. Hager had had his hair clipped in a crewcut and dyed black and his eyes were covered by wrap-around sunglasses. The alterations in the appearances of both men were sufficient to let them pass unrecognized by anyone who had only known them casually—specifically, the guards at the Museum. The disguises were not essential to the plan, in any event, but were an added precaution.

The three reached Grand Central Station a little after 3:30 P.M. They had coffee at the counter in Liggett's Drugstore at the station. They didn't do much talking. Everything had been said, their plan was now under way. Before they left Grand Central, each of the men synchronized his watch with the station clocks. Outside on Forty-Second Street, they hailed a taxi and rode to Madison Avenue and Eighty-Third Street. It was another steaming, overcast day.

After the cab had dropped them at Madison and Eigthy-Third, they separated, although each remained in sight of the other. De Angelo went first, walking west on Eighty-Third, followed a quarter of a block behind by Hager, and then Conant, another quarter of a block. When Conant crossed Fifth Avenue and reached the foot of the stone steps leading up to the Museum, De Angelo was already out of sight inside, and Red Hager was just going through the door. Conant glanced at his watch. It was ten minutes past four. The Museum would close for the day in exactly fifty minutes. They had had to allow themselves the extra time in case they ran into any delays. Conant could feel the rapid beat of his heart as he went up the steps and through the door.

There was the usual crowd inside the Museum. Conant paused inside the entrance until he spotted De Angelo going up the wide staircase to the second floor. He waited until De Angelo was almost to the top of the stair and then crossed and followed him up. Hager was nowhere in sight, but Conant knew he was wandering around the first floor somewhere, killing time.

At the top of the stairs, Conant began to browse through the galleries. To look at him no one would have guessed that he was actually making a final check of the five paintings they were going to steal. He had put a lot of thought into the selection of these particular paintings, choosing them as much for qualities which would show this was an imaginative robbery as for the value of the paintings, and now he moved unhurriedly from one to the other, studying each in turn.

The first painting was Pieter Brueghel's *The Harvesters*. Conant knew it was considered to be a towering world masterpiece, and that some authorities felt it was the first true landscape in Western art. On the canvas, Conant could see how the artist had painted in accurate detail a group of peasants of his time, the sixteenth century, harvesting wheat and had set them against a vast landscape stretching to infinity and dwarfing the human figures.

Conant remembered from his art studies that *The*

Harvesters had originally hung in a gallery in Vienna along with four other Brueghel paintings depicting the seasons of the year. In 1809 when Napoleon's army conquered Vienna, *The Harvesters* and a second Brueghel painting from the series were seized as booty and shipped to the Louvre in Paris. After Napoleon's final defeat in 1815, the Louvre returned the second Brueghel painting but *The Harvesters* vanished from sight.

It wasn't until 1917 that *The Harvesters* reappeared and was bought by the Metropolitan from a Belgian artist and collector who had purchased it from a French collector. At that time it was thought the painting might be only a copy of the lost original, but eventually the work was confirmed to be the authentic masterpiece. In fact, Conant knew, even the frame in which the painting was mounted had been identified. All five Brueghel paintings of the series had once been mounted in similar frames; now, curiously, only *The Harvesters* in the Metropolitan was still in the original frame it had been in when it hung on the walls of the gallery in Vienna in 1809. Conant, amused, thought, once Napoleon had heisted *The Harvesters;* now it was his turn.

Conant moved on to the second painting he had chosen for the heist; Rembrandt's *Portrait of a Man,* which he knew had been done in the 1630s. He saw again why for some authorities the artist was considered the master of all masters. In this painting, as in all Rembrandt portraits, Conant admired again the remarkable achievement in chiaroscuro; of how by setting the lighted face of the figure in the portrait against a dark background, the expressive features of the face fairly leaped out from the canvas. Conant calculated that by taking this Rembrandt instead of the more renowned *Aristotle Contemplating the Bust of Homer,* he would show he had used reasonable restraint in his selection for the robbery.

Picasso's *Portrait of Gertrude Stein* had been selected

by Conant as the third painting in the haul both because he knew it was considered one of the great
masterpieces of the twentieth century and because it
added a slight literary flavor to the robbery. The portrait, done in 1906, had rested for a time in the
Museum of Modern Art, Conant knew, but had been
permanently hung in the Metropolitan in 1952.

Gazing at the painting, Conant recalled that it was
supposed to be the bridge between Picasso's earlier
conventional work and the more experimental Cubism
which for a long time preoccupied the artist. Conant
could detect the link by looking first at the work overall and then, more closely, at the face, the features of
which were slightly distorted and had been painted
after Picasso had finished the rest of the canvas.

He was reminded of Gertrude Stein's own famous
"a rose is a rose is a rose is a rose is a rose," which
was generally misunderstood by most people who were
familiar with her play, *Yes Is for a Very Young Man,*
from which the line came. In that play a character lifts
a rose, studies it and finally sniffs it while repeating,
with a sense of discovery, "A rose is a rose is a rose is
a rose, is a rose." In the same way, Conant thought,
anyone studying the Stein portrait would discover from
the features of the face that a Picasso is a Picasso is a
Picasso is a Picasso is a Picasso.

The fourth painting Conant had picked to steal was
Claude Monet's *Terrace at Sainte Andresse.* He knew
it had been acquired by the Metropolitan in recent years
and that the price paid for it was almost a million and a
half dollars. If Conant could have afforded the luxury
of stealing a painting which he could keep for his own,
the Monet would be one of two out of the five which
he would have chosen. Monet's Impressionistic work
was more to his personal taste and especially *Terrace
at Sainte Andresse* which, painted early in the artist's
career, captured what Conant was sure was the exact
ambience of Sainte Andresse at a precise moment in
time.

The fifth and last of the paintings Conant had selected for the snatch, Renoir's *Madame Charpentier
and Her Children,* was the second of the paintings he
would have chosen for his own collection. He knew
the Metropolitan had brought it in 1907 and that it
was considered to be one of the world's greatest Im-
pressionist paintings. To Conant's eye, Renoir had
the supreme gift of reproducing the intangible emo-
tional bonds existing between the subjects of his work,
just as one might observe a man and a woman walking
side by side on a street, not touching, and yet know
they were lovers.

Conant was pleased with his inspection of the paintings. He went back out into the corridor and saw De
Angelo standing in one of the galleries in the rear of
the building. De Angelo gave him a look, but Conant
shook his head. He had just seen something else; ahead
of him, coming up the stairs, were two nuns leading
a group of young children up to the second floor.
When the group turned toward the rear of the building
and entered the section where the European paintings
were hung, Conant followed along with them.

He saw that he had guessed right in following the
nuns and the children when a couple of guards appeared and stood at ease, eyeing the group. The group
would temporarily distract the guards. De Angelo had
caught on, and he came limping across the area, passed
close by Conant without glancing at him, and headed
into the south wing. Conant ambled along in the same
direction, pausing now and then to examine a painting
or a piece of sculpture, until he stood midway between
the guards and De Angelo who was now out of sight of
the guards and approaching the empty, newly painted
section of gallery closed off by the velvet rope.

De Angelo looked both ways along the corridor
parallel to the gallery when he reached the rope, then
glanced back at Conant. Conant checked the guards
and saw they were still watching the group of children.
He turned and gave a barely perceptible nod of his

head to De Angelo. De Angelo stooped, slid under
the rope, and moved swiftly to the back of the deserted
gallery. Conant, watching, saw De Angelo standing in
front of one of the paneled sections. A moment later,
De Angelo stepped forward and disappeared from
view as if he had walked through the wall.

Conant could feel the constricting tightness in his
chest. He walked slowly back toward the center of the
building. The nuns and the children were moving away
from the collection of European paintings and were
heading for the American wing on the north side of the
museum. One of the guards trailed along behind them
while the other guard walked back toward the south
side of the building, passing Conant, and continuing
on.

Red Hager came into view at that moment at the top
of the stairs. Conant, as if still browsing along the
corridor near the stairs, gave Hager a quick wink.
Hager had taken note of the guard over in the American wing. Hager passed Conant and went toward the
empty gallery in the opposite direction. This time
Conant, knowing there was a second guard somewhere
in the area, followed a few paces behind.

Hager reached the velvet rope, saw the hallway was
empty, and ducked under the rope and scurried toward
the back of the gallery. Conant was now in the corridor
outside the gallery and just in time to see the second
guard appear from around a corner about six or eight
paces away. If the guard continued on, he'd reach the
empty gallery in another few seconds. Red Hager still
hadn't had time to slide the panel open. Conant hurried
forward and stopped the guard, asking the first question that came to mind: where was the men's room?

The guard, trying to be helpful, took a couple of
steps forward to show Conant the way. Conant, desperate to detain the guard and not knowing what else
to do, let several coins from his pocket spill on the
floor. The guard helped him pick up the coins and then
they walked together on up past the roped-off gallery.
Red Hager was nowhere in sight. Both men were now

concealed in place. Conant thanked the guard and went on to the men's room, which he now really did need to use.

A short while later when Conant came out of the museum, most of the crowd of sightseers was also leaving just ahead of the 5 P.M. closing time. He walked slowly coming down the steps and onto Fifth Avenue. There was nothing for him to do for the next hour or so except wait, and he was at a loss as to how to spend the time. At the curb in front of the Museum his eye was caught by the striped awning of the outdoor cafe at the Stanhope Hotel down the street, where he'd frequently met Holly for a drink. He shrugged and started toward the cafe. Hell, he might as well kill some time with a couple of drinks.

After he had finished his drink and ordered another, he went into the lobby of the hotel and from one of the phone booths around the corner from the desk, dialed Holly's number. The phone rang and rang and rang and he was just about to hang up when he heard her voice.

"Hello. Hello? Yes, hello?"

He replaced the phone on the hook. There still was nothing he could say to her. At least he knew she must be all right. He went back out to the table and sat with his second drink, his thoughts now with De Angelo and Hager locked up inside the Museum.

The first thing the two men had had to adjust to in the cramped space was the darkness. It had seemed to press down suffocatingly around them, made worse of course by the very real fact of the poor ventilation. Gradually, however, they had begun to see the faint outlines of light around the panel behind which they were hidden. They could also see the luminous dials of their wristwatches but nothing else was visible in the tiny area behind the wall.

They had taken sitting positions side by side which was the only way they could both fit into the space. There was no way they could stretch their legs out so

they kept massaging their leg muscles to ease the ache.
They could, by reaching out their hands in the darkness, feel the materials they had stowed in the hiding
place.

Soon after the Museum closed at 5 P.M. they could
hear the sound of the guards talking now and then as
they made their rounds. After a while, it grew silent
beyond the panel. The minutes passed agonizingly slow.
The time set for them to leave their hiding place was
anywhere from 5:45 to 6 P.M., depending upon whether
or not they heard the guards nearby. The first half-hour
of the wait was bad enough but from 5:30 to 5:45,
the minute hands on their watches seemed not to move
at all.

Finally, at long last, it was 5:45. At the exact
moment the second hand on De Angelo's watch swept
around to threee-quarters of the hour, he cautiously
eased the panel back. Both of them felt they couldn't
endure the confinement another instant. They strained
their ears for any sound of the guards and when they
heard nothing, De Angelo crawled out from behind the
wall and, on his heels, came Hager.

The overhead lights in the museum had been turned
to dim, but the illumination still hurt their eyes. They
were both drenched with sweat. It took them several
minutes, when they stood, to get the kinks out of their
muscles. Then they began to methodically and silently
prepare for the robbery, retrieving from the hiding
place the materials which they had smuggled into the
museum during the past weeks.

First, they removed some gray canisters with yellow
markings, two dozen of them, and lined them up across
the floor. Next they took out sheets of tarpaulin and
sheets of glassine paper, folded them flat, and laid them
on the floor next to the canisters. Finally, they took out
two oxygens masks, two firemen's rubber raincoats,
two pairs of high rubber boots, and two firemen's helmets.

The complete firemen's uniforms had been stolen
from Engine Company 222 on East Eighty-First Street,

a few blocks away from the Museum, one month earlier and smuggled into the hiding place. The heist of the firehouse had been carefully planned by Conant. On that night, they had phoned in a false alarm and while the engines were out on the call, De Angelo, Hager, Chilton, and Kroger, wearing stocking masks and armed, had slipped into the firehouse. They had quickly subdued the one fireman who was always assigned housewatch when the rest of the company was on call and who sat in a tiny cubicle at the front of the firehouse. They had stolen four complete firemen's uniforms and oxygen masks and slipped away without incident.

Now in the Museum, De Angelo and Hager quickly dressed in the uniforms and fitted the oxygen masks over their faces. Then they took from the raincoat pockets surgical gloves and put them on. Each checked the other's appearance before they proceeded.

Ready to move on, each of them gathered up an armful of the canisters and crept silently out of the empty gallery. They moved quickly in the subdued light across the second floor to the head of the marble stairs. They stood there for a moment listening and, when they heard nothing, went down the stairs soundlessly. When they were at the bottom, each man set one of the metal canisters on the step.

The metal containers were smoke bombs. The men had constructed them at the house in Bronxville, following instructions prepared by Conant. The smoke bombs were absurdly easy to make—a mixture of sodium bicarbonate, sulfur flour, hexachloroethane, potassium chlorate, zinc dust and zinc ash, all ingredients easily obtained by De Angelo and Hager in the city and taken to the house in Bronxville and then later, as smoke bombs, smuggled into the Museum.

De Angelo and Hager knelt and popped the tops on the two canisters they'd placed on the bottom step. Twin clouds of thick, white smoke immediately boiled up into the air.

De Angelo and Hager retreated back up the stairs,

pausing on every sixth or seventh step to repeat the
process of activating more of the smoke bombs as they
went. By the time they reached the top of the steps
a swirling curtain of smoke enveloped the staircase
from the first floor to the second. They paused to adjust the oxygen intake in the masks that covered their
faces. Then they hurried back to the empty gallery,
collected the remaining smoke bombs, and returned to
the head of the stairs. They placed the canisters in a
row strung out across the floor for several yards on
either side of the stairs and set off the smoke bombs
one by one.

Now they could hear shouts and the sounds of running down on the main floor. By that time the smoke
all around them was so thick they could only see a foot
or two in front of them. While Hager went back to get
the sheets of tarpaulin, De Angelo took from his
pocket a diagram of the second floor of the Museum
which they had torn from their copy of the *Guide to
The Metropolitan Museum of Art.* Conant had marked
in red crayon the locations of the paintings they were
to steal and had written in the names of each. Hager
returned with the sheets of tarpaulin and glassine paper
while De Angelo was studying the diagram. Together
they went to the spacious gallery of European paintings
in the center rear of the building.

The first painting marked on the diagram was Rembrandt's *Portrait of a Man.* De Angelo found it and
motioned to Hager. They were both trembling as they
took their places, one on either side of the painting.
De Angelo took a deep breath, nodded to Hager and,
in unison, they lifted the painting from the wall. Somewhere in the distance an alarm bell began to ring.
Whether it was a fire alarm or a burglary alarm, they
didn't know. Nor was there time to pause and think
about it.

They lowered the painting to the floor. De Angelo's
hand shook as he reached into his raincoat pocket
and took out a switchblade knife, snapping the
sharpened blade open. He remembered Conant's re-

peated admonitions to him: *Goddamn it, Vince be careful with those paintings. Do what you have to do, but treat them tenderly so nothing spoils them. We're not barbarians, and we want to return them unharmed.*

De Angelo steadied his hand, plunged the blade of the knife into the canvas at the edge of the inside of the frame, and skillfully stripped the painting out. He and Hager carefully wrapped the canvas in glassine paper. Conant had explained to De Angelo that the glassine paper, which was a chemically treated, see-through material with a dull outer surface, was used by art experts to safeguard fine paintings while they were being moved or in storage since the covering protected the canvasses from moisture, dust, and strong light. De Angelo and Hager placed the wrapped Rembrandt next to one of the sheets of tarpaulin lying on the floor. Conant had warned them again and again to be absolutely certain that the paintings be protected from water damage in case the firemen who would be arriving shortly at the Museum got trigger-happy with their hoses and started indiscriminately spraying water all over the place. As De Angelo and Hager moved on toward the second painting they were going to steal there came the sound of sirens from outside the building.

At that moment, in the drive in front of the Museum, the first of the fire engines to respond to calls from the Metropolitan, arrived on the scene. Smoke was pouring from the entrance to the building, obscuring the whole front of the Museum. Most of the guards had staggered out from the building, coughing, tears streaming from their eyes. A hook-and-ladder and two pumpers pulled up in front of the steps. There were more sirens in the distance. The firemen on the trucks pulled on their oxygen masks before clambering down from the sides of the vehicles and unreeling their hoses. Several police cars had also reached the Museum, and the police had piled out and were trying to clear the heavy traffic off Fifth Avenue so the emergency equipment speeding to the scene could get through. Hidden in the shrubbery at the side of the building, Joe Conant and Eddie Chilton watched the frantic activity taking place at the Museum entrance.

Just thirty minutes earlier, Conant had left the outdoor cafe at the Stanhope Hotel across the street and walked south on Fifth Avenue to Seventy-Ninth Street. Following their pre-arranged plan, he had stood on the northeast corner of Fifth and Seventy-Ninth until, at precisely 5:40 P.M., Augie Kroger and Eddie Chilton had picked him up in the car they had rented and driven in from Bronxville. Conant had slipped into the back seat of the car. Kroger was driving and in the car were the other two complete firemen's uniforms and oxygen masks they had stolen from the Manhattan firehouse a month earlier.

Kroger had turned south on Fifth Avenue, driven for a couple of blocks, and then turned into Central Park. As they wound their way through the Park roads north again, Conant and Chilton had slipped on the firemen's uniforms except for the helmets and oxygen masks. Kroger drove slowly up and around behind the Museum, in the Park, until they heard the first sirens headed toward the Metropolitan. By the time they had circled around the Museum and come down the road north of the building, the fire engines were approaching the Metropolitan and the three men could see the smoke billowing out through the front entrance. Kroger had stopped the car, Conant and Chilton, carrying their helmets and oxygen masks, had slipped out and taken cover in the shrubbery at the corner of the Museum, and Kroger had driven away.

Now, still hidden, Conant nudged Chilton and they both slipped on their oxygen masks and helmets. They were at that moment completely outfitted—as were De Angelo and Hager inside the Museum—in the same uniforms as the firemen on the scene, from Engine Company 222, wore. As Conant had known, the first engine company to respond to the alarm came from the firehouse, a few blocks away, where they'd heisted the uniforms.

In all the confusion, nobody noticed when Conant and Chilton, who looked like all the other firemen milling around the entrance, ran around from the side of the building and fell in alongside the firemen struggling with their hoses and chemicals. The two men even hoisted up a section of fire hose and helped haul it inside. Just before the smoke, enveloped them Conant glanced at his watch. The time was 6:12 P.M., which was still within the time schedule he had set for the completion of the robbery.

CHAPTER ELEVEN

Max Kauffman had gone directly from the 16th Precinct to his regular barbershop in Times Square at Forty-Seventh Street late that afternoon. There had been no further progress on the case during the day. None of the detectives he'd sent out to Flushing to look for the man described by Warren Griffith had turned up anything, Griffith himself had added no new information to the case. The police still had the ex-con busy going through the mug-shot files and he was becoming increasingly surly at being kept at the tiresome chore when he'd probably thought he was going to be allowed to lie around in his cell and take it easy.

The Inspector was, in addition, becoming sensitive to ordering alerts similar to the two of the previous day. He'd already learned that most of the cops out in the prowl cars were making jokes about the code name of the operation, Pandora's Box.

One precinct commander had called him earlier and said, "Hey, Max, my boys tell me they have been examining broads all over the precinct and they can find plenty of snatches, but none of the broads are named Pandora." The caller had rung off with a loud guffaw. When this call was followed by several others from other precinct commanders, all making jokes about the sexual connotations of the name of the operation, the Inspector began to do a slow burn.

Later, the Commissioner had called asking if there

were any new developments in the case and Max Kauffman said no and then mentioned that some of the precinct commanders seemed to be treating the whole
operation as some kind of joke just because of the
name he had chosen for it.

"Don't let them get under your skin, Inspector," the
Commissioner said. "They're probably just trying to
have a little fun with you. I think you'll find them
responding fast enough when you call upon them. At
least they damn sure better or they'll have me to answer to." There were no more departmental calls rib-
bing him after that and Max Kauffman decided the
Commissioner must have sent out the word.

The Inspector was due to have dinner with his
parents at 6 P.M. and later he planned to see Catherine
Devereux—thank God, her sister had gone back to
Washington that afternoon—so he left the office at
4:30. His driver had waited for him at the barbershop
while he got a trim, a shave, a facial massage, and a
shoeshine, and changed into the fresh shirt he had
brought with him from home in his attaché case that
morning. Afterwards, Detective Lukin had driven him
to his parents' apartment on Park Avenue in the
Eighties and Max Kauffman had told the driver he
wouldn't need him any more that night.

Max Kauffman's mother and father still lived in the
same twenty-two-room apartment where he'd grown
up, in one of the older cooperatives on Park Avenue.
Once space had been almost too small to contain all
the family members who lived there—his parents, both
pairs of grandparents, himself and his sisters, Rachel
and Bernice. Now with his grandparents dead and his
sisters and himself married and with their own homes,
the apartment was much too large and too empty for
just his mother and father and the cook-housekeeper
who lived in. Max Kauffman had often tried over the
years to get his parents to move into a smaller place
which would have been more practical, but, as always,
his father was stubborn and wouldn't budge.

Riding up in the elevator, the Inspector began to gird

himself for the strain of the next few hours; secretly, ever since he became an adult, he had thought of these Friday-night dinners as the weekly family gathering to kiss his father's ass.

When the housekeeper, Mrs. Hillsman, let him into the apartment, Max Kauffman saw that the rest of the family was already seated in their usual places at the at the table in the dining room. His parents usually dined later in the evening during the other days of the week but on Fridays, when the family gathered, dinner was promptly at 6 P.M., a custom which dated back to the time Asa Kauffman, Max Kauffman's grandfather, was alive.

Much of the apartment's furnishings, too, dated back to the time of Max Kauffman's grandparents. The predominant furniture was massive and dark, of rosewood or mahogany, with the chairs and sofa cushioned in tufted satin. The effect might have been gloomy, except that Max Kauffman's mother, in her periodic redecorations of the apartment over the years, had always chosen bright fabrics for the reupholstering of the furniture and selected wall paper with cheerful prints. Adding more color were the paintings on the walls, mostly of sunlit landscapes and seascapes, all of which were original oils, even if the artists remained unacclaimed.

Covering the waxed hardwood floors were rich Turkish carpets, and the dining room table was always set with Tiffany silverware and Haviland china, although the Spode and Meissen china was kept locked away behind the glass panes of the mahogany breakfront which stood against one wall of the dining room. On top of the mahogany sideboard, which stood against the opposite dining-room wall, were photographic portraits of all the members of the Kauffman family for four generations. For as long as Max Kauffman could remember, the apartment had smelled of cooking odors which air fresheners and open windows could never completely dispel.

Max Kauffman's father, Aaron Kauffman, sat at the

head of the table, his mother, Sara, at the opposite end. There were several empty chairs down either side of the table from his father; these were where Max Kauffman and his family always sat. The other chairs were all filled with Max Kauffman's sister, Rachel, her husband, Marvin Katz and their two daughters, Andrea and Betsy, on one side of the table and, on the other, his sister Bernice, her husband, Seymour Greene and their son, Sammy.

Max Kauffman kissed his mother and sisters and took his seat next to his father. His father was in the middle of one of his usual long monologues about what was wrong with the garment industry, which he interrupted only long enough to nod to his son and say, "How's the cop business?" then went on with his dire recounting of the ills of the family company before Max Kauffman could reply.

Aaron Kauffman was seventy-six years old, a huge man with a belly as big as a nine-month pregnant woman about to give birth to twins. He had only a few strands of hair combed back across his melon-like head but the hair was still black, as were the thick beetle brows across the gray eyes set deep inside hollow sockets on either side of his flared nostrils.

Each week the old man had a different theory about what was ruining the garment business: the unions, the rising cost of machinery, foreign competition, the designers. This week, Max Kauffman learned as he listened with half an ear, his father was bitter because one of the Fifth Avenue stores had canceled an order it had placed earlier for a line of Fall dresses. The dresses had already been made, the store which had ordered the line was normally a good customer, so the company had to go along with the cancellation for the sake of future business and, therefore, stood to lose $50,000 unless the merchandise could be unloaded elsewhere.

Kauffman and Son, as the business was called—Max Kauffman had once joked to his sisters' husbands, both of whom worked for Aaron Kauffman, that the name

should be changed to Kauffman and Sons-in-Law—
specialized in making copies of higher-priced dresses,
which made this present complaint of his father's more
reasonable than was usually the case. Not that the
company was in any danger of losing money, Max
Kauffman knew. Hell, they were probably raking it in
by the yard, as they always had been since his grandfather, Asa, had first started the business before he was
born.

Sitting at the table now listening to his father
harangue his two brothers-in-law, who had to appear
respectful to, and interested in, the old man's every
word if they ever expected to inherit from him, Max
Kauffman was once again eternally grateful to Grandfather Asa.

It had been Asa Kauffman, who, without Aaron
Kauffman's knowledge or consent, had left Max Kauffman a full one-third of the business in his will when
he died. Old Asa Kauffman had always been proud of
his grandson's scholastic achievements, had lived long
enough to see Max Kauffman graduated from Harvard
Law School magna cum laude and win his Rhodes
scholarship, and must have suspected the young man
had no talent or liking for the garment business.

At first, Aaron Kauffman had had no objections
when his son decided he wanted to take a couple of
years out on his own before joining the family business.
Aaron Kauffman had even approved when Jacob
Schulman, Max Kauffman's uncle on his mother's side,
who headed his own prosperous law firm and had
strong political connections in the city, managed to
place the young man as an assistant in the District
Attorney's office.

Max Kauffman was beginning even then to vaguely
consider making some kind of law enforcement job,
perhaps continuing in the DA's office, or in some
similar agency, his life's work. But he did not confide
this fact to his father. For the next year, while he was
employed by the DA, at a nominal salary, Max Kauffman had his first personal contact with the working

members of the police department. He was often present in station houses when prisoners in cases to which he was assigned were brought in, he usually listened in on the questioning of such prisoners, and he put together evidence extracted from the prisoners to be used in their prosecution.

In that one year, Max Kauffman was involved, often in a minor role, in some ten cases ranging from robbery to homicide and one investigation of police corruption. Curiously, despite his training and achievements in the study of law, he soon found himself to be far more interested in the police procedures of tracking down and apprehending criminals rather than in helping to prepare the legal cases against them.

As a boy and young man, Max Kauffman had been so preoccupied with his books and studies that there had been little time for sports or other physical activities. Now that he was in close contact with working policemen and detectives, he discovered the best of the officers were those who drew equally upon their physical and mental abilities. This concept—of needing the ability to function intellectually while under the pressure of physical danger—fascinated him and made him want to test himself in a similar manner.

As the same time there were other elements in police work which attracted him: the opportunity to play a direct role in dealing with a major problem of society, crime, as well as the sense of personal power, which came with the badge and the gun, inherent in the job. Much later, when he was more mature and had achieved a certain amount of self-awareness, Max Kauffman realized his power as a police officer was equal—or perhaps superior—to the power of the Kauffman money and so had allowed him to escape domination by his father.

From the DA's office, at the end of the year, Max Kauffman had taken the city police exam, placed among the top three out of the thousands of applicants who took the test that year, and entered the Police Academy. That was when Aaron Kauffman almost had

apoplexy, especially when Max Kauffman also decided
to sell his shares of stock in the family company. His
father had raised the money to buy Max Kauffman's
shares but for a long time afterwards relations between
the two had been strained.

As soon as Max Kauffman graduated from the Academy, while he still had a silver shield, he was assigned
by his superiors to the Internal Affairs Division (IAD)
and sent as an undercover agent to investigate corruption in the city's 16th Precinct. Working as part of a
four-man team, with two sergeants and a lieutenant
who were also undercover, the investigation led to the
bringing of a variety of misconduct charges against
the ranking officers of the 16th Precinct, and their
removal. Max Kauffman received his detective's gold
shield. Although he was offered other assignments
which might have led to faster promotion, he had
found a working home at the 16th and had stayed on
there through the years until eventually he had been
given command along with the rank of deputy chief
inspector.

Through the years as Max Kauffman had begun his
rise in the police department, he found his father was
no longer so critical of the decision he'd made to join
the force and he'd even heard—although his father
would never tell him—that Aaron Kauffman often
boasted to his friends of the exploits of his son, the
Inspector.

Now, sitting at the dining table, Max Kauffman
silently watched one of the rituals of the Friday-night
dinners which never varied; as each member of the
family finished eating, always leaving some portion of
the dinner on the plate since his mother invariably had
too much food prepared, his father would glance down
the table and say to each person in turn, "If you don't
want the rest of that food, pass it up here." The plates
would be handed along, one by one, and his father
would eat whatever remained on them. At the end of
the meal, all the plates would be stacked at one end
of the table in front of his father.

"I miss Belle tonight," his father said to Max Kauffman at one point during the meal. "She's a good
woman. Like your mother. Women who enrich life.
You miss her, Max?"

His father was peering at him with narrowed eyes.
Max Kauffman felt a flutter in his stomach. Did his
father know something, suspect something, about him
and Catherine Deuvereux?

"Yes, Papa, I miss her," Max Kauffman said.

"Good," his father answered, nodding. "A woman
like that needs to feel she's missed."

His father smiled then, surprising Max Kauffman, a
smile which clearly had in it great love for his son, a
love the old man would never, probably could never,
put into words or gestures.

Max Kauffman suddenly felt a rush of guilt for all
the unkind thoughts he so often had about his father,
mixed with a surge of affection. His father was a stubborn, opinionated, ruthlessly domineering old s.o.b, but
that was his way, probably the only way the old man
knew, to live, to survive, to command respect. Max
Kauffman knew he himself had some of the same
traits.

Max Kauffman searched for some small gesture he
might make to his father, to try to express something of
what he felt at that moment, and the signal beeper in
his pocket began to buzz.

"What the hell is that?" his father asked, startled.

"I've got to make a phone call," Max Kauffman said,
pushing back from the table.

He went to his parents' bedroom and used the phone
to call headquarters. He identified himself and the dispatcher said, "Inspector, we have a report of a fire
at the Metropolitan Museum. A bad fire, looks like."

Max Kauffman ordered, without hesitation, a PB-O-
O alert and directed that the closest squad car pick
him up at his parents' apartment immediately. He
hurried back through the apartment, explained to his
parents he had to leave at once on police business,

and by the time he rode the elevator to the street, the
prowl car was waiting out front.

"Let's go, let's move!" Max Kauffman said brusquely,
sliding into the back seat of the patrol car.

Traffic was heavy on Park Avenue, almost bumper-
to-bumper the length of the thoroughfare. It had momentarily slipped the Inspector's mind that this was an
early Friday evening in summer, and that the streets
everywhere in Manhattan would be clogged with cars
as most of the city's inhabitants hurried, at almost the
same hour, to get home or out of town for the weekend.

The driver of the prowl car bore down hard on the
siren and the cars in front tried to move to clear a
path but they were all jammed in together on the street.
Over the police radio came the staccato voice of the
Headquarters dispatcher: "PB-Zero-Zero! PB-Zero-
Zero! This is a positive! PB-Zero-Zero! All cars! Metropolitan Museum of Art, Fifth and Eighty-Second! All
units! Repeat: PB-Zero-Zero! All units!" The prowl
car moved in a series of jerking starts and stops.

"Jesus! Come on, come on!" Max Kauffman urged
impatiently. The car had gone less than a block.

The patrolman at the wheel was sweating and the
officer next to him was leaning out the window, shouting at the vehicles ahead and banging on the side of
the prowl car. As they approached the corner of Eighty-
Eighth and Park, this patrolman jumped from the car
and ran ahead, in and out between the crawling line
of vehicles blocking the street. At the corner he stood
in the middle of the intersection waving his arms to
move the traffic out of the way so the prowl car could
make a turn.

Max Kauffman was clutching the seat in front of
him. "Goddamn it!" he raged at the driver. "Can't we
go any faster?"

The patrolman at the wheel turned a strained, white,
sweating face to glance at the Inspector. "Sir," he said
in a hoarse voice, "if this thing had wings I'd try to fly
it!"

Finally, he managed to swing around onto Eighty-Eighth Street and Max Kauffman groaned. The traffic on the side street was even worse than it had been on Park. The Inspector guessed that traffic on all the streets in the area was now hopelessly backed up because of the emergency equipment which would be converging on the Metropolitan over on Fifth Aveune and Eighty-Second Street, two blocks west and six blocks south. The patrolman who had jumped from the prowl car was now moving ahead of it on foot across Eighty-Eighth Street, trying to clear space for the police car to proceed. But the Inspector could see it was an impossible task.

"I'm getting out," Max Kauffman said, shoving the door open. "I can walk it faster. Follow me on over."

Max Kauffman hit the pavement running, darted between the cars lining the street, and dashed for the sidewalk. He ran west to Madison Avenue, turned and ran south on Madison, loosening his tie with one hand as he ran, while with his other hand he jammed his .38 revolver securely into place in the shoulder holster under his coat.

He was soaked with sweat and panting for breath when he reached Madison and Eighty-Second Street and turned the corner toward the Museum a block west. He was aware that people on the sidewalks along the way had turned to watch him as he ran past.

His breath was coming in ragged gasps when he came within view of the Metropolitan at the end of the block on Fifth Avenue and saw there a line of fire engines parked in front of the building and several police cars.

A blanket of white smoke billowed out through the doors of the Museum and rose skyward. More fire equipment was arriving, along with the police van and additional squad cars. Firemen with hoses and equipment were moving up the steps and disappearing into the smoke. Several television camera crews from the various networks had pulled up in the street and the technicians were busy setting up their cameras which had been trained on the entrance to the Museum. Max Kauffman could hear a helicopter approaching from the east. Out of habit, he glanced at his watch. It was 6:35 P.M.

CHAPTER TWELVE

Inside the Metropolitan, Joe Conant and Eddie Chilton had groped their way through the blinding smoke to the second floor, at the top of the stairs, and made contact with Vince De Angelo and Red Hager. Several tarpaulin-wrapped bundles lay on the floor at their feet. De Angelo nodded to Conant. Leaving Hager and Chilton with the bundles, Conant and De Angelo hurried over into the south wing of the building. When they reached the rear panel in the empty gallery behind which De Angelo and Hager had hidden, Conant glanced inside, gave an "okay" signal to De Angelo, then pulled out a length of rope and tossed it to De Angelo. Conant then stood and carefully eased the sliding panel back in place. He and De Angelo both double-checked to see that the wall again looked solid.

Leaving the empty gallery, the two men crossed to a window in the next section of the Museum. It took their combined efforts to raise the window. Once it was up, De Angelo tossed one end of the rope out the window and let the other end drape over the window sill and onto the floor inside. Conant was satisfied with the effect; this would make it look like they somehow gained entry by coming down the rope from the roof and in through the window. It would give the police enough to puzzle over to keep them occupied for a good many days, he'd bet.

Hager and Chilton were still waiting by the stairs

when Conant and De Angelo returned. Conant jerked
his thumb over his shoulder. The men picked up the
tarpaulin-wrapped bundles and started groping their
way through the smoke and down the stairs, Conant
in the lead. They bumped into several firemen in the
dense smoke while making their descent but there was
so much confusion, no one even gave them a second
glance; figures wearing rubber raincoats, boots, and
oxygen masks were all over the place.

The firemen were still looking for the blaze which
was causing so much smoke. Conant's greatest worry
at the moment—because he cared so much about the
priceless treasures in the Metropolitan—was that the
firemen might cut loose with their hoses and damage
the art in the Museum. It struck him as ironic that if
that did happen, the only paintings which were absolutely safe were those which they had carefully protected before they were stolen.

The confusion was even worse on the main floor
where everybody was bumping into everybody else
in the blinding smoke and hoses snaked across the
floor. Conant picked his way carefully, followed by
De Angelo and then Hager and Chilton, and finally
they were at the door and moving out onto the great
stone steps.

As they came down the steps at the entrance to the
Museum and emerged from the smoke, Conant was
momentarily stunned by the sight spread out below
him: the whole area was jammed for blocks with vehicles and people, dozens of police cars and fire engines
—Jesus, even a police helicopter which had set down,
rotor blades still twirling, on the island of pavement
between the Museum driveway and Fifth Avenue. How
in the hell, he wondered briefly, had so many police
gotten there so quickly? He hadn't counted on that.
But there was nothing to do except go on with the plan.
Police and firemen were everywhere, running back and
forth, without direction. Then he spotted the television
cameras trained on the entrance, on them, as they came
out through smoke. It was an eerie feeling. For a mo-

ment he felt sheer panic, knowing it was possible they were being filmed. Then he remembered that the four of them in their firemen's uniforms and oxygen masks were completely disguised; let the crews film all they wanted.

Conant felt De Angelo, behind him, stumble and almost fall. Conant turned his head sharply and De Angelo straightened up. Conant led them at an angle down the remainder of the steps and paused for a second at the bottom to let Hager and Chilton catch up.

Conant looked around him for a moment, saw that the police had set up barricades along Fifth Avenue to divert traffic and let the emergency vehicles through, then glanced again at the other three men and jerked his thumb. They moved swiftly now, not quite running but at a trot, out to the curb—just as they'd planned— and to one of the fire engines, a pumper, which stood deserted, front end pointed out toward the street.

They quickly hoisted the bundles up into the back of the pumper and Eddie Chilton ran around and jumped into the driver's seat while Conant, De Angelo, and Hager climbed over the sides. There were shouts behind them and several firemen began running toward the pumper as its engine roared to life with Eddie Chilton at the wheel. They were already rolling fast and Eddie Chilton bore down hard on the siren as they shot out onto Fifth Avenue. Up ahead, a couple of policemen directing traffic obligingly pushed a wooden sawhorse to one side to clear the street for them and the pumper streaked past, still accelerating, siren shrieking, and sped down Fifth Avenue.

Max Kauffman was slow to react when he heard the first outcries from two or three firemen who were standing near the curb waving their arms as the pumper pulled away from the Museum. Just a minute or so before, one of the policemen under his command had handed him a still-smoking metal canister which a fireman had brought out of the building. A smoke bomb. Before then, the Inspector hadn't been able to get any information at all about what was going on inside the Museum. Mass confusion prevailed. The Inspector had been on the point of commandeering an oxygen mask for himself and going inside when his attention was attracted by the uproar at the curb.

By the time he had reached the yelling firemen and learned that three or four men dressed in firemen's uniforms and oxygen masks, had stolen a fire engine and driven away, the flashing lights of the pumper were half a block down Fifth Avenue, twisting in and out of the snarl of traffic. One of the firemen who had witnessed the getaway informed the Inspector that the men had loaded several bundles into the vehicle before they took off. The Inspector told the firemen to report to the battalion chief that the fire was probably a fake to cover a suspected robbery and that he guessed there were only smoke bombs inside. The man hurried off. Max Kauffman knew, at that moment, this was the robbery he had been planning against for the past several days.

His problem now was how to give chase. At this hour of a Friday afternoon, the streets of Manhattan were still clogged with rush-hour traffic. He'd order in other units from all over the city to try to head off the fleeing fire truck, but it wouldn't be easy to coordinate the chase by radio through all the traffic. He was already pretty certain that the perpetrators had deliberately set the time of the robbery to coincide with the rush-hour traffic so it would be harder to apprehend them.

He'd use the standby helicopter to plot the chase, and the radio to direct the ground units in pursuit. Turning, he ran hard for the waiting helicopter, and vaulted inside. "Get this thing into the air," he ordered the pilot. "Straight down Fifth Avenue."

As the overhead rotor blades began to twirl, the Inspector snatched up the helicopter transmitter and bellowed: "All units! All units! PB-One-One-One-One. Repeat! PB-One-One-One-One! All units! Intercept fire engine pumper traveling south on Fifth Avenue in the

Seventies, Sixties. Fire engine carrying three or four men believed to be perpetrators of robbery of Metropolitan Museum of Art. Repeat—"

The voice of the Police Headquarters dispatcher cut in incredulously: "A fire engine? Who is this?"

"Goddamn it! This is Inspector Kauffman!" Max Kauffman roared. "And this is a PB-One-One-One-One. All units!"

The helicopter had started to lift off. Max Kauffman got on the radio again, this time to one of the squad cars, with two patrolmen in it, still parked in front of the entrance to the Museum. "Unit Seventeen, come in! Come in, Seventeen! K."

There was a brief blast of static on the helicopter receiver and then a voice said: "Seventeen Adam responding PB-One-One-One-One. K."

"Seventeen Adam," Max Kauffman said, "check inside Museum. Verify possible robbery. Report, urgent! K."

"Seventeen Adam," the voice came crackling back. "Will investigate."

As the helicopter shot into the air, the Inspector could see the two patrolmen from Car 17 climbing out and running for the Museum steps. The helicopter rose higher and Max Kauffman could see other policemen everywhere on the street scrambling to their cars in response to his call for pursuit of the stolen fire engine. As the helicopter swung around and moved southward, several police cars below had roared out into the heavy traffic on Fifth Avenue and were trying to get through. Other units farther downtown were reporting in by radio to the Headquarters dispatcher, acknowledging their response to Code PB-One-One-One-One. With any luck, the Inspector thought, they'd head off the perpetrators.

Max Kauffman had been following the flashing lights of the stolen fire engine as it threaded its way through the heavy Fifth Avenue traffic in the distance. The pumper was still about eight or nine blocks ahead of the helicopter, somewhere in the Sixties, the Inspector

estimated, when suddenly he lost sight of its flashing
lights. He got on the transmitter again, yelling, "Fire
engine to be intercepted now believed to be moving
eastward or westward from Fifth in the Sixties or Fifties! All units move in! Intercept!" The pilot took the
helicopter higher to give them a sweeping view east
and west.

Jesus Christ, Conant thought, clinging to the sides
of the swaying pumper, this was it! There'd never been
anything like it! He felt drunk with exhilaration. He
could tell by the glitter in the eyes of De Angelo and
Hager that they felt the same way as they tried to hang
on and balance themselves in the racing fire engine.

Eddie Chilton, at the wheel, had been weaving the
fire engine back and forth across the wide avenue to
get through the streams of cars. A path had opened up
ahead and Chilton went streaking through it, then
turned east off Fifth at Fifty-Ninth Street. They took
the corner on two wheels, the siren wide open, and
cars all along the narrow side street swung into the
curbs to clear the way. Two blocks over, at Park
Avenue, they made another screaming turn and went
roaring south again.

Traffic was even worse on Park Avenue than it had
been on Fifth. The street, divided down the middle by
a wide, iron-fenced island beautified by flowers and
shrubs and under which ran the Penn Central Railroad
tracks out of Grand Central Station, was clogged with
cars moving uptown on the east side of the island
divider and downtown on the west side, in the direction
the fire engine was headed. Eddie Chilton bore down
hard on the siren and traffic parted, leaving an opening not much greater than the width of the pumper,
but he expertly maneuvered the vehicle through it.

Up ahead the traffic light was against them at the
Fifty-Seventh Street intersection, and there were cars
crossing from both directions. Chilton, hunched over
the wheel, headed straight into them, siren howling.
Most of the cars accelerated out of the way. One car
stalled midway across Park Avenue and the pumper hit

it on the rear fender and sent it skidding across the street.

A block beyond, they sideswiped another car and Eddie Chilton almost lost control but managed to swing the engine straight again and they went careening down Park Avenue, the wind whipping at them. As they shot past the side streets in the Fifties and Forties, they could see the flashing lights of police cars headed in toward Park Avenue from both sides, but temporarily blocked by the cars which had pulled over to let the fire engine past. From the rear of the pumper, Conant could see the blinking lights of a helicopter in the sky several blocks away and closing in fast.

In the helicopter, Max Kauffman had his eyes fixed intently on the stolen pumper only a couple of blocks ahead. It was still headed down Park Avenue and had almost reached Forty-Sixth Street. South beyond Forty-Sixth Street the back of Grand Central Station, and the lofty Pan Am Building, straddled the avenue and the only way south was over the narrow ramps running around the sides of the buildings, one uptown, one down. He was certain now they could catch the perpetrators once the fire engine was on the ramp. He got on the transmitter again, shouting: "Perpetrators moving south on Park toward the ramp at Grand Central Station! Head them off south on the ramp!"

Below him in the streets as the helicopter swept over, the Inspector could see the flashing red lights on the roofs of countless squad cars converging from all directions, like the lights on a switchboard suddenly gone berserk.

Some of the squad cars, hopelessly trapped in the side streets leading into Park Avenue, had been abandoned, doors still swinging open. Many police officers, some with drawn guns, continued the chase on foot, dodging in and out between the stalled cars out in the middle of the street. To make matters worse, in all the confusion the careening fire engine had left behind, there had been a three-car collision at the center

of the intersection of Fifty-Fourth Street and Park,
blocking most of the Avenue to the south.

Meanwhile, he could see the fire engine racing closer
and closer to the ramp up ahead. By God! he thought
exultantly, we've really got them! Then, once again
to his amazement, the pumper abruptly swung off Park
Avenue and came to a stop. From that distance away
in the helicopter, it looked as though the fire engine
had run up onto the wide island in the center of Park
Avenue at the end of the last block before the ramp.
The Inspector thought the fire engine had probably
crashed.

Even though Conant, De Angelo, and Hager had
been expecting Eddie Chilton to turn and stop before
they reached the Grand Central ramp, they were almost thrown off the pumper when he swung it around
at the corner of Forty-Sixth Street with a blare of
sirens to scatter the pedestrians standing on the crosswalk on the island in the center of the street. As the
people fled back across the opposite side of Park
Avenue, Chilton ran the fire engine up on the crosswalk and cut the motor. Now that they could hear the
screams of sirens coming at them from all directions,
the sound was deafening.

Conant, De Angelo, and Chilton quickly jumped
from the fire engine. Hager passed down the tarpaulin-
wrapped bundles to De Angelo and Chilton. Right next
to the pumper, Conant was kneeling at the grating atop
an emergency exit leading to a Penn Central Railroad
tunnel beneath Park Avenue. The sweat was pouring
off him as he pounded on the grating and yelled,
"Augie! Augie!"

For a moment there was only silence and then
slowly, protestingly, the metal grate swung upward and
Augie Kroger's face peered up at Conant from inside
the tunnel. He was there in place, just as they'd planned he'd be when he'd left Conant and Chilton at the
Museum. And he knew all about the workings of the
emergency exits and the tunnels beneath from questions he'd asked his uncles who had worked for the

railroad. All he'd had to do was slide back the bolt which opened the exit from inside the tunnel.

Conant ducked into the dark opening, bracing himself on the metal ladder. De Angelo and Chilton swiftly passed the bundles to Conant. Conant handed them down to Kroger. Then De Angelo, Chilton, and Hager scrambled into the opening, ducked down the ladder, and yanked the grating shut with a loud clang as police cars from both directions on Park Avenue were braking to a stop on the street up above.

The helicopter carrying Max Kauffman arrived over the spot within seconds of the time the first squad cars got there. As the helicopter hovered dangerously near the street crowded with pedestrians, policemen, and squad cars, the Inspector was screaming into the transmitter: "What the hell's going on down there? Where the hell are they? Where the hell are they?"

One of the policemen standing just beneath the helicopter leaned into a parked squad car at the curb and, using the radio, reported: "Sir, it looks like they've gone down one of the emergency exits to the tunnel. The exit opens from inside and they've jammed the bolt back into place. We can't get it open."

"Shoot it open!" Max Kauffman yelled. "Get it open and get down there! I want those men!" The Inspector glanced at the clock set in the north face of the Grand Central Building several stories above street level. The time was 6:50 P.M.

As the men below struggled with the exit grating, Max Kauffman up above in the helicopter could clearly see in his mind's eye the vertitable labyrinth of tunnels and passages leading into and out of Grand Central Station.

There were, he knew, entrances and exits on all four sides of the station, and on several levels; direct exits to the street on the Forty-Second Street side, the Lexington Avenue side, the Vanderbilt Avenue side as well as connecting doors from the station to most of the buildings surrounding it, the Pan Am Building, the

Graybar Building, the Biltmore Hotel, the Commodore, and even an underground passageway leading to the Roosevelt Hotel a couple of blocks north. Also there were doors from the main concourse of the station into almost all the shops and stores in the same building. In addition, there were the subway entrances and exits connecting the station with Forty-Second Street, Lexington Avenue, and Madison Avenue. At a rough estimate, he figured there must be twenty or more such ways for the perpetrators to escape from the station.

While he was still pondering the problem, a report came in over the helicopter receiver: "Unit Seventeen responding PB-One-One-One-One."

"Come in, Unit Seventeen," Max Kauffman answered.

"Unit Seventeen reporting investigation possible robbery at Metropolitan. Robbery affirmative. Repeat, affirmative robbery of Metropolitan. Five empty frames have been found. There may be more. The fire was a hoax. Smoke bombs were used. K."

"Continue investigation, Unit Seventeen," the Inspector replied. "And get the Museum director or somebody in authority to verify what's missing. Otherwise the Museum is to be kept secure until the crime boys have a chance to go over it."

Now that he had conclusive evidence that paintings had been stolen from the Museum and that by this time the perpetrators were probably moving through the tunnel beneath the street into Grand Central Station, the Inspector knew there was only one action he could take. "PB-One-One-One-One to all units!" the Inspector ordered over the transmitter. "Urgent! Perpetrators now inside Grand Central Station! Move in and seal off all exits from station!"

Even before he had finished his message, he could see most of the officers below on Park fanning out in different directions to surround the station. They were coordinating their efforts via walkie-talkies, which each man carried.

CHAPTER THIRTEEN

As the helicopter continued to hover over the Park Avenue crosswalk, the Inspector had already recognized the brilliant cunning displayed by the robbers in choosing to use the emergency street tunnel to enter Grand Central Station. Once in the tunnel, as they were now, they would be unobserved when they removed and discarded their firemen's uniforms and oxygen masks, which had served as disguises. When they entered the station itself, there would be nothing to set them apart from the rest of the hundreds of commuters inside. Except, Max Kauffman reminded himself, for the stolen paintings they'd be carrying.

But there was the rub, he thought sourly. If the gang had been clever enough to pull off this job the way they had so far, he wouldn't put it past them—as soon as they discovered the police had bottled up Grand Central—to try to ditch the stolen art somewhere in the station and retrieve it later. It was at least a contingency he had to consider. That being the case, he knew there were other actions he'd have to take, all in rapid succession, in conjunction with closing the station's exits. All of these actions could present serious legal consequences for the Department later, he realized, but he had to exercise his own judgment the way he saw fit; he had been given responsibility for Operation Pandora's Box and, by God, he intended to use his authority.

He immediately contacted the headquarters dispatcher direct over the helicopter transmitter and ordered all available units citywide to close in on Grand Central Station to back up the police who were now sealing up the station. No other civilians were to be allowed into the station, to add to the crowd, and no one who was inside allowed out. All entrances and exits were to be continued to be manned until further notice, he instructed, while the additional police were to begin a search for the four, possibly five perpetrators of the robbery of the Metropolitan who were known to be inside the station. It was possible, he advised, that the men had five stolen paintings in their possession. Very likely the paintings would be rolled-up oil canvases.

At headquarters, the dispatcher, who knew that a PB-One-One-One-One signal took top priority, was already feeding into the most modern communications system in the world the data being given to him by Max Kauffman. Almost as swiftly as the information was fed into the communications system, it was coded and relayed to dozens of small computer screens, resembling compact TV sets, in the headquarters communications center. Each of these small computers was, in turn, manned by a radio dispatcher who also worked from an illuminated map which told him the location of various squad cars in the city at that precise moment. Scanning both computer screen and map, each radioman began dispatching units, those already in the Grand Central Station area as well as others scattered throughout the city, to the scene with orders to surround the station.

Max Kauffman had not yet concluded his orders to the dispatcher and now he said tersely: "In addition to conducting a search for the perpetrators, I want the officers who enter the station to demand from each individual found inside proof of identity and the individual's address. Each officer is to keep a careful record of this information and it is to be turned over to me. If an individual cannot produce proof of identity and an address, I want that individual removed to the 16th Precinct and held there until such proof is satisfactorily established. The authority for this action will be Section One-Forty-Point-Five-O of the Criminal Procedure Law."

Max Kauffman was well aware he might be on shaky legal ground in employing Section 140.50 of the Criminal Procedure Law, which was titled: "Temporary Questioning of Persons in Public Places; Search for Weapons," and was also popularly, or unpopularly, known as the controversial Stop and Frisk Law. He could quote the Section, which was in two subdivisions, from memory:

ONE—IN ADDITION TO THE AUTHORITY PROVIDED BY THIS ARTICLE FOR MAKING AN ARREST WITH-OUT A WARRANT, A POLICE OFFICER MAY STOP A PERSON IN A PUBLIC PLACE LOCATED WITHIN THE GEOGRAPHICAL AREA OF SUCH OFFICER'S EMPLOY-MENT WHEN HE REASONABLY SUSPECTS THAT SUCH PERSON IS COMMITING, HAS COMMITED, OR IS ABOUT TO COMMIT EITHER (A) A FELONY OR (B) A CLASS A MISDEMEANOR DEFINED IN THE PENAL LAW, AND MAY DEMAND OF HIM HIS NAME, ADDRESS AND AN EXPLANATION OF HIS CONDUCT.

TWO—WHEN UPON STOPPING A PERSON UNDER CIRCUMSTANCES PRESCRIBED IN SUBDIVISION ONE, A POLICE OFFICER REASONABLY SUSPECTS HE IS IN DANGER OF PHYSICAL INJURY, HE MAY SEARCH SUCH PERSON FOR A DEADLY WEAPON OR ANY IN-STRUMENT, ARTICLE, OR SUBSTANCE READILY CAPABLE OF CAUSING SERIOUS PHYSICAL INJURY AND OF A SORT NOT ORDINARILY CARRIED IN PUB-LIC PLACES BY LAW-ABIDING PERSONS. IF HE FINDS SUCH A WEAPON OR INSTRUMENT, OR ANY OTHER PROPERTY POSSESSION WHICH HE REASON-ABLY BELIEVES MAY CONSTITUTE THE COMMIS-SION OF A CRIME, HE MAY TAKE IT AND KEEP IT

UNTIL THE COMPLETION OF THE QUESTIONING, AT
WHICH TIME HE SHALL EITHER RETURN IT, IF
LAWFULLY POSSESSED, OR ARREST SUCH PERSON.

The Inspector additionally ordered the headquarters
dispatcher to alert all available police helicopters to
stand by, with assigned crews of five to six men, and
await further instructions.

With the sealing up of Grand Central Station now in
motion, Max Kauffman proceeded quickly to the other
actions he knew he had to take. First, he had the dispatcher put him through to the Trainmaster's office at
the command center of the Metropoliton Transporta-
tion Authority which controlled the city's subway system from a building in Brooklyn.

The Inspector quickly explained the operation under
way at Grand Central Station, and then inquired if any
subway trains were at that time in the station or approaching it. The Trainmaster, after checking with each
of the three divisions, IRT, BMT, and IND, housed in
the same MTA headquarters, reported back negative
on any subway trains in the station, but added that an
IRT east side and an IRT west side were both due in
Grand Central within four to six minutes. Max Kauffman requested the trains be halted before they reached
the station and all additional subway service into Grand
Central be suspended until further notification by the
police department. The trainmaster agreed to the request.

Max Kauffman was satisfied that he'd closed yet
another possible escape route out of the station. He
signaled to the helicopter pilot to circle the Grand Central Building so he could observe the activity on the
streets surrounding the station. At the same time he
again contacted the headquarters dispatcher and was
put through to the office of the railroad police inside
Grand Central Station. City police always worked
through the railroad police in cases involving the physical property of the station.

His radio call was taken by Officer George Cavanaugh of the railroad police. The Inspector once again explained the situation and the action he had directed be taken. Cavanaugh, in turn, promised full cooperation of the station police force. Max Kauffman then asked that his call be transferred to the chief dispatcher of the Penn Central Railroad.

While the Inspector waited for his call to go through, the helicopter was circling around through the canyons of buildings in the Grand Central area. Below, as the helicopter slowly circled, Max Kauffman could see the congested pavements of Vanderbilt Avenue and Forty-Second Street as dozens of police cars streamed into those streets and police officers ran zig-zag through the traffic and crowds of pedestrians to cover all the station's exits. The Inspector could see a surging mob of people already gathered outside the main entrances to to the station on Vanderbilt Avenue and Forty-Second Street where they were being blocked from entering by the police who had taken up positions there. All traffic in the immediate vicinity, the tail-end of the rush hour, was hopelessly backed up for blocks.

The Penn Central chief dispatcher came on over the helicopter radio at that moment. Max Kauffman quickly detailed for him the bare facts of the Museum robbery, told him the robbers had fled into the station, and that the station was now surrounded. Then the Inspector took a deep breath and added: "It's urgent that all trains which left Grand Central since six-fifty P.M. be halted enroute and remain there until the police arrive and have an opportunity to search them."

The chief dispatcher of the Penn Central worked out of an office on the fourth floor of a building at 466 Lexington Avenue, a few blocks north of Grand Central itself. This location was the master control room of the entire line and the chief dispatcher sat in front of a large console which looked something like a giant switchboard whose blinking lights indicated the location of all trains from the time they left Grand Central Station until they arrived at their destination.

The clock on the wall in the chief dispatcher's office

showed the time to be 7:15 P.M. The chief dispatcher, a man named Gil Shelby, scanned the lighted console in front of him and saw on it the various locations of the trains which had left the city since 6:50 P.M.: the 6:45 Stamford which had been late in departing, the 6:50 to Peekskill, the 6:53 to Dobbs Ferry, the 7:00 to North White Plains, the 7:05 to New Haven, the 7:05 and 7:10 to Stamford, the 7:13 to Brewster, and the 7:13 to North White Plains.

"I have nine trains enroute since that time period," Chief Dispatcher Shelby reported.

"I want them stopped, all of them stopped, and held until they're boarded by the police," Max Kauffman ordered. "And all future trains delayed until you receive further notification."

"Yes, sir, if you say so," the chief dispatcher answered. There were three methods he could use to stop the trains anywhere enroute between Grand Central Station and their point of destination: by throwing a signal switch in advance of the trains, by radioing ahead to the signal towers which were manned at intervals along the line, or by radioing directly to the engineers of the various trains. In this case, Gil Shelby decided to radio directly to the trains.

Max Kauffman called in the Police Headquarters dispatcher, who was monitoring the exchange, while the line was still open to the office of the Penn Central chief dispatcher.

"I want you to stay on the line," the Inspector instructed him. "As soon as the trains are halted, I want you to get a fix on their locations from the train dispatcher. Once you have that information, you are to deploy the helicopters and police crews standing by to each of the trains. I want the passengers and the trains searched for any evidence of the stolen paintings from the Metropolitan. And, again, I want proof of the identity and the addresses of all passengers recorded, and the information turned over to me. Any passengers who cannot produce such proof are to be removed to the 16th Precinct, in accordance with my previous orders. Section One-Forty-Point-Five-O of the Criminal Procedure Law remains the authority for this action."

Max Kauffman had decided it was time for him to go down to the station. He and the pilot discussed the problem of where to set the helicopter down at some spot in the midtown area. They knew it was impossible for the police to clear a space for them anywhere in the streets directly around Grand Central with traffic tied up the way it was. They finally agreed that the closest place around with enough room to land the helicopter was the grounds of the United Nations on Forty-Second Street and First Avenue, three blocks east of Grand Central. The Inspector briefly speculated on whether or not the action might have some international repercussions, then decided to proceed anyway.

He radioed down to one of the manned squad cars in front of the station on Forty-Second Street, told the two officers in the car what he planned to do, and instructed them to advance ahead of the helicopter to the UN grounds and advise the guards there. The squad car was to remain at the UN and take the Inspector back to Grand Central. The squad car immediately pulled away and sped across Forty-Second Street, with the helicopter trailing slightly behind it at a height above the buildings. When the squad car reached the gates to the UN, the pilot circled overhead until the two police officers had conferred with the UN guards and waved the aircraft down. The day had been overcast since early morning but, even now in the evening hours, there was still plenty of light left in the sky.

While the guards on the ground stood watch, the pilot set the helicopter down in the deserted drive in front of the UN Building. Max Kauffman jumped clear and the helicopter quickly took off again and went winging northward above the East River toward the heliport at East Sixtieth Street. The Inspector climbed into the waiting squad car and, as it swept back out through the gates of the UN, gave a wave of his hand to the guards posted there. Within minutes the police car braked to a stop in front of Grand Central Station, and Max Kauffman was out and pushing his way through the swarming crowd that had gathered outside the police-barricaded doors of the station. The crowd covered the sidewalk solidly on the north side of Forty-Second Street all the way out to the curb where additional barricades kept them from spilling into the street. They sweated and shuffled restlessly in the sweltering heat, but remained remarkably patient under the circumstances.

The Inspector had removed his billfold from his pocket with his Inspector's shield pinned to it and he held it high in front of him as he struggled through the crowds until the police guarding the station doors spotted him and cleared a path for him. As Max Kauffman struggled forward through the massed bodies, he could hear the remarks passing back and forth among the crowd:

"Somebody said they're looking for a bomb in there."

"I heard it was a gang tried to hold up the ticket-sellers."

"Hell, I thought it was just a police escort for the Mayor who was taking a train trip."

"I knew we needed more police protection in the area, but man, this is ridiculous."

New Yorkers, they were a breed apart, Max Kauffman thought with bemused affection, as he went through the doors and into the station, the city instilled in them, for the most part, a remarkably good-humored resiliency, God bless them.

CHAPTER FOURTEEN

Inside the enormous, cathedral-like interior of Grand Central, Max Kauffman was surprised and pleased to find that his police officers, with the help of their railroad counterparts, had already begun to establish some semblance of order. The police had cleared the lower level of the station of all persons and had directed the crowd collected on the main level to form long lines in front of each of the staircases leading to the lower level. A group of four policemen stood at the top of each of these staircases and checked and recorded the identity and address of each individual, as well as made a search of each person, before passing them on, one by one, to the lower level where they were instructed to remain until the procedure was complete. The air on all levels of the station was heavy with a pall of choking, moist heat.

The Station Master had taken over the public address system and his words, repeated over and over again, went echoing and reechoing throughout the catacombs of the station: "Attention! Please be patient! Please cooperate with the police and assist them in obtaining the information they're seeking! You will not be detained any longer than necessary! Normal train service will resume at the completion of this investigation! Attention! Please be patient. . ."

Max Kauffman estimated the crowd in the station to be somewhere between 5,000 and 7,500 persons.

This figure included those who were continuing to arrive on the incoming trains for an evening in the city but who, unfortunately, also had to be detained and questioned since no one was allowed to leave the station and it was impossible to separate the new arrivals from those who had already been in Grand Central. Inevitably, there were some incidents.

Three men who had been herded into line by the police for questioning had, at almost the same moment, suddenly broken away and made a run for three different exits out of the station, one racing for the lower level, one trying to escape out through the door to Vanderbilt Avenue, and the third darting to the escalator up to the Pan Am Building. Police pursued all three, hesitating to draw their guns for fear of creating a panic among the rest of the crowd in Grand Central.

The first fleeing man was tackled by two policemen on the stairs to the lower level, the second man was grabbed by the collar and brought down by a police officer on the sidewalk on Vanderbilt Avenue, and the third man was stunned by a blow in the back of the neck delivered by a police sergeant and had to be carried off the escalator.

Once the men were handcuffed, subsequent questioning revealed that all three, although unknown to each other were unregistered aliens illegally in the country. One was from Greece, one from Cuba, one from Germany. Max Kauffman ordered that all three be removed and handed over to the U.S. Immigration and Naturalization Service at 20 West Broadway.

A little later Max Kauffman was summoned to confer with two plainclothesmen who were holding a well-dressed, matronly looking woman who had arrived at Grand Central on the 7:00 P.M. train from Greenwich. She had made the mistake of offering the two policemen a bribe to let her pass through the station without producing her identification.

When the Inspector reached the trio, who were

standing off to one side in the station waiting room, the woman was in tears. She had refused to reveal to the officers why she had offered the bribe and Max Kauffman walked her out of earshot of the two officers and talked to her quietly, explaining that he had to have all the information, including her identity and the reason why she had attempted the bribe. If she cooperated, he promised he would try to help her.

Finally, her cheeks flaming, she lowered her hand-kerchief and between choked sobs told him she was married, had five children, and had come in town to keep a date with a—a young man, and her husband didn't know she was in New York. She was terrified that if the police knew her name and address, her husband might somehow find out what she'd been up to.

Max Kauffman lectured her sternly on the serious-ness of attempting to bribe a police officer, and finally released her after she had produced proof of her name and address. The Inspector went back to the two po-licemen, gave them a wink, and said, "It was an *affaire de coeur*. This one time we'll mark it down to a simple misunderstanding on the part of an otherwise good citizen." It didn't hurt the Department, Max Kauff-man rationalized, to show occasional compassion to an erring civilian.

Soon after, Max Kauffman was electrified by the sound of gunfire somewhere in the station and a sud-den squawking over his walkie-talkie: "Inspector Kauffman! Inspector Kauffman! Come to Track Three! Come to Track Three! We think we have the perpe-trators! Track Three!"

Max Kauffman raced across the station to the en-trance to Track Three. A group of station police and city officers were gathered at the gate. One of the po-licemen recognized the Inspector and explained: "Four guys, carrying a bag, broke out of the police line, ran through the gate here and are out there on the tracks. When one of our men tried to follow, the suspects opened fire."

Max Kauffman looked out the gate and saw a dark,

deserted train sitting on the tracks. A shot came from somewhere behind the train and nicked off a piece of concrete at the top of the gate to the tracks. The group standing at the track entrance ducked.

"Get me a bullhorn," the Inspector ordered. While one of the policemen hurried away to get the bullhorn, Max Kauffman gave instructions to the other officers to draw their guns and, at his command, follow him out onto the tracks and deploy themselves along the near side of the train in a line. If the suspects continued to resist, or again opened fire, the police were to fire back, and, if possible, to try to shoot only to wound.

As soon as the Inspector was handed the bullhorn, he raised it and ordered. "This is the police. We are armed. If you do not give yourselves up, we're coming out shooting."

There was another shot from out on the tracks and Max Kauffman pulled his .38, nodded to the other police officers, and led the men in a crouching run out along the near side of the empty train. There were several more shots from out on the tracks, and then Max Kauffman fired his gun under the train and the other police opened up their weapons.

The Inspector reached the train steps leading to the second coach and climbed them cautiously, gun in hand. At the top of the steps he saw, through the open coach doors, a figure start to run across the tracks on the opposite side of the train. He raised his .38, took aim at the legs of the fleeing man, and fired four shots. The man fell, screaming, between the tracks. There was more gunfire between the police and the suspects and then a cry from the darkness beyond the train: "Don't shoot no more! We give up! We give up! Don't shoot!"

Max Kauffman raised the bullhorn. "This is Inspector Kauffman. Withhold your fire. Withhold your fire."

Three men, dragging a fourth, emerged out of the darkness and came toward the police. When the men were in custody, Max Kauffman asked sharply, "Who are you? What was all the shooting about?"

The four suspects remained sullenly silent. The Inspector ordered a couple of his officers to look for the bag the four had been carrying. The group of police and suspects stood on the station platform until the two officers returned with a canvas bag. One of the policemen put the bag down and opened it while the other policeman shone the beam of a flashlight into the bag. The bag was filled with money—ten-dollar bills, all looking newly minted.

Max Kauffman frowned and looked at the suspects. "What is this?" he demanded. "Where'd you get this money?"

"One of the suspects spat a wad of phlegm near the Inspector's shoe and said contemptuously, "Who you trying to bullshit, cop? You know that's funny stuff in the bag. That's why you flooded the place with fuzz."

"Shut up, Duke," another of the suspects said.

Funny stuff, Max Kauffman thought, the money was counterfeit. They'd stumbled on four passers of bogus bills. He gave orders to run the suspects in and the Inspector sent him to Bellevue under police guard. But they still hadn't found the perpetrators of the Museum robbery.

There were additional incidents, mostly involving resistance to being questioned and searched, on principle, from a few among the crowd in Grand Central, but the police moved quickly and quietly to quell these outbreaks, swiftly surrounding the offenders and hustling them out of the station and into waiting squad cars to be transported to the 16th Precinct.

A temporary police command post had been set up on the upper balcony of the station overlooking the main level and radio equipment had been brought in to back up the walkie-talkie communications system. The Inspector found that the police officers he had earlier sent down into the emergency street tunnel on Park Avenue, used by the perpetrators, had brought to the command post the evidence they had collected from the tunnel. There were four complete firemen's

uniforms and four oxygen masks as well as several
sheets of tarpaulin and sheets of a curious-looking
thin, almost opaque, paper which the Inspector did
not recognize, left behind by the robbers. But there
was no sign of the stolen art—only the evidence of
the sheets of tarpaulin in which the perpetrators had
concealed the paintings when they fled the Museum.

Max Kauffman questioned the police officers who
had searched the tunnel and sent them back down
into the bowels of the station to continue the hunt.
Then he directed other policemen to remove the firemen's uniforms and tarpaulin and paper sheets to the
crime laboratory for analysis. Either the robbers had
managed to hide the paintings somewhere within the
confines of Grand Central Station or they still had them
in their possession.

The Inspector was still optimistic that the helicopters he'd dispatched to the halted trains might yet uncover the perpetrators and recover the missing art. As
he stood on the balcony observing the tedious process
of the questioning and searching of the crowd taking
place below, he could hear some of the garbled exchanges over the radio between headquarters and the
pilots of the helicopters which had by then reached
the halted trains and were standing by while the police
crews made their investigation and search.

At 7:25 P.M., ten minutes from the time Penn Central Chief Dispatcher Gil Shelby had first received the
call from Max Kauffman, all nine trains which had
left Grand Central Station from 6:50 P.M. onward,
stood dead on the tracks at varying intervals stretching from south of the 125th Street Station to north of
Mount Vernon, New York. Within another quarter of
an hour the first police helicopters began landing alongside the tracks of the stalled trains and police crews
began going through the coaches, questioning the passengers and searching for the stolen art.

Joe Conant was feeling great. He kept chuckling
softly to himself at the slick way the robbery had gone.

Jesus, he was so excited he felt he might pop out of his skin at any moment and it was all he could do to contain himself from bursting out laughing and shouting. It was like the whole thing had been greased from beginning to end. He glanced over at Vince De Angelo in the seat next to him and gave him a big wink. De Angelo, a wide, silly grin on his face, winked back.

The five of them, Conant, De Angelo, Hager, Chilton, and Kroger had had to separate when they boarded the 7:00 P.M. train to North White Plains in Grand Central Station because the coaches were crowded and most of the seats were taken. One of the station stops before the train got to North White Plains would be Bronxville. They were all in the last car of the train where Conant and De Angelo had been able to find two seats together while the others had to sit separately in front or behind them.

Conant didn't even give a damn when the train ground to a stop while they were still four minutes away from the Bronxville station which was their destination. He figured there was just some delay on the track up ahead and his mind was so busy retracing the course of the robbery that he paid no attention to how long the train sat there until De Angelo suddenly nudged him sharply in the ribs.

"Christ, Joe," De Angelo whispered in alarm, "look out there."

Conant glanced through the train window and saw the helicopter which had just set down next to the tracks. There was no mistaking the uniforms worn by the men who climbed out of the helicopter and came aboard the train: New York City cops!

"What's going on, Joe?" De Angelo asked in a worried whisper.

Conant shook his head. "I don't know," he said softly, "but we got nothing to worry about if we just play it cool. Pass the word to the other guys."

People all up and down the coach were standing and peering out the windows on one side of the train to try to see what was going on with the helicopter. De Angelo moved casually through the aisle, leaning over each of the men, Kroger, Hager, Chilton, and whispering to them before returning to his seat next to Conant.

"It's okay," De Angelo said out of the side of his mouth. "I told them to stay calm and play dumb."

A long time went by while they fidgeted in their seats until finally four policemen entered the last coach. The policemen worked in pairs, one pair on each side of the aisle, questioning the passengers and searching them.

"Jesus, Joe," De Angelo said in a hoarse undertone, "they're searching everybody and asking them questions."

"So?" Conant answered more calmly than he felt. "We've still got nothing to worry about."

A couple of moments later two of the policemen reached the seat where Conant and De Angelo sat. One of the policemen nodded pleasantly and said, "Sorry to inconvenience you, but this is a police investigation. May I have your name and address, please, and some proof of your identity?"

Both Conant and De Angelo repeated their names and addresses which the second policeman wrote down. Then both men took out their wallets. Conant passed over his social security card and a couple of department store credit cards. De Angelo offered his driver's license, his social security card, and two credit cards. Both policemen glanced at the cards and the second policeman made check marks in the book in which he'd recorded their names and addresses and the cards were passed back to Conant and De Angelo.

"Now," the first policeman said, "I'd appreciate it if you'd step out here in the aisle for a moment."

Conant and De Angelo both stood and stepped forward. The policemen quickly frisked them—Conant didn't miss the fact that they carefully probed for anything hidden inside his shirt or trouser legs—then examined the train seat and the floor under and around it.

"Thanks very much for your cooperation," one of the policemen said. "Sorry to bother you." They moved on through the coach and Conant and De Angelo sat back down.

One man from the car in which they sat was taken from the train when he was unable to produce any proof of his identity but Conant didn't begin to breathe easy again until he saw that Hager, Chilton, and Kroger had successfully passed the police inspection. Shortly after that the police left the train, climbed back into the waiting helicopter along with nine persons they had taken into custody, and the helicopter lifted off.

After a short wait, the train proceeded on into the station at Bronxville and Conant, De Angelo, Hager, Chilton, and Kroger got off.

"Holy God," De Angelo said anxiously to Conant, "now they've got a record of our names and addresses. And they were sure as hell looking for the paintings we took. What's it all mean, Joe?"

Conant couldn't figure it out, either. He knew all right that the police had been looking for the stolen paintings and he realized they must have stopped other trains out of Grand Central and searched them. The fact was he'd been mystified by the extraordinary efficiency of the police ever since the five of them had come out of the door of the Museum and seen the force gathered there. It almost seemed as if the police had been prepared and waiting in readiness for the robbery to be pulled. Could there, somehow, he wondered, have been a leak despite his careful planning? But he said nothing of what he had thought.

"I don't know what it all means," he answered De Angelo, and the other three who were, he could see, equally worried. "The fact that they have our names and addresses means nothing. Hell, if they questioned everybody who was in Grand Central the same time we were they must have collected thousands of names and addresses. The important thing is we've done it! We've got the paintings, we got away with it, and we're going to collect our ransom. So forget it."

By the time the police completed their search of the nine trains which had been stopped, 1800 passengers had been interrogated and frisked. Of this number, fifty persons either could not produce proof of their identity or resisted the police in their investigation and were taken into custody, removed from the trains and flown back to the city by helicopter for detention at the 16th Precinct. The police search of the trains and passengers failed to produce any evidence of the prepetrators or the stolen paintings.

Gil Shelby had been Chief Dispatcher for the Penn Central Railroad for nine years now and in all that time he had never before been confronted with a situation similar to the one he now faced. As time passed, the sight of the giant console in front of him—which indicated that nothing was moving northward on the tracks out of Grand Central—made him increasingly uneasy and prompted him, finally, to put in a call to the president of the Penn Central at his home in Greenwich and notify him of the situation.

As soon as William Mather, president of the Penn Central, received Shelby's call and got as many of the facts as the Chief Dispatcher could give him, he called the Mayor at Gracie Mansion.

Mayor Andrew Forester had not, up until that moment, been aware of the robbery of the Metropolitan Museum of Art nor of the events occurring at Grand Central Station. He did not, however, acknowledge this to Mather. Instead, he said, "We're right on top of the situation, Bill. Yes, I can appreciate your concern to get the trains moving again as soon as possible and I can assure you that the police department is moving as speedily as possible. Let me try to see if I can hurry things up. I'll have someone get back to you."

The Mayor immediately called the Commissioner at Police Headquarters and was told that Commissioner

Hilliard had left earlier in the day for a weekend at
his summer home in Montauk, Long Island. When Andrew Forester phoned Montauk, he discovered Commissioner Hilliard had gone deep-sea fishing off Montauk
in a chartered boat. The Mayor then contacted
the Coast Guard and directed them to locate the chartered boat and the Commissioner and fly him back to
the city. Afterwards, Andrew Forester sent one of his
deputies to find out what the hell was going on at
Grand Central Station while he himself prepared to
visit the Metropolitan.

It wasn't until shortly before midnight that Max
Kauffman left Grand Central Station and headed over
to the 16th Precinct. He was satisfied that the police
had done all that was humanly possible in investigat-
ing those who were in the station and on the trains
at the time Grand Central was sealed up. He had ordered that the station be opened again and the trains
and subways resume normal operation although he had
left two details of police behind, one to continue a
search through the building for the stolen paintings, the
other to maintain surveillance on the people moving
in and out of the station. Word had come in from police
still at the Metropolitan, meantime, that Museum
curators had verified that only five paintings had been
stolen. Experts from the crime lab were in the process
of going over the premises for possible clues.

When the Inspector reached the station house, he
walked into sheer bedlam. Three hundred and nineteen persons had been taken into custody by the police on one charge or another, resisting an officer,
failing to produce identification, or for more serious
offenses; the Grand Central dragnet had turned up a
number of persons with illegal narcotics in their possession, five individuals who were already fugitives
from felony charges, one who had escaped from the
mental ward at Bellevue Hospital, and twenty who
carried concealed weapons on their persons. These
offenders were easy to deal with; the mental patient

was returned to Bellevue and the others were processed
through the 16th Precinct booking desk and removed
by police vans to the Tombs to await further disposi-
tion of their cases.

In addition, the police roundup had netted twenty-
two habitual vagrants, none of whom had a perma-
nent address and most of whom spent some part of
every day or night in Grand Central Station. One of
these vagrants, an old woman of indeterminable age,
wearing shapeless, shabby clothes grabbed Max Kauffman's arm as he tried to make his way up to his office.

"Help me, please," she pleaded. "I'm just an old,
old woman. I haven't done nothing bad. The police
always left me alone before. They know old Sadie don't
mean no harm. I don't want to be locked up." She
kept shaking her head, bewildered, and clutching his
sleeve. Her filthy clothes were damp with sweat from
the heat of the station house.

Max Kauffman nodded to a policeman standing near
by and said, "Bring her up to my office."

When they were inside the office, Max Kauffman
took a twenty-dollar bill from his pocket and gave it
to the woman. She started weeping.

"Get yourself a place to sleep tonight," he told her,
"and stay away from Grand Central Station." To the
officer, he said, "Release her and take her wherever
she wants to go, then report back to the desk sergeant."

The old woman, still weeping, continued to clutch
at Max Kauffman's arm until the uniformed policeman
pulled her away and led her from the office.

Son-of-a-bitch, Max Kauffman thought, he must be
getting soft in the head. Then he put the incident out
of his mind and went to check on what was happening
with the remainder of those still held in custody. Most
of these people were reasonably well-dressed individuals who simply hadn't been carrying any identification with them when they'd been questioned. Now
they were all lined up in front of phones on various
desks in the station house calling, or trying to call,
wives or friends or lawyers to come vouch for them.

The Inspector didn't look forward to the contingent of lawyers he knew he'd have to face before the night was over.

Earlier in the evening the 16th Precinct desk sergeant had begun making phone calls to try to locate all the regular station-house personnel to report for emergency duty. He wasn't able to get in touch with Sergeant Margaret O'Dell until after midnight and shortly before 1:30 A.M. she appeared at the precinct. Max Kauffman put her to work at once collating and counting the names and addresses recorded by the police of persons who had been in Grand Central or on the trains which had been halted.

By 2:30 A.M., most of those who had been brought in to the 16th Precinct from the station and the trains had had their identities established for them by friends, relatives, and lawyers, and were being released.

As Max Kauffman had been expecting all along, he got a phone call from the desk sergeant telling him that a group of lawyers demanded to see him for an explanation of why their clients' legal rights had been so grossly violated. With a sign of resignation, the Inspector told the desk sergeant to send them up.

There were nine lawyers in all in the group, about half of them representing the Legal Aid Society. Max Kauffman listened patiently while they expressed their outrage and indignation and even nodded unflinchingly when a couple of the lawyers sprinkled their complaints with such expressions as "gestapo tactics," and "police brutality."

"I understand your feelings exactly," he told them earnestly in reply. "I realize that to some of you the methods used by the police department tonight might appear unreasonable but I assure you there was no intention on the part of any officer to do more than carry out a lawful investigation into a major and serious crime. I would remind you that the law was strictly observed by the police department in this matter—"

"You call it lawful to arrest a man just because he's

unable to produce proof of his identity?" One of the
lawyers demanded.

"None of the people brought into the station house
because they could not establish identity were arrested,"
Max Kauffman pointed out, "merely detained."

Before anyone could object to his statement, he
added hurriedly, "But of course, as I'm sure you know
by now, the action taken tonight was by authority of
Section One-Forty-Point-Five-O of the Criminal Procedure Law. If you question that authority, you can
naturally register your complaints with the proper
courts."

He buzzed Sergeant O'Dell quickly and had the
group ushered out of his office.

He was seething with rage. That's all he'd needed
at a time like this: a goddamn delegation of bleeding
hearts lecturing him on the law. Suddenly, he began
to laugh at himself. What a *schmuck!* he thought,
shaking his head. Now he'd begun to think of lawyers
who were only doing their jobs as bleeding hearts. He
was getting to be as bad-mouthed as his old man.

Sergeant O'Dell had just finished tallying up the record of names and addresses of those taken into custody
from the station and trains and had laid the lists on his
desk when Police Commissioner John Hilliard walked
into the office. It was 3:15 A.M.

The PC was sunburned, his hair was tousled, and he
was dressed in rumpled sports clothes. Max Kauffman
dismissed Sergeant O'Dell, and Commissioner Hilliard
yanked a chair up to the desk opposite Max Kauffman
and sat down in it stiffly.

"I got a call from the Mayor earlier this evening,"
the Commissioner said, scowling. "He chewed me out
about this business you pulled at Grand Central tonight."

"You know about the Museum robbery?" Max Kauffman asked.

"Yes, I know all about the robbery," John Hilliard
said, biting off his words. "What I don't know, Inspector,
is why you felt it was necessary to take the action you

took, rounding up all those people, having trains and subways halted. Jesus, you'll have the whole city screaming police harassment—and for what?"

Max Kauffman leaned back in his chair. His face was gray with fatigue, his eyes bleary. "I knew," he said, his voice hoarse, "the perpetrators had fled into Grand Central Station. I know they hadn't had time to get out before we surrounded the place. So they had to be somewhere in the station or on the trains or planning to catch a subway. I suspected they might find a way to ditch the stolen paintings somewhere, in the station, or in the tunnels, perhaps. I believed we might not ever get a chance to trace them once they were beyond the station and the trains, so I decided upon the action I took; to get a complete list of the identity of everyone who was in the station at the time we sealed the exits."

"But how in God's name is that going to help us?" the Commissioner demanded.

Max Kauffman pointed to the lists lying on his desk. "There are three thousand, five hundred and sixty-three authenticated names on those lists. I would almost guarantee you that the names of the perpetrators of the robbery of the Metropolitan are somewhere on those lists." He leaned forward and rested his elbows on the desk. "Now we've got this guy, Griffith, we're holding who probably does know something about this job, and we're going to use him. But, in addition, what I thought was we'd program these three thousand, five hundred and sixty-three names into the computer down at headquarters, or even better, into the computer at the National Crime Information Center in Washington, D.C. Then we add every scrap of information we can get our hands on, about the robbery, about the Museum, and from the FBI files and our own. If we get lucky, we might pick up a cross-reference which will give us a lead to the perpetrators."

"Yes, I see, Inspector," Commissioner Hilliard said slowly. He nodded his head in reluctant agreement.

CHAPTER FIFTEEN

J. T. Spanner was awakened at 7 A.M. Saturday by a telephone call from Inspector Max Kauffman. Spanner had been out of town the previous day on an investigation for the law firm of Hogarth, Whittaker, Macauley. He had not gotten home until very late the previous night and he knew nothing of the robbery of the Metropolitan Museum of Art until he received the phone call.

The Inspector was calling from the Museum. He sounded annoyed when he found Spanner didn't know of the robbery and that time had to be wasted to fill him in on the facts. Max Kauffman had concluded the call by saying testily, "I'd like to see you up here at the Museum right away, Spanner."

Spanner had quickly showered, shaved and dressed, but stopped off, bought copies of the two New York morning newspapers, and had breakfast at a coffee shop on his way to the Metropolitan.

Both papers had the story of the robbery on the front page. The *Daily News* headline read: *MILLION $ ART THEFT AT MET*—GANG HEISTS 5 MASTERPIECES.

The photograph showed smoke pouring out of the front of the Metropolitan and the street jammed with police cars, fire engines, and emergency vehicles. The caption under the photograph was: *Where there's smoke . . . ?*

The *Times* Story was headlined: PRICELESS

PAINTINGS STOLEN IN DARING ROBBERY AT
METROPOLITAN MUSEUM—THIEVES ELUDE PO-
LICE—GRAND CENTRAL SCENE OF MASSIVE MANHUNT,
THOUSANDS QUIZZED, SEARCHED.

Alongside the story of the robbery were photographs
of the stolen Brueghel, Rembrandt, Picasso, Monet, and
Renoir.

Spanner read through the accounts in both newspapers, and then headed up to the Museum. He had a
lot of sympathy for Inspector Max Kauffman now that
he knew exactly what the police official was up against.

At the Metropolitan, the police had cordoned off the
front of the building and closed the Museum to the
public. Wooden barriers had been set up, blocking the
entrance to the building, and behind these stood several
hundred spectators who had been drawn to the scene
by the news accounts of the robbery. Spanner found a
place to park his car on Eighty-Third Street, and walked
back. It was another hot day, with the temperature well
into the eighties that early in the morning, the sky a
cloudless blue, and a hot, dry wind rattling the dusty
leaves on the trees lining Fifth Avenue. Spanner identified himself to one of the policemen on duty at the
entrance to the Museum, and explained that Inspector
Kauffman had sent for him.

The policeman went away to check and came back
and led Spanner into the building and up to the second
floor. Members of the police crime lab were all over
the interior of the building with their equipment, looking for evidence, photographing, dusting for finger-
prints, and footprints, collecting samples of dust from
the floor and taking scrapings from the walls where
the stolen paintings had hung, for analysis. Spanner
saw that the empty frames which had contained the
paintings and the smoke bomb canisters used in the
robbery still stood where the perpetrators had left them
the night before while the police experts continued
their microscopic photographing and examination of
each item.

Inspector Max Kauffman was standing with a group

of men near one of the Museum's second-floor windows which was raised, with a rope draped over the sill. One end of the rope dangled outside the window, the other end lay coiled on the floor inside. The Inspector nodded to Spanner briefly, conferred for a while longer with the group at the window, and then came over.

Max Kauffman was clean-shaven and wearing a neatly-pressed suit and a fresh shirt but Spanner could see the purple pouches of fatigue under his eyes.

"I'm having Griffith brought up from the station house," the Inspector said without any preliminaries. "He should be here shortly. There's something I want him to see and I want you to be there at the same time."

"You think this is definitely the job he had the tip on then, huh?" Spanner asked.

Max Kauffman rubbed his eyes. "If it's not, it's one hell of a coincidence."

Spanner looked around the area of the second floor. "You got it figured out yet how they did it?"

Max Kauffman shrugged. "Based on the evidence we've uncovered so far, it looks like they came down from the roof by that rope over there and in through the window. But I don't know, we're still working on it. One thing's for sure, though, they really did a sweet job of it. They stayed a step ahead of us all the way despite our best efforts."

"And now?" Spanner asked.

The Inspector grimaced. "Unless we get a make on them and fast, I guess we wait for them to make their ransom demand."

"Yeah," Spanner said, "I figured it for a ransom demand, too, soon as I read the stories in the newspapers. There's no way they could unload those paintings anywhere else in the world."

"A slick bunch of bastards," Max Kauffman said. Then his eyes narrowed. "But they're still not in the clear yet."

He left Spanner and went to check on the lab men who were examining the empty frames. Spanner wandered around the second floor for a while watching the investigation until he spotted Warren Griffith coming up the staircase, handcuffed to a plainclothesman.

Griffith's face was dead-white and his eyes kept darting nervously from side to side as the plainclothesman led him past the groups of lab technicians at work and over to where Max Kauffman stood. The Inspector motioned to Spanner to join them.

"We're going to take a ride downtown," Max Kauffman announced. "There's some additional evidence that's come in and I want us to take a look at it."

The Inspector led the way down the stairs and out the front entrance of the Museum. His limousine was waiting at the curb. A second plainclothesman joined them and he and the plainclothesman handcuffed to Griffith hustled Griffith into a prowl car parked in front of the limousine.

"Come on," Max Kauffman said to Spanner and climbed into the limousine. When Spanner explained that he had his own car parked around the corner, Max Kauffman said, "Come on, come on. You can pick it up later."

The prowl car carrying Warren Griffith pulled out, followed by the Inspector's limousine, with a second prowl car bringing up the rear. Sirens blaring, the three-car motorcade proceeded down Fifth Avenue.

"Mind telling me what this is all about, Inspector?" Spanner asked as Max Kauffman leaned back in the seat and lit a cigar.

"Mmm," Max Kauffman mumbled, drawing on his cigar, "We got a call from the TV people at NBC earlier this morning. They had a camera crew up at the Museum yesterday afternoon filming what they thought at the time was a fire. After they learned about the robbery and their film was developed, they found that it appears they may have picked up some film of the actual perpetrators coming out of the Museum. None of it has gone out over the air yet. They're going to use it on their six P.M. news program and they've offered to let us view it first. Could be interesting, especially if Griffith is able to identify the man he claims told him about the robbery."

Spanner nodded his head and the two men rode in silence as the three cars sped down Fifth Avenue, turned west on Forty-Ninth Street, and swung around and stopped in front of 30 Rockefeller Plaza. The group was met there by a man Spanner recognized as the Deputy Police Commissioner for Public Affairs and whose name, he thought, was Bob or Bill or Something Harlow, and who escorted them through the building and into the elevator up to the ninth floor. On the way, Harlow explained that NBC was making its Executive Screening Room, the Red Room, available to them.

The room was crowded. In addition to the group that had come down from the Museum, Spanner spotted the Police Commissioner himself sitting in the back of the room, along with a contingent of plain-clothesmen some of whom, Spanner would have bet, were FBI men. There were also some NBC people present.

As soon as they were all in their seats, Max Kauffman and Warren Griffith and Griffith's police guards sat down front, Spanner in a seat just behind Griffith, one of NBC men spoke briefly.

"What we're going to show you now," he said, "is all the film we shot yesterday up at the Museum, including the out-takes—that is, the stuff we won't be using on the air once we've finished editing the footage for tonight's Sixth Hour News."

Just before the lights in the room went out, Max Kauffman took a quick look at Griffith slumped down in the seat beside him. He hadn't told Griffith what this was all about before he'd brought him down from the Museum. Griffith was wetting his lips with his tongue, a puzzled look on his face.

The lights went out and the film flashed on the screen in the front of the room.

The first shot was a slow, sweeping pan of Fifth Avenue in front of the Metropolitan showing the street

clogged with private cars, police cars and vans, and
fire engines. In the foreground, firemen could be seen
unreeling their hoses and dashing toward the Museum,
which was clearly visible in the background with a
thick blanket of white smoke billowing out through the
front entrance and rising skyward.

A fireman suddenly appeared, a huge closeup as
he must have dashed almost directly in front of the
camera, his black raincoat filling the screen.

The next shot was a zoom-in to the entrance to the
Museum where great clouds of smoke rolled out, en-
veloping the firemen dragging their hoses up the massive stone steps. Slowly, the camera pulled back again
for a wide shot, revealing more emergency equipment,
firemen and police arriving in front of the Museum.
There were several seconds more of the scene in
front of the Museum and then abruptly the camera
panned upward and away from the Museum. There
were the tops of trees and the higher floors of the
apartment buildings across Fifth Avenue and, finally,
the sky. For several seconds the sky filled the screen
and then a helicopter appeared at the top of the
screen.

As the helicopter slowly descended, the camera followed it down to the island of pavement between the
museum driveway and Fifth Avenue where it sat,
rotor blades twirling. The following scene was a me-
dium closeup of the helicopter, with the Museum in
the background. Max Kauffman suddenly stirred in
his seat with embarrassment when he caught a glimpse
of himself, arms gesturing as he stood talking to a
policeman who was handing him a smoke-bomb canister. He was only in the scene for a moment and no
one else in the room seemed to have noticed, but it
had been enough to make him slightly uncomfortable.
There was another minute or so of the activity out
in front of the Metropolitan before the camera zoomed
in again for a closeup of the entrance.

In the darkness of the room the NBC man who

had spoken to them earlier said sharply, "Watch this
next sequence carefully now. We think this is it."

The front entrance to the Museum filled the screen.
The scene was framed by three or four of the top
steps leading up to the entrance, at the bottom of the
screen, and smoke still pouring out of the doorway
and beyond the frame at the top of the screen. A
couple of firemen came into view at the bottom of
the screen, climbed the steps and disappeared into
the smoke. The camera held on the scene briefly,
started to pan away, then panned back again to the
same frame-shot of the smoking entrance as a couple
of dark forms materialized in the midst of the swirling smoke.

"This is it," the NBC man said excitedly.

Max Kauffman slid forward to the edge of his seat.

On the screen, two firemen emerged from the
smoke, followed almost immediately by two more firemen. Almost as soon as they appeared, one of the
firemen, the second one in line, seemed to stumble
and almost lost his balance. The man in front turned
his head sharply and then all four of them were moving forward again. The camera held on them briefly
as they started down the steps in single file at an angle. The man in front was carrying two dark bundles,
one under each arm. The other three men each carried a similar dark bundle.

"Jesus, yes! That's them!" Max Kauffman called
out, unable to restrain himself.

The four men were only on-screen for a few seconds
more before they moved swiftly out of the frame. The
camera didn't follow them and instead held on the
smoking entrance and eventually pulled back again
for a wide shot of the front of the Museum. There
was no sign of the four men, and Max Kauffman calculated that by the time the scene they were viewing
now was filmed, the four perpetrators were in the
stolen fire engine, heading down Fifth Avenue

The shots of the four men coming out of the Museum and starting down the steps had gone pretty fast, and Max Kauffman hadn't been able to take in much about their appearances in any detail. He shifted impatiently in his seat until the reel of film ended and the lights came up in the room again.

The NBC spokesman stood at the front of the room and looked around. "Was any of the film of help, gentlemen?" he asked.

Max Kauffman half-rose in his seat. "Hell, yes," he said. "Those were the four guys all right, in that last sequence there at the entrance to the Museum. Can we see it again?"

"Better than that," the NBC man said. "We made another print of that sequence and put it on a separate loop—just in case we had what we thought we had. We can show you just that part again and over and over as often as you like."

There was a short wait with the lights still on in the room. Max Kauffman leaned over to Warren Griffith. "Now listen to me," he said in a low, curt voice, "I want you to take a good, goddamned, hard look at those four guys up there when the film is run again. And then I want you to tell me if any of them looks anything at all like this guy, Hap, you say talked to you. And I want you to tell me if there's anything familar-looking about any of the others, too. Understand?"

Griffith nodded his head vigorously. His face was once again, as it had been on the first occasion he'd met the Inspector, shiny with sweat.

The room was darkened and they ran the sequence of film again. And again. And again. Finally the projectionist stopped the reel so the film remained frozen on the screen at the exact spot where the four men coming down the Museum steps were closest to the camera.

Max Kauffman studied the shot intently. Even that close up to the camera it was impossible to identify the faces of the four men in their firemen's uniforms and oxygen masks except for their size and general build. But even that was more than they'd had before and might be helpful later on.

The Inspector leaned over to Warren Griffith. "Well, what do you think?"

"I—uh—it's, you know, hard to tell," Griffith said hesitantly. "But the second guy there, the one that sort of stumbled, it could be him. I mean the size, the shape of him, is right. Yeah, it could be him."

After the lights came up once more, Max Kauffman rose from his seat and looked around the room. "Anybody spot anything he thinks is significant?" he asked.

One of the FBI men sitting near the Commissioner said, "It's nothing particularly significant, I'm sure we all noticed it, but I assume those were genuine firemen's uniforms the four men were wearing."

Max Kauffman nodded. "Yes, I'd assume so, too. We'll have to check into that matter. Anyone have anything else to add?"

When there were no responses, Max Kauffman went over and thanked the NBC man for the showing and arranged to have photographs made of the scene where the four men were closest to the camera so the police could study it in detail. He wanted his own copies of that scene in the film even though he knew that once the film appeared on the evening news program, newspapers and magazines would soon be reproducing the photograph.

The Inspector then conferred briefly with the Commissioner before he came back, ordered the two plain-clothesmen to return Griffith to the 16th Precinct, and said to Spanner, "Come on, I want to have a talk with you."

CHAPTER SIXTEEN

Spanner sat in one of the scarred, wooden chairs outside the closed door of Inspector Max Kauffman's office at the 16th Precinct and watched Sergeant Margaret O'Dell typing at her desk. It was hot as a sweatbox in the station house. Spanner had removed his coat, rolled up his sleeves, and loosened his tie but it didn't help much. He was growing increasingly annoyed that Max Kauffman, inside his air-conditioned office, was keeping him waiting so long in the airless corridor outside.

The Inspector hadn't had much to say to him on the drive over to the 16th Precinct from NBC except to repeat that he wanted to have a talk. When they'd reached the station house, Max Kauffman had asked him for the keys to his car, asked where the car was parked up at the Museum and the license number, and had sent a couple of patrolmen up to bring it down to the 16th Precinct. They had gone on up to the Inspector's office then but, instead of taking Spanner inside, Max Kauffman had asked him to wait in the corridor. A few minutes after that, Spanner was surprised to see Police Commissioner Hilliard arrive and go into Max Kauffman's office. The two men had been in there for three-quarters of an hour now.

Spanner lit a cigarette, the sixth one he'd smoked while he was waiting, and continued his casual contemplation of Sergeant O'Dell for want of something

better to do. He'd already decided she was a pretty
good-looking little thing, take her out of that uniform,
soften up her hairdo a bit, apply a touch of makeup
here and there, a darker red shade of lipstick and a
trace of eye shadow. He knew she was aware of his
eyes upon her and it amused him that she so stu-
diously ignored him. Another time, another place, he
thought, and who knew?

A few minutes later, the Police Commissioner came
out, glanced briefly at Spanner, and went on toward
the elevator. Max Kauffman, standing in the open
doorway, beckoned Spanner into the office. The Inspector sat down behind his desk and motioned Spanner to a chair opposite him.

"We want you to do a favor for us, Spanner," Max
Kauffman said. "I'm going to release Warren Griffith
in your custody. I want you to take him out and start
beating the bushes, the bars, or whatever the fuck, and
see if he can turn up this character, Hap, he's been
shooting his mouth off about."

"Hold it! Wait a minute, Inspector!" Spanner protested, half-rising from his chair, his hands outstretched.
"No thanks. No way, no thanks."

"Sit down, Spanner," Max Kauffman said pleasantly.
He waited until Spanner was seated again and leaned
back in his own chair, his chin cupped by the fist he'd
made with his right hand.

"Spanner," he said conversationally, "I'm not going
to go into all the crap about the facts of life for a
private investigator who has to keep in the good graces
of the police department to stay in business. I'm not
going to go into all that crap because I know you already know it. Instead, I'm going to repeat what I
said before. We want you to do a favor for us, Spanner." He paused and nodded his head. "Okay?"

"Under duress, yeah," Spanner answered, "okay."

Max Kauffman got up and came around the desk.
"We appreciate your cooperation," he said. "Oh, and
one other matter I'm not going to go into because I
know you already know it. That's if you lose Griffith,

you're in big trouble. I'll leave it in your hands as to how you convince Griffith it wouldn't be worth it for him to try to get away from you."

It was mid-afternoon before Spanner left the 16th Precinct in his car with Griffith and headed out to Queens. For safety's sake, he decided to keep Griffith handcuffed during the drive. He noticed that his prisoner looked unusually glum and when they'd driven about halfway to Flushing and Griffith still hadn't said anything, Spanner asked, "What's wrong, Griffith? You got exactly what you wanted, you got your deal with the police, you're on your way to put the finger on the guy who was in on the robbery, why so gloomy?"

"I'm just kind of bugged, man. That's all," Griffith said, shrugging. "Jails do that to me."

Spanner drove on out Northern Boulevard until they reached a wooded area near Flushing Meadow Park. He turned off there onto a side street and drove on into a deserted woodland section bordering the park. Griffith was instantly alert, sitting up straighter in the seat, looking around him.

"Hey, what the hell is this?" Griffith asked, agitated. "This ain't the way to Flushing. Where are you taking me?"

Spanner didn't answer. He drove deeper into the woods for another quarter of a mile, leaving the road behind and winding around through the trees. There were no people or houses anywhere near. When they reached a clearing where, on the far side, there was a stand of elm trees, he parked the car. He got out, walked around, and opened the door where Griffith sat.

"Come on," Spanner said. "Out!"

Griffith cringed back in the seat and Spanner reached in and hauled him bodily out and prodded him roughly ahead of him. Griffith stumbled across the clearing, glancing back over his shoulder at Spanner who walked a couple of paces behind. When they stood about fifteen to twenty feet from the line of elm trees at the edge of the clearing, Spanner said, "Okay, stop here." He drew his gun from his hip holster. It was silent in the clearing. The sunlight filtering through the trees cast odd-shaped patterns of shadow on the ground. Griffith, as if mesmerized, never took his eyes off the gun in Spanner's hand.

"Listen, what are you going to do with me?" Griffith asked in a choked whisper. "Jesus, what is this?"

"Why don't you shut up," Spanner said disgustedly. "I'm not going to shoot you. I just want to show you something. Just in case you get the bright idea somewhere along the line you're going to try to get away from me."

He motioned toward the line of trees across the clearing. "Let's say that first tree over there is you on the run. I'd aim for your kneecap."

He raised the .357 Magnum, aimed quickly, and fired. The bullet slammed into the trunk of the tree a few feet up from the base, scattering pieces of bark across the ground. Spanner nodded.

"Let's say," he said, "I missed you on that first shot —even though I didn't. Let's say you'd still be running." He indicated the other trees in the line, raised the gun again, and fired four shots, pivoting slightly on his toes after each shot. Three of the bullets went into the first three tree trunks at approximately the same distance from the base of each tree, a few feet up from the ground. The fourth shot thudded into the bark higher up the trunk of the remaining tree.

"That last shot," Spanner said, shaking his head, "even with the best control you can't hit a bull's-eye every time. That one would have probably buried itself in your brain."

He pointed the barrel of the gun toward the ground and ejected the spent sheels. He stomped the empty cartridges into the dry earth with the heel of his shoe and smoothed the ground over with his foot. Then he reloaded the gun and stuck it back into his hip holster.

"Those aluminum cups they use to replace smashed kneecaps," he said, "they don't really work very well."

They walked back to the car in silence. Spanner noticed that Griffith had developed a slight tic in his left cheek. He didn't think he was going to have any trouble with him.

Max Kauffman's eyes burned and his head ached. By 4 P.M. that afternoon, Saturday afternoon, he had been up for thirty-three hours straight. After Spanner had left the 16th Precinct with Warren Griffith, Max Kauffman had gone back down to Grand Central Station where a detail of police were still searching for the stolen paintings. In the early hours of the morning the police had gotten a court order authorizing them to open up the lockers in the station. They had recovered, from various lockers, a bag of burglars' tools, a cache of cocaine, an attaché case containing a batch of pornographic pictures and film, two .38 revolvers loaded with dum-dum bullets, and a battered suitcase packed with travelers' checks and credit cards in different names, but not paintings. Now they were concentrating for the most part on the tunnels on the lower level, probing the dark ledges and crevices in the tunnel walls with powerful flashlights but so far they had succeeded only in flushing out the hordes of rats that infested the subterranean passageways.

The Inspector went into the tunnels and watched the men at work for a while. It was a hot, tiresome, dirty job and even though Max Kauffman soon began to feel claustrophobic, he stayed on out of a sense of duty until he could no longer stand it. After a few words of encouragement to the men on the detail, the Inspector fled back to the street and his limousine and told his driver to take him back to the 16th Precinct.

Max Kauffman leaned back in the seat and closed his eyes, but his mind was busy thinking about the case.

Earlier, Max Kauffman and the Commissioner had met at the 16th Precinct to discuss the lists of names and addresses of those who had been in Grand Central Station and on the trains the night before, the lists which were to be fed into the computer.

"I checked with the Mayor," Commissioner Hilliard said. "He now understands the actions you took last night. But he doesn't want to use the National Crime Information Center computer in Washington. We'll use the one at Headquarters."

"We'd get better and faster results with Washington," Max Kauffman quickly pointed out.

Commissioner Hilliard nodded. "I expect so. But you know how touchy everybody is these days about anything that smacks of Big Brother in Washington being given information about private citizens. I expect that's what His Honor has in mind."

Max Kauffman didn't need the message spelled out for him in any more detail. He knew there had already been minor furors created in a couple of places in the country over the information that had been gathered by the National Crime Information Center's computer file on private citizens. And, after all, Mayor Forester did have a liberal image to maintain.

"Okay, Okay," he said to the Commissioner. "If that's the way it has to be, it has to be. But I want you to know I'm on record as requesting that we use the facilities of the National Crime Information Center."

Soon after that when Commissioner Hilliard left the station house, he took with him the lists of names and addresses of those who had been in Grand Central Station and on the trains that evening before and by now, hopefully, that information was being programmed into the computer at headquarters. Soon, other facts, from law-enforcement files and all additional sources which could be connected in any way with the robbery, would also be fed into the computer. Officials at the Museum were also compiling lists, at the request of the police, of all persons who had been employed at the Metropolitan in any capacity during the past three years. Because it was the weekend and certain companies, such as delivery services which supplied people frequently used by the Museum, were closed, police would be dispatched to locate the heads of such companies wherever they were to obtain the names of those personnel and as quickly as the names were obtained they, too, would be fed into the computer. It was a long shot that the computer would turn up anything to give them a lead, Max Kauffman knew, but it was worth the effort.

The Museum guards who had been on duty at the time of the robbery had been intensively questioned. None of them had anything to add to the case and all of them had volunteered to take lie-detector tests which they'd passed. Another dead end.

Commissioner Hilliard had also argued against releasing Warren Griffith into Spanner's custody. "I don't like it," he told Max Kauffman. "How do we know Griffith isn't going to try to pull a trick on us? I've got a hunch that all he wants to do is find a way to escape from police custody. Besides, we don't even know Griffith has an idea of where to find the man who was supposed to be in on the robbery."

"True," Max Kauffman agreed. "Everything you say could be true. But if it is we might as well find it out as soon as possible. And if Griffith is up to something, he's damn sure more likely to try it if we release him in Spanner's custody. I think we ought to do it."

"Yes, yes, all right," the Commissioner eventually agreed. "Have it your way." And the matter had been settled.

There were several aspects to this robbery which disturbed Max Kauffman more than usual. That business of the firemen's uniforms the perpetrators had worn, for instance. One of the first things Max Kauffman had done that morning was have a check made of all the robbery reports that had been turned in city-wide for the past six months. The report of the burglary of four complete firemen's uniforms and oxygen masks from Engine Company 222 only a couple of blocks from the Museum had come to light right away. The burglary had taken place just a few weeks earlier.

If he had had that information a few days earlier, Max
Kauffman thought, it might have helped alert him to
be suspicious of the firemen on the scene at the Museum. But, at the time, the report of the firehouse
robbery was routine, one of hundreds of such reports
filed daily in New York City, and there was no reason
why anyone should have called it to his attention.

Then there were the precautions the perpetrators
had taken to protect the paintings they'd stolen. The
director of the Metropolitan, Alan Coopersmith, had
been impressed when he was shown the tarpaulin
covers and the sheets of glassine paper recovered from
the Grand Central tunnel. "Obviously," the Museum
Director said, "the thieves were exercising great cau-
tion to see that no harm came to the paintings. The
glassine paper," he went on to explain to Max Kauffman who hadn't known what the material was, "is
the most protective covering you can use to shield
valuable canvases. It would appear they used the outer
covering of tarpaulin both to conceal the paintings as
they came out of the Museum and to protect the canvases from possible excessive water damage. Also,
when the paintings were stripped from the frame,
these men appeared to be most careful to preserve
as much of the original canvas as possible. No question about it; there was considerable thought given to
keep the paintings safe."

These facts had made it easier for Coopersmith to
accept the police opinion that a ransom demand was
probably going to be made by the gang for the safe
return of the paintings.

The Director had, additionally, offered grudging respect to the thieves for the particular selection of paintings they had chosen to steal. The collective value of
the five stolen paintings was, he assured police, almost
impossible to calculate. Nor did the fact that the gang
had taken Rembrandt's *Portrait of a Man* and left
the more famed *Aristotle* escape Alan Coopersmith's
attention. "It may sound crazy," he had stated, "but
I feel these men must have deliberately passed up

the *Aristotle* to try somehow to signal us they were reasonable people."

All of which brought Max Kauffman to the crux of the matter: exactly what manner of men were they dealing with here? More to the point, exactly what manner of man was the leader, the brains, of the robbery? It was an old game the Inspector always played when he was going after an unknown culprit, or unknown culprits. Was the man who masterminded the robbery—Max Kauffman had already figured him for the perpetrator who had led the way coming out of the smoking Museum—a pro? Was it an inside job? Was it just a bunch of amateurs who got lucky?

Even though the Inspector still had no face to put on the ringleader of the robbery, he had already begun to get some tenuous impressions of the kind of man he was looking for, based on the emerging M.O. of the crime. The job had been well-planned, so his man was smart. It had also been well-executed, so he was daring. The knowledge that had gone into the selection of the paintings to be stolen suggested that he was, also, well-educated. Max Kauffman speculated that the man must, in addition, be a careful person as evidenced by the way the stolen paintings had been so protectively wrapped when they were taken from the Museum.

Another fact which intrigued the Inspector about the robbery was that the whole thing had been executed by the perpetrators without resorting to weapons or violence. In that regard, it more closely represented a typically British crime—as Max Kauffman knew from his visits to Scotland Yard and discussions with his English counterparts there—where wits, skill, and planning usually took the place of force and guns in the commission of most heists. In any event, Max Kauffman reflected, there couldn't be much doubt but that he faced a worthy adversary—whoever he might be.

The Inspector was still driving across town when a few minutes later he received a call over his car phone

from the Headquarters dispatcher telling him he was
wanted up at the Museum immediately. The gang had
made contact with the Director of the Metropolitan
and had stated the ransom demand.

Within fifteen minutes, Max Kauffman was inside the
Museum and in the Director's office where Alan Coopersmith sat at his desk, looking pale-faced and shaken
while the room filled with police officials assigned to
the case. In addition to Max Kauffman, there were
present hand-picked members of the robbery squad,
working under the Inspector's command, and several
special agents from the FBI. The FBI had no jurisdic-
tion in the case as yet but they were cooperating with
the NYPD and being kept informed of all developments as they occurred.

"The phone call came at exactly three-fifty-five
P.M.," Coopersmith said in a husky voice, glancing
down at a sheet of paper on the desk top in front of
him. "I tried to write down everything that happened
that I thought was important. It was a man speaking.
The switchboard took the call first. Then they rang
me and said there was a man on the line who stated
he had some information about the paintings that had
been stolen and that he wanted to talk to me, that is,
talk to the Director of the Museum."

Coopersmith looked up and around the room. He
was a heavy-set man in his early fifties with thick,
black hair graying at the temples, and he wore half-
spectacles on the end of his nose. On the previous
occasions when Max Kauffman had met him, the Director had had a ruddy complexion. Now it was easy
to see that the phone call had unnerved him. Max
Kauffman was sympathetic; the sordid business of crime
was far removed from the lofty, insulated world of art,
and he suspected that the Director felt somehow
soiled even by the telephonic contact he'd had with the
perpetrators. It was not an uncommon reaction among
civilians who had had no previous experience in dealing with criminals. The Inspector nodded encourag-
ingly to Coopersmith to proceed.

The Director peered down at the paper through his spectacles. "I took the call and asked the individual who he was. He said never mind that. He said he was going to tell me how to get back the Brueghel, Rembrandt, Picasso, Monet, and Renoir. Before he did, he added, he wanted me to be convinced I was dealing with the legitimate party who had the paintings. The proof of that was, he said, that the frame from which the Brueghel had been taken, which incidentally, he knew was the painting's original frame, had had a small x-mark cut into it after the painting had been removed. He said the mark had been left on the frame as identification so we would know the caller actually had the paintings. He asked if I understood. I said, yes, I did."

Coopersmith paused and looked up at Max Kauffman.

Max Kauffman nodded his head. "Yes," he said. "The lab men made a note there was just such a fresh mark on the Brueghel frame. And that information has never been revealed to the press and public. It couldn't have been a hoax call."

"I suspected as much at the time," Coopersmith said. He referred to the paper on his desk again. "The man then said if we wanted the paintings back, here's what we had to do." He paused, sighed, shook his head and continued slowly, "He said that first we were to raise three million, seven hundred and fifty thousand dollars in cash. The money was all to be in fifty- and hundred-dollar bills, all of it was to be old money, and none of the bills were to be in sequence. He repeated those instructions to me twice, and then asked me to repeat them back to him so he could be sure I had it correct. He said the money had to be ready for delivery tomorrow morning."

Max Kauffman tried to curb his impatience when Coopersmith paused again to wipe off his glasses.

"Let's see now," the Museum Director then said, again referring to the piece of paper on his desk. "Oh yes, I tried to protest that the ransom was too high but this man went right on talking as if I hadn't spoken. He said the three million, seven hundred fifty thousand dollars should be placed aboard a plane tomorrow morning, and that the plane should be completely fueled, have the money in it, and be ready for takeoff at exactly twelve noon. The plane had to be a Beechcraft King Air—he was most emphatic about the precise plane to be used. The plane should have a pilot and copilot aboard, he said, and no one else. And no tricks. He instructed that the money should be placed in a leather mail pouch and attached to a parachute. And the plane should also carry five additional parachutes."

"Yes, yes, and then what?" Max Kauffman demanded when Coopersmith paused once more.

"Well, and then," Coopersmith said, frowning, "the man said we'd have to make arrangements so that the instructions to be phoned in here, to the Museum, could be relayed immediately to the plane. He stressed that it was vitally important that communications arrangements be made so there would be constant contact with the plane not only prior to takeoff but until he instructed otherwise. He added that he'd call here again tomorrow morning between eleven and twelve noon with further instructions for the plane. Finally, he warned that if we didn't follow his instructions to the letter, we'd never see the paintings again. And then he hung up." Coopersmith swabbed his sweating face with a silk handkerchief and leaned back in his chair, removing his reading glasses.

Max Kauffman looked around the room. "Anybody here fly a plane?"

"I do," the FBI agent in charge, a man named Martin Eberhard, answered.

"You have any idea why a Beechcraft King Air should have been specifically chosen?" Max Kauffman asked.

"Just as a guess," Eberhard said, "I would suppose they wanted that model Beechcraft used because it has the necessary seats, usually carries a pilot and copilot, is equipped with communications, can climb to sixteen to eighteen thousand feet, has a bit of radar, a turboprop engine and, perhaps most important, it has a door which can be opened while the plane's in flight."

Max Kauffman nodded absently. "I figured it was something like that, so they could make their jump with the money, if that's the plan."

"Wait a minute," Alan Coopersmith interrupted, puzzled. "What do you mean, make the jump with the money? Do you think they're going to be on the plane when it takes off?"

"No, I don't think that," Max Kauffman said. "But there's nothing to prevent them from instructing the plane to land and pick them up somewhere, and then make their jump. I'm just theorizing aloud, based on the facts we know, that they asked that there be five parachutes on the plane, in addition to the parachute with the money. And of course we don't know where the plane is headed till they tell us. Let's put that aside for now." He looked at the Museum Director. "What did this man sound like? I mean, young? Old? Was he calm? Excitable? Tough-sounding? Any particular accent or peculiarity in his speech."

"I'd say," Coopersmith said, "that he didn't sound *old*. If anything, his voice sounded completely flat. He was quite calm, not particularly tough-sounding. I remember thinking in the middle of the conversation how matter-of-fact he sounded, as if we were having an ordinary, everyday business discussion. It struck me quite forcibly how very odd it all seemed."

Well, there it all was, Max Kauffman thought, glancing over the notes he'd made while the Museum Director talked. Now that they knew what the ransom demand involved, they'd have to begin making a whole new set of contingency plans to deal with the problem.

Alan Coopersmith interrupted his thoughts at that point, saying, "Inspector, what do we do now? I mean, what is the police position on this matter? Do you advise we pay the ransom, or what?"

Max Kauffman hesitated for a moment before he

answered. "I'm afraid the decision will be up to you, up to the Board of Directors of the Metropolitan. Either way, of course, our investigation will go forward. If you do decide to pay, it's very possible we will still break the case meanwhile. Naturally we'd like to know the decision you make, as soon as possible so we can plan accordingly."

Coopersmith nodded. "I've already been in touch with most of the members of the Board since I first received word last night of the robbery. This time of year the Board members are scattered all over the country, but I'm hoping they'll all be back in New York for a meeting here later today. I don't know this for certain, but I would assume, given the priceless quality of the stolen paintings, the vote will be to pay the ransom."

Max Kauffman ended the meeting then, his mind churning with all the preparations that had to be made in short order. And first among these was to set up a communications center here in the Museum. He'd have to contact the telephone company, and bring in some of the police communications experts as well and—he stopped suddenly and thought: *My God! Kit! I forgot all about Kit!* It was the business of the telephones which had reminded him of her. Ever since last night when the robbery had occurred, he'd been meaning to call her but something else more urgent had kept distracting his attention.

Now, he decided, as soon as he had made the arrangements with the telephone company to start running extra lines into the Museum, he'd call her. Hell, for that matter he could even see her briefly while he was waiting for the communications set-up to be completed. On his trips to and from the Museum over the last two days, he'd noticed an outdoor cafe just down the street, at a place called the Stanhope Hotel. He'd call her and she could meet him there for a drink.

CHAPTER SEVENTEEN

An hour later when Max Kauffman left the Museum and strolled down to the Stanhope Hotel two blocks away, he was surprised when he didn't find Catherine Devereux waiting for him at one of the outdoor tables under the striped awning. He knew she should have had time to get there by now and he was mildly irritated because he had specifically told her that they wouldn't be able to spend too much time together. Most of the tables were occupied and as he looked around for a place to sit, he heard Kit calling his name. He turned and saw her sitting on a lounge just inside the door of the lobby.

When he reached her, she took hold of both of his wrists with her hands, pulled him toward her, and kissed him quickly on the lips. She was wearing a pale yellow, knee-length, halter dress which left her arms and back bare, no hose, and pale gold, flat sandals. Just looking at her made him feel grubby in comparison.

"Come on," he said, pulling her toward the entrance, "Let's have a drink."

She shook her head. "I have a better idea," she said. "Let's go into the bar inside where it's cooler."

She led him around through the front of the lobby and into a small bar which was deserted except for one other couple. The windows of the bar looked out on the sidewalk cafe and Fifth Avenue in front, and on Eighty-First Street and up Fifth Avenue toward the

Metropolitan Museum on the side. Max Kauffman chose a corner table, across the room from the other couple, and from which he could see the front of the Museum up the street. They both ordered Scotch mists.

Earlier, when he had talked to her on the phone, he had apologized for not calling her the night before when he'd broken their date but he hadn't explained the reason why he hadn't called. Now she had noticed him glancing out the window of the bar toward the Museum, and she said, "You're working on the robbery at the Metropolitan, aren't you, Max?"

He nodded his head. He'd always made it a firm rule never to discuss his cases with anyone outside the Department, including his wife and Catherine Devereux.

"I thought that was what had happened," she said, "when you didn't show up and when I heard about the robbery on the news late last night and then read about it in the papers this morning. You're sure it's all right for us to be having a drink here? I mean an awful lot of people you work with must be right up there at the Museum now."

He smiled at her. "It's all right, Kit," he said. God, he reminded himself, when would he ever learn to stop underestimating this woman? It was a mistake he was always making with her. The reason she had chosen the bar inside the hotel for them to have a drink, instead of the outdoor cafe, was because she knew it was more discreet for him, with all the fellow police there were in the neighborhood. And, of course, as always, she was right; it was just something to which he had given no thought, with all the other matters he'd had on his mind.

"Max," she said, her voice low, "I know you don't like to talk about your work. But may I ask you a question, just this one time?"

"Yes, Kit," he said. "What is it?"

Her face was troubled. "They're not going to get away with it, are they, Max? Nothing is going to happen to those beautiful paintings, is it? It would be so terrible."

He patted her hand "Darling, you mustn't worry

about such things. No, no, they're not going to get away with it. And the paintings will be all right, just don't you worry about it."

They talked about other things then, she told him he looked so tired and that she wanted him to get some rest, he told her that he was going to be busy for a while but that he'd try to phone her regularly and they'd be together as soon as he could wind up the case.

"I'll be waiting for you, darling," she said. "Don't worry about anything. Just concentrate on what you have to do. And let me know when you're free."

Afterwards, when he'd put her in a cab and started walking back up to the Museum, he thought about what he'd told her; that the perpetrators weren't going to get away with it and the paintings would be all right. He wished he could be as sure of that as he had made himself sound when he told her. He felt a sharp, stabbing pain at the bridge of his nose which made his eyes suddenly tear. He stopped at the curb across Fifth Avenue, took out his handkerchief and rubbed the spot on his nose as if he could wipe the pain away. He wished he could catch a few hours' sleep, but he knew he had a long evening ahead of him.

"Inspector Kauffman, could you come in now, please." Alan Coopersmith stood in the doorway of the Museum conference room and beckoned to Max Kauffman.

The Inspector entered the room, glancing at the men seated around the table in the center of the room, and took a chair set back against the wall at the foot of the table. He had already been introduced earlier to the other men in the room, members of the Board of Directors of the Metropolitan, before the meeting, from which he was excluded, had begun. The meeting had lasted for several hours and it was now 8:30 P.M. He was curious as to the decision the Board had made, but he could tell nothing from the faces of the men seated at the conference table.

Coopersmith nodded at the man sitting at the head

of the table, and said, "Inspector, I think Mr. Shefford would like to inform you of the conclusions we reached at our meeting."

George Shefford, the chairman of the board of the Metropolitan, was in his sixties, and had a long, angular face bronzed by the sun from a vacation in Maine which had been interrupted by the previous day's robbery. He put a hand to his dark blue silk tie which matched the color of his suit, frowned, and said, "Inspector, as I'm sure you must have anticipated, the board of directors of this Museum feel that the stolen paintings are infinitely too valuable to risk losing if there's any possible chance they can be recovered. We have, accordingly, voted unanimously to pay the ransom in full. Tomorrow, Sunday, the money will be prepared for delivery. You may proceed accordingly and we shall await your instructions as to exactly how the money is to be transported from the bank to the airport."

"Yes sir, fine," Max Kauffman answered. "I'll be in touch with you tomorrow through Mr. Coopersmith."

Since the Inspector knew that George Shefford was also chairman of the board of the National Deposit and Savings Bank, one of Manhattan's largest banks, and that two other members of the Museum's board of directors present, Alfred Wentward and Richard Lloyd Gibbons, were also presidents of two other of the city's banks, he didn't have to ask how the money would be raised over the weekend. George Shefford had said the money would be ready and Max Kauffman knew it would. The Inspector nodded to the men still assembled in the conference room and left and went to the Metropolitan's Grace Rainey Rogers Auditorium. The Museum officials had decided to let the police use the auditorium as an operations room, and telephone company men and the Department's communications specialists were already busy at work there running in extra lines and cables and installing a switchboard.

Max Kauffman, several of the Police Intelligence officers assigned to the case, and FBI Agent Eberhard

and some of his men, sat on chairs on the auditorium
stage making preparations to deal with the ransom demand the following day. Now that they knew the money
was going to be paid, there were the logistical problems
to be solved, of locating the specified plane to be used,
picking the pilot and copilot, and procuring the parachutes. After much back-and-forth discussion and many
phone calls, they discovered that just about everything
they wanted could be obtained at the suburban Westchester County Airport, in White Plains, New York.

An aircraft charter service operating out of the airport had available a Beechcraft King Air and agreed,
at the FBI's request, to have it serviced and ready for
takeoff the following morning. In addition, there were
U. S. military personnel, members of the New York
State National Guard, stationed at the Westchester field
who had and were willing to provide the necessary six
parachutes.

Since the ransom payment operation was to be a joint
NYPD-FBI effort, Max Kauffman picked one of the
men from the department, Lieutenant Dan Pope, an
experienced and skilled pilot, and Agent Eberhard chose
the other, FBI man Charles "Chuck" Greaves, also a
seasoned pilot. The two men were summoned to the
Museum, briefed on their unusual assignment and sent
home to sleep with orders to report to the Westchester
County Airport early the following morning. Before the
meeting ended, Agent Eberhard put through a phone
call to the National Flight Center in Washington, D.C.,
to alert them of the flight. The Washington center would
coordinate all radio communications between the
ground and the plane while it was in flight the next day.
Direct lines between the National Flight Center in
Washington and the operations room at the Metropolitan would be kept open at all times. When the
meeting concluded, even though it was past midnight,
Max Kauffman drove back to the 16th Precinct.

He was surprised to find that Sergeant O'Dell was
still on duty. He shook his head at her and said, "You
didn't have to stay, Sergeant."

"I know, sir," she said. "But I appreciate how important this case is to the Department and I thought perhaps there might be some last-minute work you'd want me to do."

"As a matter of fact," Max Kauffman said, heading into his office, "I would like to prepare a report of the day's activities for the Commissioner."

For the next half hour, the Inspector dictated his report to Sergeant O'Dell. Just as he finished his dictation, J. T. Spanner knocked on the door and Max Kauffman said, "Sergeant, could you make up a pot of coffee, please? And then I want you to go home. You can type that report tomorrow. And I don't want you in here until after noon tomorrow. That's an order." He motioned Spanner into a chair in front of his desk. "Well, how did it go with Griffith?"

"Negative," Spanner said, shaking his head. "Griffith led me around for five or six hours out there, but he couldn't find this guy, Hap. Most of the bartenders in the places we visited knew Griffith all right and a couple of them even said, when Griffith prompted them, that they thought they knew the guy he was talking about but they weren't sure and, anyway, they hadn't seen anyone they thought might be him around lately. But what they said might not mean anything."

"How's that?" Max Kauffman asked.

Spanner lit a cigarette. "The impression I got was that none of the bartenders were likely to break an arm or leg to help Griffith. They'll serve him booze and take his money, but you get the feeling that they'd be just as happy if they never saw him again. I'd guess he's probably gotten out of hand a few times and caused trouble. Whatever, they just don't warm to him, I'd say. In fact, the reason I brought him back a little early tonight was that he'd had several drinks and I could tell he was beginning to get an edge on. We did have to order drinks in some of the places we visited. Anyhow, I didn't want him to get a half a load on and try to do something foolish and I'd have to shoot him."

Max Kauffman grunted. "Did he try to give you any trouble?"

"Oh, no," Spanner said. "On the way to Queens I stopped off in a deserted area and gave him a short demonstration of my marksmanship. He was properly respectful after that. But I didn't want to take the chance of having too much booze build up any false courage in him."

"So where do we stand now?" Max Kauffman asked.

Before Spanner could answer, Sergeant O'Dell returned with a pot of coffee which she brought over to the desk along with two cups and saucers. Max Kauffman thanked her and so did Spanner and she said good night and left. The Inspector got up and went to a cabinet behind his desk and took out a bottle of Napoleon brandy and two pony glasses. He put the bottle and the glasses on the desk, sat down again, and poured himself some brandy and a cup of coffee. He pushed the bottle and the other glass over to Spanner. "Go ahead," he said, "have a brandy."

Spanner could scarcely contain his surprise as he filled his glass and poured himself a cup of coffee. It was the first even halfway-human gesture he could ever remember the Inspector making to him in all the time he'd known him. Usually, the Inspector appeared to Spanner to be a man besieged; under constant fire and hunkered down in the trenches, from which, from time to time, he lobbed out a grenade and caught everyone by surprise.

"So where do we stand now?" Max Kauffman asked again.

"Well," Spanner said with a weary sigh, "we didn't cover all the places out there by a long shot. So I guess we haul ass out there again tomorrow for another go-round."

Max Kauffman twirled his brandy glass between his palms. "What do you make of this guy, Spanner, now that you've been with him for a night? You know, your cop's instinct."

Spanner took a sip of brandy and washed it down with coffee before he answered. "You said it best once yourself, Inspector. You never know what a sneaky son-

of-a-bitch like that has in mind. But I'll be damned if
I can figure out what he thinks he'd gain if it was all
a lie. Besides, he did know there was going to be a big
job pulled before the Museum was robbed."

"Yeah, there is that, all right," Max Kauffman admitted. He took a swallow of his brandy. "Anyhow, at
this point we've got to go with all we've got." His voice
dropped lower, "For your information only, the gang
made their ransom demand this afternoon."

"How much?" Spanner asked.

"Three million seven hundred and fifty thousand dollars."

Spanner whistled softly.

"They got a cute method all worked out for the ransom delivery, too," Max Kauffman said. He told Spanner most of the details of what had gone on that
afternoon. By that time, the Inspector was pretty well
convinced that Spanner hadn't been in on the plot but
if it turned out that he did happen to be involved he'd
certainly be anxious to pass on the confidential information that the ransom would be paid—and the police
still had taps on his phones.

"So, as of this moment," he added, "Griffith's aid, if
he really can lead us to one of the perpetrators, is all
the more important."

"Yeah, so we'll keep trying," Spanner said. He
finished his brandy and coffee and started to rise. "So
tomorrow I'll be back and pick up Griffith and we'll go
out and beat the bushes some more. Thanks for the
brandy and coffee, Inspector."

Max Kauffman nodded toward the bottle. "How
about another one, for the road?"

Spanner hesitated for a moment. He sensed that the
Inspector wanted him to hang around simply so he
wouldn't be alone and he realized he was seeing Max
Kauffman in a rare and vulnerable mood. But he was
tired and beginning to feel the drinks he'd had, and the
final glass of brandy had almost done him in. It was
apparent, too, that the Inspector was exhausted. Spanner
shook his head. "No thanks, but I'd like to take a

rain-check," he said. "And you look beat, Inspector. You'd better get some rest."

"Yeah, yeah, you're right. You, too, Spanner."

After Spanner left, Max Kauffman poured himself another finger of brandy. He'd missed eating dinner again but he wasn't hungry and the coffee and brandy he'd already drunk lay in the pit of his stomach like a hard, indigestible lump. He took a sip of brandy. He knew he ought to be at home in bed asleep. There was nothing else he could do tonight. But the day's events had left him feeling both restless and depressed.

He rubbed his eyes and got up and went to the window of his office and opened the drapes. To the north, in back of the 16th Precinct, many of the houses and buildings in that area of the West Side had been razed and he had an unobstructed view for several blocks. The streets were deserted at that hour of early Sunday morning, a few minutes past 2 A.M., except for a garbage truck collecting the day's refuse one block over and, a block beyond that, a sanitation truck spraying down the still-simmering pavements. Max Kauffman had lived and worked in these streets almost all of his life and had often observed Manhattan in the dead hours of early morning without particularly noticing it. Now, however, the silent city somehow reminded him of a vast, empty arena being scoured of the excrement, blood and death left behind by one day's combatants and in preparation for the next.

"A fanciful thought, that," he mused aloud, scoffing at himself. He walked back to his desk on stiff legs, washed both brandy glasses and put them and the bottle away, and went down and got his chauffeur to drive him home.

CHAPTER EIGHTEEN

At 8 A.M. Sunday morning, less than six hours after Max Kauffman had left the 16th Precinct, he was back in his limousine again which stood, motor idling, at the curb in front of the National Deposit and Savings Bank on Park Avenue in the Fifties. Directly in front of Max Kauffman's car was an armored truck with two guards standing at its opened rear doors. There was a squad car pulled into the curb ahead of the armored car and a second squad car parked directly behind his limousine. Both of these cars also had their engines running. A detail of six blue-helmeted motorcycle police sat astride their bulky machines in front of the lead squad car and an additional detail of the same number of motorcycle police was lined up behind the rear squad car.

Max Kauffman fidgeted impatiently in the rear seat of the limousine, his eyes on the entrance to the bank where two armed guards paced back and forth. What the hell was holding things up? Max Kauffman thought fretfully. His greatest concern was making the round-trip run to the Westchester County Airport in time to be back at the Metropolitan Museum of Art when the morning's ransom call came. Technically, of course, there was absolutely no valid reason why he had to go along on the delivery of the money to the airport. But this was his case, and he intended to be in on every aspect of the operation possible when he felt it was

his responsibility, as he did now in the case of the delivery of the money.

He'd only had a little over four hours' sleep but he
was refreshed and alert even though his eyes felt puffy.
Also he'd fixed for himself and eaten a large breakfast
that morning before he left the apartment and that too
put him in better spirits. Now if they'd only bring the
money out and load it into the armored truck.

At that moment, a group of men came out of the
entrance to the bank, two uniformed guards carrying
a large, obviously heavy, mail pouch, among them. Max
Kauffman had earlier learned from George Shefford that
the total weight of the ransom money, fifty stacks of
five hundred one-hundred one-hundred-dollar bills, five
hundred stacks of five hundred fifty-dollar bills, would
be a little over one hundred pounds. The group advanced to the edge of the curb and the two guards, with
the help of the other two armored guards waiting in the
street, hoisted the mail pouch into the rear of the truck.
Three of the guards then climbed inside with the money
and the rear doors slammed shut. The fourth guard
went around and climbed into the front of the armored
truck next to the driver.

Up in front of the line of vehicles, one of the motorcycle policemen raised his hand, then let it drop. There
was a roaring crescendo as the police gunned their
engines, the sound reverberating in the still air and
scattering into flight a flock of pigeons which had been
nesting under the eaves of a building across the street.
The convoy pulled out, a phalanx of six motorcyclists
in the lead, followed by the squad car, the armored
truck, Max Kauffman's limousine, the second squad
car, with the other six police motorcyclists bringing up
the rear. The motorcycle escort and the two squad
cars used their flasher lights, but kept their sirens off
since there was little traffic on the streets.

The motorcade sped swiftly up Park Avenue, cut
across town to the West Side Highway, and was soon
beyond the city, heading up to Westchester County. It
was another hot, cloudless day. Max Kauffman relaxed

in the back seat of the car, lit his first cigar of the day, and enjoyed looking at the profusion of foliage which grew along both sides of the suburban expressway. The trip was swift and uneventful and much sooner than the Inspector had anticipated, the convoy had turned off the highway and into the Westchester County Airport.

The forward motorcycle escort led the procession of cars across the tarmac and brought the convoy to a halt alongside an airstrip where the Beechcraft King Air sat, gleaming silver in the sun. Since the multi-million-dollar ransom would be transferred to the plane well before takeoff, the FBI had requested the New York State Police to provide security and the aircraft was ringed by State Police cars and troopers along with a detail of FBI men.

As Max Kauffman climbed out of his limousine, the two men who would pilot the plane, FBI agent Chuck Greaves and Police Lieutenant Dan Pope, came out of one of the hangars, sipping coffee from cardboard containers.

"How's it going?" Max Kauffman asked.

"A-okay," Agent Greaves answered. "The parachutes are aboard, she's all fueled up, and now that the money's here, we're ready to go as soon as we get the word."

The three men stood by the side of the airstrip watching as the guards from the armored turck unloaded the leather mail pouch containing the ransom money and carried it aboard the plane. Then Max Kauffman, Greaves, Pope, and a couple of other FBI agents in attendance also entered the plane and stood by while a National Guardsman who had been brought in by the Federal Bureau attached the mail pouch to one of the parachutes.

Afterwards, Max Kauffman shook hands with Agent Greaves and Lieutenant Pope out on the airstrip and wished them luck. In parting, he cautioned them again that they were not to try to apprehend the perpetrators of the robbery. Their only responsibility was to see that the ransom was successfully passed on. From then

on it would be up to the police and FBI to actually
apprehend the gang—hopefully after the paintings had
been returned.

The police motorcycle escort led Max Kauffman's
limousine and the two squad cars back to Manhattan,
and without the armored car to slow them down, they
made the trip in a little over half the time it had taken
them to drive out to the airport. By 10:18 A.M., the Inspector was entering the Metropolitan Museum of Art
where he went directly to the Grace Rainey Rogers
Auditorium.

Overnight, the auditorium had been transformed into
a fully-staffed communications center, complete with its
own switchboard and other sophisticated communications equipment including an amplifying system and
recording devices. The instruments were manned by a
combination of NYPD and FBI specialists as well as
some personnel who had been recruited from the U.S.
Army Signal Corps.

A single red phone had been set aside from the other
equipment. It was plugged into the Metropolitan's
switchboard to take the call for the Director from the
gang. This particular line had also been tapped into
by additional lines. One of these tap lines would allow
a man wearing earphones to eavesdrop on the conversation and take it down in shorthand, and a second
line, which was connected to one of the room's recording
devices which operated automatically as soon as the
receiver on the red phone was lifted, would tape the
full exchange.

Also, any use of the phone on this line would flash
an instant alert to the nearest telephone exchange and
a trace of the call would begin immediately. If the phone
conversation lasted long enough for the incoming call
to be traced, that information would be swiftly trans-
mitted to unmarked police cars standing by at various
locations in the city. Those cars would then speed to
the point of origination of the call and hopefully pick
up the trail of the perpetrators.

There were also direct lines which would be kept

open at all times between the Washington Flight Center
and the Museum. The Center had supplied one of its
air traffic controllers to work with the authorities at the
Museum. He would pass on the flight instructions received from the gang. The Washington center would
then relay the instructions over direct phone lines to
various flight centers across the country which would,
in turn, radio-transmit the instructions to the plane.

Finally, aside from all the electronics equipment in
the room, a large, detailed aerial map of the United
States covered one wall of the auditorium. It would be
used to chart the course of the plane once it was in
flight.

Max Kauffman found Alan Coopersmith, the Museum Director, seated at a desk in front of the red
phone.

"Nothing yet, huh?" the Inspector asked.

Coopersmith shook his head. He looked around the
room and observed, "The place looks like the control
room for one of those NASA space shots."

"At least you can't say we're not giving you service,"
Max Kauffman answered.

While they waited for the phone call to come in,
there was work for the Inspector to do. Lists were still
being completed, in the Museum, and in various companies around the city, of people who had worked in
the Metropolitan or had had frequent access to the
Museum during the past three years. As soon as each
list reached Max Kauffman, he dispatched it by patrol
car to the chief computer programmer-analyst at Police
Headquarters for comparison against the names of those
who had been questioned in Grand Central Station and
on the outbound trains the night of the robbery.

At a couple of seconds before 11:45 A.M., the red
phone rang. It had been equipped with a high, piercing
ring which served as a warning to the rest of the people
in the room to maintain silence until the call was completed.

Max Kauffman could see Alan Coopersmith's hand
trembling as the Museum Director lifted the receiver.

"Yes, this is the Director," Coopersmith said. "I've been expecting your call. Go ahead." Coopersmith listened intently, the police intelligence officer, wearing the earphones and eavesdropping on the line, scribbled in shorthand as he listened and the tape recorder tapped into the line twirled slowly, making an electronic transcript of the conversation. After several seconds, Coopersmith tried to say something—he had been instructed to try to keep the man on the line as long as possible—then replaced the phone in the cradle, shaking his head and saying,. "He gave me the instructions and hung up before I could say anything."

While the tape recorder was being rewound, one of the men in the room monitoring a line to the telephone exchange, said: "We'll have the results of the attempted trace of the call in a couple of minutes. Also, after we've listened to the recording, we'll have voiceprints made of the tape."

The police intelligence officer who had intercepted the call was busy typing up his shorthand notes of the conversation when the rewound tape recorder began to play back the exchange, with the volume turned up so that all in the room could hear it:

VOICE:	Hello, hello, is this the Director?
COOPERSMITH:	Yes, this is the Director. I've been expecting your call. Go ahead.
VOICE:	Now listen carefully if you want the paintings back. I'm not going to repeat this and it's very important that you follow these instructions precisely. The plane you have standing ready is to take off at exactly twelve noon. It is to maintain a speed of two hundred forty knots and is to proceed to Stanton Intersection on Vector Sixteen North and Vector Eleven East, Memphis, Tennessee VOR-

> TAC. At that point, approximately
> three hours from now, you will re-
> ceive further instructions.

COOPERSMITH: Could you repeat—

There was the sound of a sharp click and the line went dead.

"He must have guessed he was being taped and the call was being traced," Max Kauffman said to no one in particular.

The air traffic controller, a man named Howard Comfort, who had come up from Washington was already on the phone to the Washington Center, relaying the instructions that had been received. Max Kauffman wandered over to the aerial map on the Museum wall and stood studying it until the man from Washington completed his call. The Inspector beckoned him over.

"I didn't understand much of those instructions," Max Kauffman said. "It sounded like a lot of garbled 1984 Newspeak. Where's this Stanton Intersection he mentioned? Is there an airport there?"

The air traffic controller smiled. "Not likely, Inspector. Stanton Intersection is a point in midair in the Memphis, Tennessee, VORTAC. That 1984 Newspeak, as you call it, was given in radio-navigational terms. The VOR in VORTAC stands for Visual Omnidirectional Range and the TAC stands for TACAN which provides the Distance-Measuring-Equipment to the aircraft. The DME—Distance-Measuring-Equipment—receiver actually permits the pilot, while he's in the air, to read the mileage to the station transmitting to him. Consequently, once the plane is within radio range of the Memphis Center, these two pieces of equipment combined as VORTAC means that the pilot receiving broadcasts in megacycles and on TACAN and DME channels will know when he's precisely at Stanton Intersection, Vector Sixteen North and Vector Eleven East, Memphis, VORTAC."

"It still sounds like a lot of Newspeak to me," Max

Kauffman said, shaking his head. "But I guess the real question I have is how will the pilot be able to find his way to this, uh, navigational point in midair?"

"It's simple," the air traffic controller said. "The National Washington Center will be actually controlling his flight and relaying instructions to the various flight centers through which he will pass; first, the New York Center, then Washington, Indianapolis, Atlanta, and on to Memphis. Each of these centers will, in turn, be in radio contact with the plane for approximately thirty-six to forty minutes as it progresses from one to the other and will guide its flight."

"Then if I understand all this correctly," Max Kauffman said slowly, "the gang's purpose in giving these instructions in navigational terms is that even after the plane is in flight, headed for a precise point in midair, there's still no way we can determine its true destination."

The air traffic controller nodded. "That would certainly seem to be the purpose. The next call we get could order the plane to set down anywhere enroute between here and Memphis, or land in Memphis, or proceed beyond, or turn back."

"Real Machiavellian stuff," the Inspector grunted, shaking his head.

Eberhard, the FBI agent, had joined the two men and now he said, "It looks like somebody who knows a lot about navigation is calling the shots on this one."

"It looks that way," Max Kauffman agreed.

"I'll have to alert all the Bureau field offices along the way," Eberhard said, "Indianapolis, Atlanta, Memphis—down the line. When we do get orders for the plane to set down, there probably won't be enough time for anybody to reach the location before they take off again. But at least we'll have to give it a try."

As he started to turn away, there was a squawking sound over the room's amplifying system and Howard Comfort, the air traffic controller, said, "Sounds like our plane's about to take off."

Max Kauffman knew that one of the direct lines from

Washingon was hooked into the amplifying system set up in the Museum auditorium. The Washington Center, in turn, had various direct lines to Westchester Airport, the New York Center, and the Indianapolis, Atlanta, and Memphis Centers. Washington would be monitoring and recording the exchanges between the plane and each of these centers and as fast as the recordings were made they would be relayed into the room's amplifying system, with only seconds lost in time lag. Over the amplfying system he heard now:

"Westchester Airport, this is One Hundred Quebec Papa. I have a special-instrument clearance to Memphis VORTAC."

Howard Comfort had explained to the Inspector that the plane had been designated, in keeping with the International phonetic alphabet, as 100 Quebec Papa.

"Roger, One Hundred Quebec Papa, this is Westchester Ground Control. Altimeter set three-zero-zero-two. Runway Thirty-Four. Wind three hundred sixty degrees, light and variable. Cleared taxi to runway. We understand the special nature of your flight."

A period of static followed over the amplifying system. The police officer who was on the line to the Museum's telephone exchange checking the results of the attempted trace on the phone call which had come in earlier beckoned to Max Kauffman.

"Yeah, what've we got?" the Inspector asked, crossing the room.

"They managed to trace the point of origination of the call," the police officer said, "but it was terminated before they could dispatch a car. The call came from an outdoor phone booth at Broadway and Forty-Fifth Street."

"Well, that's something anyway," Max Kauffman said.

"They're putting the phone booth under surveillance," the police officer said, "although chances are he won't try to use it again."

"Yeah, good," Max Kauffman said.

In the background, there was another exchange over the amplifying system:

"One Hundred Quebec Papa. This is Westchester Ground Control. ATC clears One Hundred Quebec Papa to Memphis VORTAC via flight-plan route. Maintain sixteen thousand."

"Roger, Westchester Control. Understand ATC clears One Hundred Quebec Papa to Memphis VOR-TAC via flight-plan route. Maintain sixteen thousand. One six thousand."

"One Hundred Quebec Papa, this is Westchester Ground Control. You are cleared via the Patterson Six Departure. Maintain runway heading to one thousand feet, then turn heading to ninety-five degrees for Vector to Solberg Radio Sixty-One and then to Solberg VORTAC. Maintain seven thousand via flight-plan route. Upon clearance contact Departure Control One Hundred Twenty-Decimal Five Five, Squawk Code Three Three Three Three. Center advises this will be your special code due to the nature of your flight. . . ."

Max Kauffman was so engrossed in listening to the exchanges between the plane and the Westchester Airport Tower that he didn't at first hear the police officer who had come up and was speaking to him.

"Yes, what?" Max Kauffman said.

"I said, sir," the police officer answered, "there's a phone call for you from Headquarters."

Max Kauffman went over to one of the desks and picked up the phone. The conversation between the plane and airport tower continued in the background.

"Inspector Kauffman here."

"Inspector, this is Paul Benedict, Chief Computer Analyst, Headquarters. I have a match-up for you."

Max Kauffman could feel his heart beating faster. He picked up a pencil and pad from the desk. "Let's have it," he said.

"It's a Brian—that's B-R-I-A-N—Turnett—T-U-R-N-E-Double-T. Address Forty-Two Central Park West, Manhattan. Information has him questioned

aboard the six-fifty-three Dobbs Ferry train, Friday
P.M. A list received from the Metropolitan today shows
a Brian Turnett, same name, same spelling, same address, Forty-Two Central Park West, Manhattan,
worked there as a curator until eight months ago."

"Thanks very much, Benedict," Max Kauffman said.
"We'll get on it right away and bring him in for questioning."

As Max Kauffman hung up the phone, he heard
over the amplifying system:

"Westchester Departure Control, this is One Hundred
Quebec Papa. Level at One Six Thousand."

"One Hundred Quebec Papa. Westchester Tower
Control. You are now cleared to switch to New York
Center One Hundred Twenty Decimal Six Eight. Have
a good day, sir."

On the opposite side of the auditorium, Howard Comfort, the air traffic controller from Washington, said,
"Well, gentlemen, our ransom payment is in the air
and Memphis VORTAC bound."

Max Kauffman remembered a philosophical He-
brew phrase his grandfather, Asa Kauffman, used at
times when events appeared to be beyond his control
and the Inspector repeated the phrase to himself now,
Tzi bashert; it is fated.

CHAPTER NINETEEN

Brian Turnett was a tall, five feet, eleven inches, maybe six feet, thin man with stooped shoulders. He had a narrow face with rather esthetic-looking features, a finely-chiseled nose, thin lips, blue eyes with delicate lashes, an angular but firm chin. His age was somewhere in the forties, probably late forties. He was wearing a brown-striped seersucker suit, white shirt, tie, and wing-tipped brown shoes. He was obviously nervous but tried to conceal it. The two plainclothesmen Max Kauffman had sent out to pick him up had brought him back to the Museum conference room where the Inspector prepared to question him.

Max Kauffman had already had a discussion with Alan Coopersmith about Turnett. The Museum Director had remembered him as a conscientious employee, knowledgeable in the field of Egyptian art, a member of the staff for five years who had resigned to take a position with one of the art galleries on Fifty-Seventh Street.

"Inspector—Kauffman, is it?" Turnett asked. "Could you please tell me what this is all about?"

"Yes, just a moment please, Mr. Turnett," Max Kauffman said. The two of them sat on either side of the conference table, in chairs across from each other. The two plainclothesmen were lounging by the door at the head of the table. After a moment, the door to the room opened and another plainclothesman, a sergeant, came in with a pencil and stenographic pad in his hand. He took a seat next to Max Kauffman and the Inspector, with a nod of his head, dismissed the two plainclothesmen by the door.

Max Kauffman cleared his throat. "Mr. Turnett, I have to advise you that you have a right to a lawyer before you make any statement. If you don't have a lawyer, we'll provide you with one. And you must clearly understand that anything you tell me can also be used against you in court."

"In court?" Turnett asked, agitated. He made a frantic motion in the air with his hand. "I don't even understand why I'm here. What do you want of me?"

"What did the officers who picked you up at your apartment tell you I wanted?" Max Kauffman asked, more for the sake of the record which the sergeant, sitting next to him, was taking down in shorthand.

Turnett swallowed hard. "They said, uh, said that you'd like to have a talk with me about the robbery here at the Museum night before last."

"And you agreed to come?"

"Yes. But I thought you probably wanted to ask me some questions about the time I worked here at the Museum, general information. Nobody said anything about what I'd say being used against me in court."

Max Kauffman looked at him steadily. "Well, do you want a lawyer, Mr. Turnett?"

Turnett looked confused. "I—uh, don't know why I should need a lawyer. Of course I don't know what you're going to ask me yet."

Max Kauffman leaned back in his chair and said, "Don't you remember being questioned by the police on Friday night while you were aboard the six-fifty-three train to Dobbs Ferry?"

The Inspector thought it might have been his imagination but Turnett grew so pale it seemed he was in danger of passing out.

"Yes," Turnett said faintly, "that's so. But they only

asked for my identification, I supplied it, I assumed that was the end of the matter."

"Later, then, when you read the newspapers," Max Kauffman pressed on, "surely you knew the police who had boarded your train were searching for the men who robbed the Museum, that the police had your name and address, and you knew you had once worked at the Metropolitan? Didn't it occur to you we would be interested in the coincidence of those two facts?"

"Quite honestly, Inspector," Turnett said, a bit more strongly, "it never crossed my mind that the two things would even be linked together."

"Well, now," Max Kauffman said, "now that the two things have been linked together, I would like you to tell me how you happened to be on that particular train on that particular night."

Turnett had gone pale again. "Oh, I'm afraid I can't do that."

"Why not?" the Inspector asked. "If your explanation is satisfactory, that's the end of the matter."

"I was going to visit at the home of a friend," Turnett said, faintly again, "in Dobbs Ferry."

"All right, good. Now may we have the name of your friend?"

Turnett grew briefly agitated once more, looked all around the room, and back to the Inspector finally. "If it's necessary for me to answer that question," he said, in a low voice, "could we talk in private, just the two of us?"

Max Kauffman, without yet knowing why, was beginning to feel sorry for the man under examination. "No, I'm afraid that's not possible," he said in a more gentle voice. "There has to be another witness, the sergeant here, present. If the information you have to give is not related to the robbery, it will be kept strictly confidential."

"And I won't be in the papers, will I, nor what I tell you? My wife doesn't have to know?"

"If you have no connection with the robbery, no, I can assure you of that."

"All right, then," Turnett said, but still reluctantly, "my friend is—is this man." He looked up, away from Max Kauffman's eyes and flushed. "I—I'm married, you see. My wife doesn't know where I was that night. The name of my friend in Dobbs Ferry is Ralph Jenner. I can give you his phone number and address." He swallowed hard. "Actually, you probably already have it since he was on the train with me that evening and also identified himself to the police."

Turnett suddenly leaned forward and the words came pouring out of him. "You understand, I'm under the care of a psychiatrist. I'm trying to get help. I don't want my wife to know—"

The Inspector had tuned him out. Lord, it seemed once you started digging into the backgrounds of private individuals you uncovered some pretty bizarre behavior. He passed no moral judgments; it was only that it made his job more difficult.

Max Kauffman stood. "Sergeant," he said, "will you check this out, please? And if everything's satisfactory, will you please see that Mr. Turnett gets home."

The Inspector felt deflated after he left the conference room. It was personally distasteful to him that on occasion a necessary investigation intruded, as he was sure it had in this instance, into an individual's privacy. And led only to another dead end.

The next call with instructions for the ransom delivery came into the Museum at 2:49 P.M. The plane was, by then, two hours and forty-nine minutes out of Westchester Airport and in radio contact with, and approximately twenty minutes away from, Memphis International Airport, approaching the designated position of Stanton Intersection, Vector 16 North and Vector 11 East, Memphis VORTAC. Max Kauffman and the others assembled in the Museum auditorium had been following the course of the flight over the amplifying system. As soon as the red phone rang, all sound in the room was killed. This time, Max Kauffman used the earphones on the tapped-in line to eavesdrop on the call.

The voice was the same as on the first call. Only now it sounded more hurried.

"You're doing fine there, Mr. Director," the voice said to Alan Coopersmith who had taken the call. "Here are your new instructions: plane is to land and refuel at Memphis International Airport, which it is now approaching. Plane is to take off again immediately after refueling and proceed to Okmulgee VOR-TAC, Tulsa, Oklahoma, maintaining previous speed of two hundred forty knots. At Okmulgee VORTAC, plane is to commence holding pattern. If at that point you receive no further instructions, plane is to land, refuel and take off immediately for Shelbyville VOR-TAC, Indianapolis, Indiana, proceeding at established speed of two hundred forty knots."

There was a sharp click on the line, ending the call. Max Kauffman yanked the earphones off his head and exploded. "What the hell kind of crap are these guys trying to pull!"

Howard Comfort, the air traffic controller, was replaying the tape recording of the conversation and feeding the instructions over the phone line to the Washington center to be passed on to Memphis International Airport.

At the same time one of the police officers was on the line to the telephone exchange, waiting to see if they'd had any luck this time in attempting to trace the ransom call. The officer looked up after a minute or so and shook his head at Max Kauffman. "The same problem again, I'm afraid, sir. They were able to locate the point of origination again, all right, but he was off the line well before they could dispatch a car. The call came from another phone booth, this one at Broadway and Fiftieth Street. That's the best they could do."

Max Kauffman went to confer with Howard Comfort and FBI Agent Eberhard, who were standing over by the wall aerial map.

"It looks like we're in for a long wait," the air traffic controller said to Max Kauffman and Eberhard and pointed to the map. "The plane's got a three- or four-hour flight out to Oklahoma and if we don't receive another call, a three- or four-hour flight back to Indianapolis.

"And anywhere along the way," Eberhard put in, "we could receive instructions for the plane to land?"

"Correct," Howard Comfort agreed.

"So we still have to continue to alert the Bureau field offices all along the way," Eberhard said glumly.

Howard Comfort nodded.

Max Kauffman left the two men and went to confer with the police officer he had assigned to verify the alibi given by the possible suspect, Brian Turnett. The police officer had just walked into the auditorium alone.

"I'm sorry, Inspector," the officer told him. "Turnett's story checked out. His friend, that fellow, Jenner, backed up everything Turnett told us. I put him in a patrol car and sent him home. The poor bastard was so shaken by everything that had happened he had all but turned green with fear. But I did take the precaution of putting a tail on his apartment for the time being. Just in case."

Max Kauffman patted the officer on the shoulder and nodded; there was nothing to be said.

The Inspector stood alone for a moment, listening to the droning of voices over the room's amplifying system between the pilot of the plane carrying the ransom money and the tower at Memphis International Airport.

Then Max Kauffman mentally turned out the sound. That aspect of the operation had now passed beyond his control and was in the hands of the FBI. Meanwhile, however, there were matters he could, and should, handle on his end of the investigation. Information was coming in to him from the lab on the materials which had been examined and photographed the previous day, in connection with the robbery, and the materials which the gang had left behind in the Museum and in the tunnel in Grand Central Station; the smoke canisters, the empty frames from the paintings, the rope, the uniforms, and other equipment. Also, there was a detail of men who were continuing to search the station, and sending reports in to the Inspector. Earlier, he had brought Sergeant O'Dell up from the 16th Precinct, after she had finished typing the summary he had dictated to the Commissioner the night before, and she was at one of the desks in the auditorium, trying to organize the various communications.

The Inspector briefly rifled through the sheaves of paper Sergeant O'Dell had prepared for his inspection. There wasn't much there to cheer him up. The lab technicians had turned up a couple of smudged finger-prints from the canisters and the frames which they weren't sure were usable, even if they turned out to be-long to a member of the gang, and were running further analysis on the rope to try to determine if they could get a lead on where it might have been purchased. The men in Grand Central Station had had no better luck, either; so far there was no indication that the stolen paintings had been stashed in the station, but the search was continuing.

Max Kauffman handed the papers back to Sergeant O'Dell and shook his head.

The Sergeant, in turn, was worried by the Inspector's appearance; he looked so exhausted and perturbed.

"I can't believe they'll get away with it, sir," she said.

"Perhaps not," Max Kauffman answered, smiling wryly. "But even I have to admit they've been doing a pretty good job of it so far, despite our best efforts." Then he noticed the very real worry on her face and knew it wasn't because she cared whether the gang got away with the robbery or not, but because she cared that he was upset.

"No, you're right, Sergeant," he said, smiling more confidently. "They aren't going to get away with it."

On sudden impulse, he strode to one of the phones at the front of the room where no one could hear his conversation and called Police Commissioner Hilliard through the Headquarters switchboard. The Commissioner was back out at his summer home on Long Island. As soon as he answered the phone, Max Kauffman gave him a terse account of the day's proceedings and added, "Sir, I consider it absolutely vital to the successful investigation of this case that we use the National Crime Information Center computer in Washington. We simply are not getting fast enough results from Headquarters. This is an urgent request."

"All right, Inspector," Hilliard replied slowly. "I'll check with the Mayor again and call you back."

It was another hour before the Commissioner phoned Max Kauffman at the Museum. "His Honor is very unhappy about this," Hilliard said, "but he's given his okay to start programming your lists through the National Crime Information Center."

Max Kauffman was pleased and immediately contacted Headquarters and instructed Chief Computer Analyst Paul Benedict to forward all the lists compiled by the police and by the Metropolitan to the Washington Crime Information Center. The Inspector was regretful that they'd lost a full day's use of the national computer but he was still hopeful that now perhaps they'd turn up something they could use.

Then, since there was nothing more he could think to do at the Museum and since it seemed they were going to have a long wait until they received further instructions on the ransom delivery, he sent Sergeant O'Dell home and went home himself to sleep, leaving instructions that he was to be called if there were any further developments in the case.

CHAPTER TWENTY

"It's been a son-of-a-bitch of a night," air traffic controller Howard Comfort said in greeting to Max Kauffman when the Inspector returned to the Museum just before noon on Monday morning. Earlier, Max Kauffman had been at Headquarters checking to make certain that all the information on the case was being forwarded to the National Crime Center in Washington.

"Look here," Howard Comfort said, waving a hand at the aerial map on the wall. "Pick almost any spot you want on the map and our plane carrying the ransom money has been there during the night. For instance, at twelve-thirty A.M. it was up over Lake Superior. We almost notified you then. We thought perhaps they were going to order the plane to land over the border in Canada. But the next call sent the plane to Chicago, where it refueled and took off again."

"And where is it now?" Max Kauffman asked.

"Headed back down south again," Howard Comfort said bitterly. "This time to Biscoe International, Pine Bluff, Arkansas, VORTAC. You'll notice that's not far west of Memphis International Airport."

"And Memphis International was their first destination point yesterday," Max Kauffman said, puzzled.

Howard Comfort nodded. "Right. Those bastards have had that plane crisscrossing the U.S. for twenty-four hours now, completing a giant circle. And Eberhard and the FBI field offices are going out of their

217

minds with all the false alerts they've had to deal with."

"Which is exactly what the gang is counting on," Max Kauffman said. "So, again, all we can do is wait?"

"That's about it," Howard Comfort said. "All we can do is wait."

Three hours passed before the red phone rang again. Max Kauffman once more eavesdropped on the earphones plugged into the line. He recognized the voice of the caller as the same he had heard on the previous day.

"Your plane should now be in the Pine Bluff, Arkansas VORTAC," the voice told Alan Coopersmith. "You will now instruct it to land and refuel at the Pine Bluff airport and proceed immediately after refueling to the Hudspeth VORTAC, Albuquerque, New Mexico Center. It is to continue to maintain a speed of two hundred forty knots. At Hudspeth VORTAC, plane is to commence holding pattern. At that point, approximately three hours from now, you will receive further instructions."

As soon as the call ended, Max Kauffman hurried over to the police officer who was on the line to the telephone exchange attempting to trace the call. "He was too quick for us again," the officer said to Max Kauffman, "but we did verify the call came from a phone booth at Broadway and Forty-Fourth Street."

Max Kauffman frowned. "Our man must be holed up somewhere around Times Square, then. And he has to call again."

"Yes, sir," the police officer answered. "The only thing is, there are dozens of public phones in the area. Apparently he's smart enough to use a different one each time since he knows we're trying to trace the calls. I don't see how we can put taps on all of the phones in Times Square."

Max Kauffman, who was thinking, said slowly. "No, we haven't got the time to do that. But I have an idea that just might work. Suppose we plaster two-thirds of those phone booths in the area—two out of every three

—with out-of-order signs—you know, those yellow out-of-order stickers the phone company pastes over the coin slots so you can't deposit your money for a call. And then we try to put taps and surveillance on as many of the others, which he'll be forced to use, as we can manage within the next two to three hours before he's supposed to call again."

The police officer nodded. "You know, it just might work."

"Good," Max Kauffman told him. "I'm giving you the assignment."

The Inspector moved on across the room to where Howard Comfort was standing at the aerial map, calling to him and to Eberhard, the FBI agent in charge.

"Well, my friends," the air traffic controller said, "I'd say the pattern behind the flight instructions we've been getting is beginning to emerge more clearly. I want to show you something here on the map. Our new destination point, Hudspeth VORTAC." He stabbed the map with a finger, touching a blank spot in West Texas. As far as Max Kauffman could see the only places marked on the map anywhere near where Howard Comfort's finger rested were two mountain ranges, the Guadalupe Mountains to the east, and to the west, the Finlay Mountains and beyond them was the Texas-Mexican border. "The Hudspeth VORTAC is approximately here," he said.

"In midair, I presume," Max Kauffman said drily.

Comfort nodded. "And once here, the instructions were that the plane was to assume a holding pattern."

"Convenient to the U.S.-Mexican border," Eberhard remarked. "What would you calculate the distance to be, Mr. Comfort?"

"To the border? Roughly forty miles, I'd say."

"And if," Eberhard asked, "they planned to have the plane pick them up across the border, where would the next instructions likely order the plane to put down for refueling? El Paso?"

The air traffic controller nodded. "That would seem likely, yes. By the time the plane gets to the holding pattern at Hudspeth VORTAC, he's going to be running low. He'll be close enough to El Paso that they could order him to set down there and then hop over into Mexico. Looking back, it appears now the reason they routed the plane to Pine Bluff was so it could refuel there for the flight west."

Eberhard looked at Max Kauffman. "I guess I'd better get on the horn to the El Paso office, tell them to alert the border patrol, and to get in touch with the Mexican authorities, and request their cooperation in case the pickup is planned, as it looks like, to take place in Mexico."

The inspector nodded.

It was then 3:23 P.M. and Max Kauffman could hear, over the amplifying system, the tower at Pine Bluff Airport in radio contact with the plane:

"One Hundred Quebec Papa. Pine Bluff approach Vector Zero Three Four."

"Roger. Vector Zero Three Four."

"One Hundred Quebec Papa. You are now cleared to descend and maintain four thousand."

Sergeant Margaret O'Dell who had returned to the Museum that morning was now signalling frantically to the Inspector from her desk.

"It's a call from Washington, something I think you'll want to hear," she said excitedly and handed him the phone when he hurried over.

It was a man named Kendrickson, a computer analyst at the National Crime Information Center in Washington calling.

"I hit a lucky double for you, Inspector," Kendrickson said. "Two match-ups. You ready?"

The Inspector didn't feel the same excitement as he had the first time when there had been a computer match-up for Turnett; once burned . . . but, picking up a pencil from the desk, he said, "Okay, let's have it."

"The first name is Vincent De Angelo. V-I-N-C-E-N-T, capital D—little E—capital A-N-G-E-L-O. The address is Six Eleven Perry—P-E-R-R-Y Street, Bronxville, New York. The second name is George L.

Hager—H-A-G-E-R. His address is 29 Alden—
A-L-D-E-N—Lane, in Bronxville. The police report
has both men questioned aboard the seven P.M. White
Plains train out of Grand Central, Friday P.M. Do you
have all that, Inspector?"

"Yes, I have it," Max Kauffman said.

"Here's the rest of it," the Washington computer
analyst said, pausing to draw a breath, "according to
information the Metropolitan supplied, a construction
firm recently did some work renovating the inside of
the Museum. In fact, they finished up a week ago Friday.
Now, that firm, Givens Brothers Construction Corporation, compiled a list of their personnel who worked
on the renovation. Among the names are Vincent De
Angelo and George Hager and their addresses, both
in Bronxville, correspond to the addresses given by the
two men of the same name aboard the train."

"Sounds like there may be something there, all right,"
Max Kauffman said. "We'll get on it, and thanks again,
Kendrickson."

"My pleasure, Inspector."

Max Kauffman handed the phone back to Sergeant
O'Dell and told her to call the police station in Bronxville and that he wanted to talk to the ranking officer
on duty. She put the call through and he talked to a
Captain Abernathy. The Inspector explained that he
was in charge of the investigation of the robbery at the
Metropolitan, which the Bronxville police officer knew
all about from news reports, and asked that the Bronxville police pick up the two men, De Angelo and Hager,
at the addresses which he supplied, and hold them for
questioning.

Captain Abernathy replied that he would be glad to
oblige and would radio a pickup order on the two men
to one of his cruising prowl cars and report back, hopefully, within thirty minutes to an hour. Max Kauffman
gave him the number of the temporary switchboard in
the auditorium and added that he would send two men
up to return De Angelo and Hager to Manhattan if
the Bronxville police were successful in locating them.

The Inspector then instructed Sergeant O'Dell to stay at the phone until the Bronxville police called back, while he went to have a talk with the Museum Director.

Alan Coopersmith seemed puzzled when, after Max Kauffman told him about the two names, the Inspector asked to be shown the area of the Museum where the renovation had taken place, but he led him up the stairs to the south wing which housed the new collection of Mexican art. Max Kauffman could smell the paint, which was still fresh.

"Show me now," he asked Coopersmith, "exactly what was done up here."

They walked along the hall parallel to the galleries while Coopersmith explained, "Before the renovation, there were four small, separate galleries here and we wanted three somewhat larger ones in their place. So, the construction company knocked down three of the old walls and put up two new ones. And that meant, of course, that a portion of the ceiling had to be replaced and some new flooring put in as well. Essentially, that was the whole project."

"I see," Max Kauffman said, nodding his head, and frowning.

"What is it, Inspector?" Coopersmith asked. "What concerns you?"

Max Kauffman shrugged. "I don't know. Probably nothing and anyway we'll wait until we see what we hear from the Bronxville police about those two guys."

They went back downstairs and Max Kauffman prowled restlessly around the auditorium, trying not to listen to the reports coming in over the amplifying system from the plane carrying the ransom money as it flew west. He didn't want to keep being reminded that time was slowly running out for them.

The return call from the Bronxville police didn't come in until after 5:30 P.M. Captain Abernathy in Bronxville apologized for the delay and then said, "I'm sorry to have to tell you, Inspector, we struck out on both of those men you asked to be picked up."

"Struck out? How?"

"It looks," the police captain said, "like they've flown the coop. At least we couldn't locate either one of them at the addresses you gave me. My men found a cooperative superintendent at one of the apartment buildings, where this Hager's supposed to live, and he let them into Hager's apartment. Most of his clothes and personal stuff were gone. They haven't been able to get into the other fellow's place, but they questioned people around the neighborhoods of both men, in the bars and such, and nobody remembers seeing them recently. I'm afraid we haven't been of much help, but we'll keep on it."

"You may have been of more help than you realize," Max Kauffman told him. "If they did skip, chances increase they were in on the job, and even if we haven't got them, it gives us a lead. I really appreciate your help."

The Inspector hung up the phone and stood for a moment, thinking. Then he went over to Alan Coopersmith and said, "The Bronxville police can't locate those two construction workers who were here in the Museum and on that train Friday night, and there's evidence they may have skipped town." He paused, thought for a moment, and added, "If they were in on the job, it could explain one thing about the robbery that's been puzzling me more than anything else."

"What's that?" Coopersmith asked.

"Well," Max Kauffman said, "We all agree the Museum security was tight on the night of the robbery as well as on other nights. And I've always been bothered by the question of how the perpetrators managed to bring all that equipment in here at one time on that night, firemen's uniforms, oxygen masks, smoke bomb canisters, the lot."

"But we found the rope from the roof and the open window," Coopersmith pointed out.

"Yes," Max Kauffman agreed, "they probably came in that way, all right. But suppose all the stuff they used was here, right inside the Museum, all the time? Smuggled in, a piece or two at a time, by those two construction guys."

The Museum Director shook his head slowly. "I don't follow you. Smuggled in, yes, but then what? Where was it all the time before the night of the robbery?"

"They had a hiding place for it, here in the Museum," Max Kauffman answered quickly. "My guess would be somewhere in the area of where they were doing the renovation work. Yes, that's it! That's got to be it!" He stopped talking suddenly and then his next words were almost a shout: "My God! They *did* have a hiding place. I'm positive, and not only did they hide some of the stuff there, but the gang hid there, too, the night of the robbery. Or maybe some of the gang hid inside, before the Museum closed, and then came out and set off the smoke bombs. And then when the firemen arrived the rest of the gang, dressed in firemen's uniforms came in to help carry the paintings out. My God, that's it!"

Max Kauffman turned away and hurried to the desk where Sergeant O'Dell sat. Alan Coopersmith followed anxiously behind him, grabbed his arm, and asked, "What are you going to do now, Inspector?"

"We're going to find that hiding place," Max Kauffman said. "We're going to get some men up here with the proper tools and take that gallery apart."

"I can't permit that, Inspector," Coopersmith protested.

"I'm not *asking* you," Max Kauffman all but roared. "I'm *telling* you! If we find that hiding place we may find additional evidence, fingerprints, they overlooked." The Inspector nodded to Sergeant O'Dell. "Call the precinct. Get me some men with strong backs up here and some crowbars and sledgehammers."

He turned back to Alan Coopersmith while Sergeant O'Dell was talking to the desk sergeant at the 16th. "Now look here," Max Kauffman said reasonably, "if I'm right about this and we find it out, not only may we uncover fresh evidence, but it'll also get your guards off the hook for any blame of negligence. That ought to be worth something. And you can direct the removal of all the art from there before we start looking for the place."

"The desk serveant said the men and equipment are on the way," Sergeant O'Dell interrupted, "And he wants to talk to you for a minute."

Max Kauffman took the phone.

"Inspector," the 16th desk sergeant said, "J. T. Spanner's here to take that Warren Griffith out to Queens again. Is it okay?"

"Yeah, okay," Max Kauffman said. "Only be sure to notify Sergeant Rojas before Spanner and Griffith leave."

The Inspector ended his call just as the police officer he'd put in charge of arranging to place out-of-order signs and taps on the phone booths in Times Square walked up.

"Inspector," the officer said, "your instructions about the phones have been carried out. Two out of three phone booths in Times Square are, as far as the public knows, out of order, and most of the other phones there have taps and surveillance on them. The next time our guy calls, we should have a better-than-average chance of nabbing him."

Max Kauffman grunted. "The rest of the gang are probably already over the border in Mexico, and this character making the calls from here in the city probably expects to join them. Oh, how I'd like to get him!"

CHAPTER TWENTY-ONE

Vince De Angelo dawdled over his cup of coffee at the Nedick's stand on Broadway, now and then glancing at his watch. It was the sixth cup of coffee he had drunk since noon. He had also sat through two movies in a couple of the fleabag theaters on Forty-Second Street, all to kill time between the phone calls. Every nerve in his body had been stretched out so tight he felt like he was hopped up to the eyeballs.

He was momentarily bitter that Conant had insisted he'd have to be the one to phone the ransom payment instructions in to the Museum. Especially after Conant had warned him the calls would probably be recorded and traced. It was a goddamn eerie feeling to know that your every word was being permanently recorded and would be pored over and listened to by all kinds of law-enforcement people in the country. But Conant had also told him not to worry about it as long as he kept the calls brief and quickly left the phone after he'd made his calls. They'd decided outdoor phone booths would be safer since there would be fewer people around who would notice him and still be there to give a description of him in case the police did manage to trace the calls after he'd left. And every call was to be placed from a different phone booth, for added safety.

There was another worry, too; he kept thinking he'd misread the instructions Conant had prepared for him and passed on incorrect information to the Museum and

the whole ransom delivery thing would get screwed up.
Hell, he didn't even understand what the instructions
meant, all those terms, VORTAC, Vector, Stanton Intersection, Hudspeth. But Conant had seemed to know
what he was doing when he'd worked the whole thing
out. And, in fairness to everybody, De Angelo had to
admit that he was the logical person to make the calls.
It was just that it was so miserably nerve-racking. Jesus,
he'd probably sweated off twenty pounds in fear. The
only consolation was that now it was almost over. He
glanced at his watch again and saw he still had plenty
of time. But he paid his check and wandered slowly
up Broadway; he liked to at least be near a phone booth
in plenty of time ahead of when he planned to call.

There were quite a few strollers out along Broadway
despite the early evening heat, which must have been
close to 90. The usual mixture of people drawn to
Times Square—what looked like tourists, a number of
family groups, couples who looked as if they'd taken
the subway in from the Boroughs, and the inevitable
freaks in their outlandish costumes. Recently, the police
had done a good job of clearing the area of so-called
undesirables which, De Angelo reflected, was a good
thing, since all he'd need now was to have some nut
draw a gun or a knife on him and steal the instructions
Conant had made for him and he carried in his pocket.
It struck him as suddenly ironic that here he was, in
the midst of a gigantic caper, expressing gratitude to
the police for protecting him from a possible holdup.
He laughed to himself.

He spotted a phone booth at the next corner, he was
a couple of blocks uptown from the booth from which
he'd placed his last call, and he approached it. He was
still a little early, but the booth was empty and he decided to grab it. He could make some calls, to the
Weather Bureau, to get the correct time, to Dial-A-
Prayer, and keep the phone to himself until it was time
to make his call. He was all the way into the booth before he saw the yellow sticker over the coin slot: Out
of order.

De Angelo shrugged and crossed Broadway and

walked for a block until he found another phone booth.
He started into it and then stopped when he saw this
phone, too, had an out-of-order sign on it.

"Son-of-a-bitch," he muttered and started walking
faster up Broadway in search of a phone that worked.
He still had enough time not to have to worry, but
he was damn annoyed. The next-closest phone booth
was on the opposite side of Broadway, he saw, and he
crossed back over again. He hurried faster when he
saw the phone booth was empty. Now all he needed
was to find that this phone, too, was out of order.

When he was a few paces from the booth, he was
able to see there was no sign on the phone, and he
walked faster. When he was almost to the door of the
phone booth, he thought, for no reason at all, that it
was damn peculiar how the other phones had been
out of order. Suddenly, he veered away from the phone
booth. He didn't know how but, all at once, instinct
warned him that things were not as they appeared to
be. There was something going on with these phone
booths. *He could feel it.* He studied the street around
him casually but carefully. There was a car parked a
couple of feet from the phone booth. A man was sitting
in the car smoking a cigarette. Another man stood on
the sidewalk opposite the parked car, thumbing
through a magazine.

De Angelo felt the fear running through him. He
knew as surely as if the two men had been wearing
full uniforms and badges that they were cops. He
didn't try to puzzle the whole thing out, he just knew
that somehow the police had traced his calls to this
area, and were trying to force him into making a call
from one of the booths which they were watching and
had probably tapped. He realized it all seemed incredible and might be temporary pananoia on his part,
but he was absolutely positive he was right. And he
had come that close, a foot or two away, from walking
right into their trap. The plan would have to be
changed, there wasn't that much time left, and he
turned off Broadway and walked quickly east. He'd

pick a hotel—the Taft a block over ought to be all
right, and make the call from a phone booth in the
lobby.

He was slightly out of breath by the time he walked
into the lobby of the Taft Hotel a few minutes later
and made his way to the row of telephone booths in
the rear of the lobby. He picked out a booth where
there was no one near. He closed the door, took out
the sheet of instructions Conant had given him, and
dropped a dime into the slot.

At that same moment, at the Museum, Max Kauffman and FBI Agent Eberhard were both restlessly
pacing back and forth across the auditorium, Alan
Coopersmith sat expectantly in front of the red telephones as he had been doing for the past half hour, and
Howard Comfort was hunched over the phone on the
direct line to the Washington Center. It was now past
7 P.M., more than three hours had passed since the last
call giving ransom instructions, and still the red phone
remained silent. The only sound in the room came
from the amplifying system:

"Calling Albuquerque Center. This is One Hundred
Quebec Papa. Still Holding Hudspeth Five-Three. Estimated fuel remaining another thirty minutes. Do you
have further clearance?"

"This is Albuquerque Center One Hundred Quebec
Papa. We read you. Stand by for further clearance."

For the past several hours the Inspector and the others in the auditorium had listened as the plane passed
from the Pine Bluff Center to the Forth Worth Center,
proceeded to Texarkana, continued on beyond Mid-
land, Texas, and, finally, when it was within radio
range of the Albuquerque Center, had gone into the
holding pattern at the Hudspeth VORTAC.

Max Kauffman glanced over at the silent red phone.
"Jesus!" he exclaimed. "Why doesn't he call?"

Nobody answered and the Inspector went on pacing. All his earlier excitement of believing he had
figured out that the robbers had had a hiding place

inside the Museum was gone. Upstairs on the second
floor, at this very moment, the guards were removing
the last of the Mexican art from the renovated gallery
and a crew of five policemen from the 16th Precinct
were standing by with sledgehammers and pickaxes
with orders from Max Kauffman to take the floors,
ceilings, and walls apart to try to find if such a hiding place existed. Meanwhile, the Inspector had lost all
interest in that project. After all, what the hell difference did it make what they found if, thousands of
miles from here, the ransom delivery was somehow
going to be screwed up? What the hell had happened
to the anonymous caller? And then he had a terrible
thought: suppose, somehow, they had scared him off.
In that case they'd never get the stolen paintings back.

There was another exchange beginning over the amplifying system:

"Albuquerque Center calling One Hundred Quebec
Papa. Come in, come in. Urgent. Come in for further
clearance."

"This is One Hundred Quebec Papa standing by."

"You are now cleared to Pinon VOR. Descend and
maintain twelve thousand. Report."

There was a moment of stunned silence in the room
and then Eberhard shouted, "What exactly is going
on out there? Where'd the tower get those instructions?
What's happening?"

"Wait a minute!" Howard Comfort yelled from the
phone where he was talking to Washington Center.
"They're trying to tell me something they just heard
from Albuquerque."

Eberhard hurried over and Max Kauffman followed
him. Comfort handed the phone to Eberhard and said,
"This is one for you, sir."

The FBI agent took the phone and Max Kauffman
watched the growing amazement on Eberhard's face as
he listened silently and then said, "Yes, yes, tell them
they're to comply, with my authorization."

Eberhard stepped away from the phone and looked
at Max Kauffman with a shocked expression on his

face. "It's incredible!" he said in a hoarse voice. "Washington was just advised by Albuquerque that their control tower received an anonymous long-distance phone call with final instructions for the plane. The caller identified himself as a maker of picture frames—the code—and Albuquerque wanted to know if they had FBI authorization to radio the instructions to the plane. I said yes. What else could we do?"

"But what were the instructions?" Max Kauffman asked.

"Listen!" Eberhard said, pointing to one of the amplifying speakers. "Here they come now."

"One Hundred Quebec Papa. This is Albuquerque Center. You are now cleared to proceed present position direct to position ten miles northeast of the Pinon VOR on the Zero-Six-Zero Radio and at that point to release parachute with special baggage. Then proceed to Cavern City Air Terminal and land. Do you read me?"

"Roger, Albuquerque. We are to proceed present position direct to position ten miles northeast of the Pinon VOR on the Zero-Six-Zero Radio and at that point to release parachute with special baggage."

"What is your weather?"

"We are now in thin overcast which began at fourteen thousand and we do not know to what lower altitude the overcast extends."

Max Kauffman shook his head. "It was as easy as that. The son-of-a-bitch simply called Albuquerque direct with the last instructions."

"And they want the money dropped, miles away from where we've got any men waiting," Eberhard said. The FBI man looked at Howard Comfort. "Where's the drop point? And how far is the plane away from it?"

"Washington says the Pinon VOR is in the New Mexico desert," Comfort said. "They estimate the plane is approximately seven minutes away from the drop point."

"Let's get over to the map," Eberhard said to Comfort. "Show me the area we're talking about, I'm still going to try to get some men in there."

Max Kauffman hadn't moved from the spot where he'd been standing when the events had begun to take their last surprising twist. The truth was he was as much stunned by a kind of grudging admiration for the cleverness of the perpetrators as he was by the events themselves. He looked up when he heard someone calling his name, and saw one of the men he'd assigned to the detail to search for a possible hiding place in the upstairs Museum gallery.

"Inspector," the man called to him, "we think we've found something. You'd better come take a look."

"Yes, yes, all right," Max Kauffman answered. To himself, he thought, so what? Even if I'm right again, and I have been a few times in this case, the gang is always a step ahead of me. Even so, however, as he reluctantly crossed the room to go up to the second floor, he said, when he passed Alan Coopersmith, "Perhaps you'd better come up with me. The men seem to have found something."

In the south wing on the second floor of the Museum, Max Kauffman and Coopersmith found the men from the 16th Precinct and a couple of the Museum guards bunched around an open, gaping hole in one wall near the back of the renovated gallery. The Inspector was relieved to see that the men hadn't had to do all that much damage to the gallery; there were a couple of holes punched in the ceiling, a four- or five-foot section of floor ripped up and, of course, the larger hole in the wall in the back of the gallery.

"All right," Max Kauffman said. "You did a good job, men. Now step aside and let us take a look."

The hiding place looked to the Inspector's eye to be approximately seven feet high, a half a dozen feet long, and close to five feet deep.

One of the men on the detail said, "Sir, when we tapped on the wall along here, we could tell there was a hollow space behind it. Actually, as it turned out we think part of the wall was a panel that you could probably slide back and forth. But we didn't know that until we'd already busted it in. It looks like they left some stuff behind, too."

Max Kauffman could see several metal canisters identical to the ones the thieves had left scattered around the Museum on the night of the fire, as well as several rolled-up sheets of tarpaulin, also similar to those they had used to cover the paintings they took with them when they left the Museum, as he remembered from the television news film and as had later been recovered from the tunnel in Grand Central Station.

"Well, Inspector, it looks like you were right about a hiding place," Alan Coopersmith said as Max Kauffman knelt and halfheartedly lifted a couple of canisters to see that they were still full and then indifferently picked up one of the cylindrical sheets of tarpaulin and began to unroll it.

A moment later, Alan Coopersmith gasped, "Oh my God!" and Max Kauffman threw himself backwards from the now flattened-out sheet of tarpaulin as if it had opened to reveal a poisonous snake. Inside the tarpaulin, covered by a layer of glassine paper, was an oil painting of a face, the features of which were slightly distorted.

Even as Max Kauffman recognized the painting, Coopersmith was babbling hysterically, "It's the Picasso! Oh my God, it's the Picasso! The Gertrude Stein Picasso!" He snatched up the painting, clutching it to his chest, while saying, "See what's in the other rolls. "Hurry!"

Max Kauffman could hardly catch his breath as he fumbled clumsily with the other rolled-up sheets of tarpaulin, not stopping to pause after he'd unrolled one before starting on another until there, miraculously, laid out in front of him on the floor, were Pieter Brueghel's *The Harvesters,* Rembrandt's *Portrait of a Man*, Renoir's *Madame Charpentier and Her Children* and Claude Monet's *Terrace at Sainte-Andresse.*

Max Kauffman was astonished. All five of the stolen

paintings were right there in front of his eyes, here in
the Museum, carefully wrapped and protected. My
God! he thought, the paintings had been here all the
time, they'd never left the Museum! It took a moment
for the significance of that fact to sink in: no wonder
they hadn't been able to find them anywhere in Grand
Central Station or on the trains they'd stopped. The
perpetrators had never removed them from the Museum. All that other business of the five men in firemen's uniforms leading them on the chase in the stolen
fire engine and then leaving the empty tarpaulin and
glassine paper in the tunnel of Grand Central had
been a deliberate misdirection of the eye. A bit of
hocus-pocus to convince the police they'd escaped
with the stolen paintings. Otherwise, Max Kauffman
slowly reasoned, the perpetrators figured that if the
police weren't totally convinced the paintings had actually been spirited away, they'd have taken the interior of the Museum apart to search for the stolen
art. The hiding place would have been uncovered even
sooner and there would have been no ransom payment.

Ransom payment! Max Kauffman struggled to his
feet. Now that the paintings had been recovered, they
could stop the payment of the ransom—if there was
still time. He went lurching out of the gallery like a
drunken man and down the staircase, taking the stairs
two or three at a time, barely managing to maintain
his balance.

Bursting into the auditorium, Max Kauffman
shouted to Howard Comfort: "Get Washington on the
line! Tell them to instruct Albuquerque to order the
plane not to drop the ransom! Do it, man, hurry!"

As Howard Comfort, bewildered, swung around to
the phone, Eberhard was racing toward Max Kauffman.

"What are you doing?" he demanded. "Why are
you countermanding—"

"The paintings have been recovered!" Max Kauffman shouted back. "We've got the paintings, all five
of them, they're here, they're safe!"

In what seemed like only seconds after Howard Comfort began to speak to the Washington Center, there was a squawk of static over the amplifying system and the voice of the air traffic controller at Albuquerque came in:

"Calling One Hundred Quebec Papa! Urgent! Come in! Urgent! Revised instructions! Top urgent! Where are you?"

There was a long, agonizing moment of silence and static and then:

"One Hundred Quebec Papa calling Albuquerque. Position fourteen miles northeast of Pinon VOR on the Zero-Six-Zero Radio. Have just dropped parachute with special baggage. Proceeding Cavern City Air Terminal. Fuel running low. Advise new instructions. Roger."

In the otherwise dead silence of the auditorium, the only sound was what appeared to be a loud snort or groan from Max Kauffman but was actually a half-smothered, bitter horselaugh at himself as, head averted, he hurried from the room before he collapsed into a fit of hysterical laughter. It was either that or weep.

Several thousand miles west of Manhattan, Joe Conant stood in the overcast, early twilight and watched the billowing parachute slowly descend from the slate-gray skies above the white sands of the New Mexico desert.

"Practically plumb dead on target," he said and laughed softly. "Did you ever see a prettier sight?"

Eddie Chilton, standing beside him, shook his head silently, his eyes glued to the bulky leather pouch swinging gracefully back and forth at the end of the parachute's lines.

The two of them had stayed hidden behind a pinon rock, their car a good distance away and camouflaged by yucca bushes, until the plane had flown over, dropped the chute, and disappeared into the clouds to the northeast.

Now they hurried toward the chute as it finally touched down, flopping in the sands, the heavy leather pouch helping to anchor it to the earth. Both men grabbed a handful of line and Conant hacked the pouch free with a knife he had taken from his pocket. It took the combined strength of the two of them to lift the pouch and lug it across the sands to where they'd left the car. The parachute, blown free, gusted off across the dunes like a big, broken kite trying and failing to take flight.

Both men were silent as they loaded the pouch into the back seat of the car, a Chrysler, and Conant crawled in behind the money bag while Chilton went around and got into the front seat behind the wheel.

Conant fought down his natural impulse to urge Chilton to hurry up and get them out of there; he knew there was nothing he had to say to Chilton. Chilton already had the Chrysler in motion and the car leaped forward, the rear end slewing around, then straightening out as Chilton accelerated and they shot out across the sands. Their position at that moment was north of Pinon, New Mexico, just beyond the edge of the Lincoln Natural Forest, almost directly due southeast of Alamogordo, the site of the explosion of the first A-bomb.

Conant knew the region well; in the days when he was being trained by the Air Force as a navigator, he had made numerous dry-runs over this very area, practice bombing runs for which he had to plot the navigation for drops on imaginary targets. That's why, knowing the desolation of this section of the country, he had chosen and plotted the ransom drop for the Pinon VOR.

"Is the money in there?" Chilton asked.

Conant was still trying to get the leather pouch open and he hadn't seen inside yet. But he answered confidently, "You can bet on it. Much as they have to want those paintings back, they wouldn't screw around for the sake of a measly little old three million, seven hundred fifty thousand dollars."

A few minutes later he had the pouch open and had lifted out a bundle of one-hundred-dollar bills. He leaned forward and dangled the stack in front of Chilton's face. "Man," he said laughing, "just look at all those faces of old Ben Franklin. And just think, every face is worth a hundred bucks."

"Jeez, I haven't got my dark glasses on, Conant," Chilton complained jokingly. "You're dazzling me with the sight. We'll wind up in a ditch!"

Conant sat back laughing. He felt good. He began rapidly transferring the bills from the pouch to the two empty suitcases they'd brought along after he'd first counted through one of the stacks and found it contained five hundred bills: $50,000. From then on he counted each stack as he placed it in the suitcase.

So far everything had gone right on schedule, but they still weren't out of the woods. This was the most dangerous part of their trip, from the drop point east to Roswell, New Mexico, seventy miles distant. There was always the possibility they'd run into a police roadblock but he didn't think it likely. Unless he'd miscalculated in his planning, the authorities were probably concentrating chiefly on the roads southwest, to Mexico. So, heading in the opposite direction as they were, they should have a good chance of making a clean run of it, especially since he was pretty damn sure they had a good thirty minutes' to an hour's start on any police who would be pouring into the Pinon area.

The police would have to think they were complete idiots to be that close to the Mexican border and not be planning to go across it and lose themselves on the other side. Surely nobody would guess they'd be crazy enough to be heading straight across the country back to New York again after they'd successfully retrieved the multi-million-dollar ransom.

Actually, Conant thought, there was nothing he'd rather do than hightail it to Mexico—God, how easy it would be, a hop-skip-and-jump away—and go on from there. But that wasn't the way he'd planned the job from the beginning. Getting their hands on the money didn't solve everything. He had to make sure De Angelo and Hager got out of the country safely. They were going to be tied into the robbery by the police as soon as the call was made to the Museum revealing the hiding place of the paintings. If they got caught, Hager, especially, might talk and implicate him, Conant, before he made his own safe getaway. De Angelo, he felt sure, would keep his mouth shut. Although, even with him, you couldn't be certain.

So he'd had to plan that part of the operation, too. And these days it wasn't that easy to leave the country with three-quarters of a million dollars in cash. But they'd managed to work that out, and Tuesday morning, if all went well, both men had arranged and signed on—with the help of some guys De Angelo knew who could arrange such things—to ship out as deckhands on a Venezuelan tanker, carrying their loot with them. Once they were gone—and Conant wanted to be there to make damn sure of that fact, which was why he felt he had to return to New York—Conant would call the police and tell them where to find the paintings.

Then he'd take off, too, into Canada and from there, with the aid of a buddy he'd flown with in the Air Force who was now a pilot with a Canadian airline, to France and on to Costa del Sol. He hadn't had to worry too much about Chilton and Kroger. Neither of them should be tied into the robbery, and both of them planned to stay in the country and live it up. Besides, neither of them really knew very much about him, and even if they got caught after he'd gone, it didn't seem important. He could risk that but he couldn't risk having De Angelo and Hager picked up within the next few days. So, back to New York it had to be to split up the money.

He and Chilton were retracing the exact journey they'd just taken the day before, only this time going from west to east. Yesterday, Saturday, they'd flown from New York to Oklahoma City, where they'd checked into a hotel and rented the Chrysler for the drive to New Mexico. Before that, however, while they

were still at the airport, they found a charter flight
service and, posing as businessmen, had hired a plane
and pilot to fly them back to New York at 10 A.M.
Monday. They couldn't use a scheduled commercial
plane for the flight back because they'd be carrying the
ransom in their suitcases and the luggage would be
searched as part of the anti-hijacking precautions.
Conant had figured that Oklahoma City was far enough
away from the New Mexico drop point that nobody'd
be checking all its outbound flights on Monday—hell,
there must be close to a hundred or more such charter
services operating in the same area of the Southwest.

The drive from Oklahoma City to Pinon, New Mexico, was approximately five hundred miles and they'd
left before dawn that morning and, spelling each other
at the wheel of the rented Chrysler, were well in place
on the desert before the plane arrived.

Now on the drive back, Conant finished transferring
the money from the pouch to the suitcase. Fifty stacks
of five hundred one-hundred-dollar bills, or $2,500,000,
and fifty stacks of five hundred fifty-dollar-bills, or
$1,250,000, a grand total of three million, seven hun-
dred and fifty thousand dollars. Conant carefully wiped
the empty pouch clean of prints and flung it from the
speeding car into the underbrush alongside the road.

He leaned back in the seat, a vastly satisfied man. He
could feel in his guts they were going to make the trip
back safely, on into Roswell, and from there a hundred
miles to Clovis, New Mexico, another hundred to Am-
arillo, Texas, and two hundred more across to Oklahoma City. In less than eight hours, at a conservative
sixty miles per hour, they'd be in Oklahoma City. Then
at 10 A.M. tomorrow morning they'd take off for the
flight back and should be touching down in the late
afternoon at the airport he had decided upon because
it was close to Bronxville—the Westchester County
Airport in White Plains.

CHAPTER TWENTY-TWO

On Tuesday the temperature in Manhattan set a new record for that date in August, rising to 102 degrees at 11 A.M. Con Edison, whose generators supplied most of the electricity to the city, had cut back on the power an hour earlier because of the increased demand on its facilities and issued periodic warnings that if electricity wasn't conserved there was the possibility of a citywide blackout.

Max Kauffman sat alone at the desk in his office, staring into space. Because there was only one light on in the office, most of the room was in shadows, and although the air conditioner was turned up full, the room wasn't—because of the cutback in power—really cool.

The Inspector had again been up for most of the previous night, clinging to the desperate hope there'd be some word from the West that the perpetrators had been apprehended. The word had never come, and finally he had given up, gone home and slept for a couple of hours.

To make matters worse the day, so far, had been even worse than the previous night. Starting at 8 A.M., there had been a two-and-a-half-hour meeting at the Mayor's office, which had been little more than one long session of heated postmortems and recriminations at the failure of the police to solve the robbery before the multimillion-dollar ransom had been paid. Present at the meeting had been the Mayor, the Police Com-

missioner, the Deputy Police Commissioner for Public
Affairs, FBI Agent Eberhard and a couple of his men,
and Max Kauffman.

After both Eberhard and Max Kauffman had made
verbal reports on all their activities of the previous day,
Commissioner Hilliard had shaken his head and remarked, "Gentlemen, what it all boils down to is that
your—our—efforts just weren't good enough. By God,
we had the whole thing right there in the palm of our
hand, the paintings safe right there in the Museum, the
ransom undelivered, and we failed. A little more foresight, and we'd not only have had the paintings and the
money but we could have kept the perpetrators dan-
gling long enough to swoop in and nab them on the
spot."

Max Kauffman kept his silence but he was grateful
when Eberhard spoke up. "I'm not sure, sir," the FBI
agent pointed out to Commissioner Hilliard, "that it
was a question of lack of foresight which hurt us in this
case. Leaving the Bureau out of it altogether, I'd say
Inspector Kauffman here performed admirably and
certainly displayed remarkable foresight, as you term
it, in suspecting there might be a hiding place in the
Museum which led to the safe recovery of the paintings.
Otherwise, we could be sitting around here today, having paid the ransom, and still wondering where the
paintings were."

"Yes, yes, I know all that," Commissioner Hilliard
said, "but we still have the trustees of the Metropolitan
to deal with, and I can assure you they would very
much like to have their millions back." He frowned and
added, "In fact, if anything, they're more unhappy
about having paid the ransom when, as we now know,
the paintings were in the building all along."

Department Public Affairs Deputy Commissioner
Harlow had interrupted at that point to say, "Speaking
of the recovery of the paintings, I understand that fact
is still being withheld from the news media."

"That's correct," Max Kauffman said, "on my orders."

"I think it's a mistake not to release the information," Harlow said. "It would help take some of the heat off the Department for letting the ransom and the perpetrators get away from us. Commissioner?"

The Commissioner nodded slowly. "Yes, I'm inclined to agree. It shows we didn't completely bungle the job. And I really can't see what purpose is served by keeping those facts secret, compared against the best interests of the Department."

"The purpose is twofold," Max Kauffman said quietly. "One—at this point, the perpetrators don't know that we know the identity of at least two members of the gang and that there's a nationwide pickup order out on both of them. If they find out we've discovered the hiding place and the paintings, they'll certainly know we were smart enough to connect these men, De Angelo and Hager, to the job. Secondly, as long as they don't know we have the stolen art, they're probably still planning to let us know where the paintings are. That gives us at least the possibility, however tenuous, of one more contact with them."

"I understand all of that quite clearly," the Commissioner answered, "but I'm still not certain it outweighs the benefit to the Department of having some positive facts about this investigation made public."

Max Kauffman had to struggle to control his temper. "Sir, since you put me in charge of this investigation, I feel I have to recommend with the strongest conviction possible that we continue to withhold the information that the paintings have been recovered. And you do remember, don't you, that I urged from the beginning that we use the facilities of the National Crime Information Center in Washington? If we had, chances are we'd have nabbed the gang before this."

Commissioner Hilliard flushed angrily and for a moment Max Kauffman was sure he had gone too far and was about to be relieved of the case. To hell with Hilliard, Max Kauffman thought, police commissioners came and went with each change of mayors and sometimes more often. Max Kauffman had survived others,

and he'd survive Hilliard. He was taking no more crap
from Hilliard. But before anything else could be said,
Mayor Forester had quietly interceded, saying, "Inspector Kauffman, I assume that when you plead for a
delay in the release of this information, you're speaking
of a delay in hours, is that correct?"

Max Kauffman nodded. "I would think so, sir. Or of
a day or so, at the very most. I would suppose until the
perpetrators feel they're all safely away from the danger of immediate apprehension. It's our judgment at
the moment that most of the gang are probably already
out of the country and they may be waiting until they're
all in the clear before contacting us again."

"In that case, Commissioner," the Mayor said, swinging toward Hilliard, "I think you'd agree the Department can survive for such a brief interval."

That had ended the argument in Max Kauffman's
favor. There had then followed some discussion about
any leads which might yet be supplied by Warren
Griffith, who was still being held at the 16th Precinct.
Max Kauffman explained that he had read a report on
Griffith, as given by J. T. Spanner to Sergeant Rojas
when Spanner had returned Griffith to the jail after
another night of touring Queens, and the report was
negative. "Frankly," Max Kauffman told the Commissioner and the others gathered at the Mayor's office,
"I've reluctantly concluded that although Warren
Griffith somehow came by advance knowledge of this
robbery, or possibly just lucked into a wild coincidence,
it's highly doubtful he can provide us with any help at
this point in the investigation. I intend to continue to
hold him as a possible material witness for the moment,
but I do not intend to send him out again with Spanner
on another wild goose chase to Queens."

Shortly after that the meeting had ended and Max
Kauffman had returned to his office, a very unhappy
and discouraged man. He had, he knew, alienated the
Commissioner, perhaps temporarily, perhaps permanently. He had probably also damaged his own career,
again perhaps temporarily, by letting the perpetrators

escape with the ransom. And yet—and yet—he had
the personal satisfaction of knowing that he had tried
his damnedest and it was truly no fault of his that the
gang—granted they had been clever and methodical—
had seemed to be favored by good luck.

Although the Inspector had no appetite, he decided
he had to have some lunch. Since it was unbearably
hot outside, he ordered a cold salmon platter which he
ate at his desk. Later, he called Catherine Devereux
and told her he'd like to see her that evening and
that he planned to leave the office early and be at her
place between 6 and 6:30, if that was all right with
her, which it was. The combination of lunch and the
expectation of being with her that evening put him in
better spirits and for the next two hours he worked
hard on catching up on the paperwork which had
again accumulated during his absence at the Museum.

He didn't think he'd be putting in any more time
up at the Metropolitan. Most of the communications
equipment there had been dismantled and removed,
although he had left a couple of men up there to await
and record a possible future call from the gang, and
the Museum officials had decided to keep the building
closed to the public for another day or two.

It was after 3 P.M. when Sergeant O'Dell buzzed
him to say that J. T. Spanner was on the phone.

"Just checking in, Inspector," Spanner said. "I heard
the news that the ransom was paid, so what do you
want to do about Griffith?"

"Knowing the possible penalties for the use of ob-
scenity over the telephone, I hesitate to tell you what
I want to do about Griffith," Max Kauffman answered.
"But if you want to know what I want you to do about
Griffith, I think we might as well forget about any more
tours of Queens in search of the elusive Hap. I do want
to thank you for your help though, Spanner."

"Inspector," Spanner said cheerfully, "you have
just made me a very delighted individual. I think you
may have been right about him all along when you
once said he could be a psychopathic liar. Last night

when I had him out in Queens, he came up with a new twist. Something he said he'd just happened to remember; that this guy, Hap, had a girlfriend and that he might be hiding out at her place. Griffith claimed he went with Hap to the girlfriend's house once—now get this, some new geography—in Bronxville. He thought tonight we should go up there and look for her place. Give you a laugh, Inspector? The guy keeps trying. Fast as we exhaust one suburb, he comes up with another.''

"Listen, Spanner," Max Kauffman said slowly, "are you sure he said this place was in Bronxville?"

"Yeah, Bronxville. I'm sure. Why?"

Max Kauffman thought for a moment and then said, "Look, I'm sorry but you and I have to have a talk. Can you come in? Now, as soon as possible."

Spanner sighed. "I thought I was getting off the hook too easy. Yeah, I'll be there in a half hour or so."

The Inspector went back to his paperwork but his mind was distracted. What in the name of God, he thought, could account for Griffith's suggestion of making a trip to Bronxville? Could the miserable son-of-a-bitch really have some knowledge of the robbery, after all?

Spanner arrived a short time later and Max Kauffman waved him into a chair, saying, "I want to ask you one more time, and it's important, you're sure Griffith said this Hap's girlfriend lived in Bronxville and that he wanted you to take him up there for a look around. I mean, did he at any time ever mention any other suburb?"

"Just Bronxville," Spanner said, "and last night was the first time he ever mentioned it."

Max Kauffman worried his lower lip with his teeth for a moment and then said, "I'm going to tell you something, Spanner, that only a handful of people know. And the information has to stay with you, understand?"

Spanner nodded, his eyes curious.

"Yesterday we tied two guys to the robbery, names of De Angelo and Hager. They were part of a construction crew working up at the Museum until a week ago. We also recovered the paintings." The Inspector quickly gave Spanner all the details of the recovery of the stolen art.

"Well, I'll be damned," Spanner said.

"Yeah, but here's the rest of it," Max Kauffman said. "We traced those two guys to the addresses where they'd lived up until a week ago. Two different addresses. It looks like they've both skipped. But they both lived in Bronxville."

"Oh yeah," Spanner said, "I see why you wanted to talk to me. Last night, out of the clear blue, Griffith mentions Bronxville. H'mm."

"How about it?" the Inspector asked, holding up a finger. "One more favor? It still might not come to anything, but—"

"Okay, okay," Spanner said, shifting around in his chair, "Call the keepers and get him ready and we'll do the Bronxville tour."

The Inspector went downstairs until Spanner and Griffith left the station house. Then he went back to his office and began clearing away his work in preparation for leaving for Catherine Devereux's apartment. He was damned if he was going to be cheated out of another evening with her. He'd leave word with Sergeant O'Dell that if he was urgently needed, he could be reached through a call to Headquarters which could signal him on the beeper he still carried; Operation Pandora's Box was still in effect. Much as he was looking forward to an evening with Kit, he couldn't help but wonder exactly what the hell was going on up in Bronxville.

In the house in Bronxville, Vince De Angelo was standing in front of the refrigerator popping the top off a beer can. He could hear the voices of Red Hager and Augie Kroger arguing in the living room.

Bitch, bitch, bitch, De Angelo thought, gulping

down the cold beer, that's all the two of them had done since Friday night. They were worse than a couple of old maid broads complaining about everything under the sun from the heat to the sounds one or the other of them made when they breathed. And like a couple of old maid broads neither of them would spit out what was really bothering them. Which was that they were suffering a bad case of nerves. For that matter, all three of them were suffering a bad case of nerves, waiting, waiting, waiting for Conant and Chilton to show up with the money.

The only difference between the way the three of them were suffering, De Angelo thought, was that Hager and Kroger didn't trust Conant. And that worried him. Worried him bad. Not only did the two of them suspect, without voicing it, that Conant was going to double-cross them, probably kill Chilton, and they'd never see him again, but also, De Angelo knew, Hager and Kroger were secretly afraid that if Conant did come back, he might try to kill them as well. The reason he knew that was because, quite by accident, he'd discovered that both of them were packing guns —contrary to the orders he'd given them. They still didn't know that he knew they had guns, and he wasn't going to mention it. But he'd been worried enough about it so that he'd dug out his own .45 which he'd picked up in the service and had tossed it into his suitcase along with bullets when he'd left his apartment. Now he wore the .45, loaded, inside his belt under his shirt and *they* didn't know he was packing it. Now, if they tried to give Conant any trouble when he got back, he, De Angelo would be able to cool things with his .45.

Crazy, he thought, here they all were about to cash in on the biggest bundle in their lives—the ransom had been paid, they knew that, from the news reports in all the papers and on television and radio—and when they should be holding a celebration they were, instead, holding a wake. He finished his beer and walked back into the living room. As he passed one of the front windows, he couldn't help glancing out, hoping he'd see Conant and Chilton approaching the house. They should have been here by now. And it was nuts to think Conant would try to double-cross them.

Or was it?

CHAPTER TWENTY-THREE

One of the troubles with bars where you don't know the regular customers, Spanner thought, is that if you don't look outside you don't know whether you're in Queens or Bronxville. Or sometimes, even if you *do* look outside, you still don't know.

He and Warren Griffith were in a bar in Bronxville. It was now 7:30 P.M. and they had driven all to hell and gone around Bronxville in search of the house where Hap's girlfriend was supposed to live. They hadn't found the house and they had wound up in the bar when Griffith claimed that he thought it looked like the one where Hap's girlfriend had taken him and Hap the night he supposedly visited Bronxville.

Spanner was fed up with Griffith anyway and, curiously, letdown. For a while there he'd really thought the ex-con might actually lead him to Hap. And he was surprised at how much he was anticipating the encounter. But now it looked like the whole thing was just another of Griffith's concoctions, naturally. He'd gone along with Griffith's suggestion that they try the bar and see if this girlfriend showed up only because he needed a drink himself. Two, three drinks they'd have and then he'd pack Griffith in the car, haul him back to the lockup and hope to hell he'd never see or hear of him again in his life.

"Hey! Hey!" Griffith said suddenly in a low, urgent voice. "I saw him! I'm sure I saw him! Hap! He

just went into that house there across the street."
Griffith was pointing out the front window of the bar
to a single-story house directly opposite the bar.

"I don't see anybody," Spanner said.

Griffith was out of his chair and standing. "He just
went in, I told you. Come on!"

"Hold it. Wait a minute," Spanner said. "Let's take
it easy now. If you're sure that's him, I'll go call Inspector Kauffman. He'll make arrangements to have
him picked up."

Griffith was fairly dancing up and down. "No, no,"
he said. "He could leave. We could lose him and I'd
lose all my chances of making a deal. Come on, nab
him." He stuck out his wrists. "Put the cuffs on me,
I'll lead you over there. He'll open the door for me.
You got a gun, you can take him."

Spanner was surprised at how easy he was to convince. Hell, he *did* want to take this guy himself, he
admitted to himself. For the very first time since he'd
met up with Griffith, he was absolutely certain Griffith
was telling the truth. And it was possible the guy
would go out the back door.

Spanner pulled out the handcuffs and put them on
Griffith. There were only three other people in the
bar and neither they nor the bartender even seemed
to notice Spanner and Griffith. Spanner took his gun
out of his holster and transferred it to his coat pocket.
"And if you try anything, anything at all," he warned
Griffith, "you get a bullet."

They went across the street, Griffith in the lead, and
up the front steps of the house. Griffith banged on the
door. There was silence in the house.

"Hey, it's me, Griff. Warren Griffith, Griff. Let me
in. I know you're in there—Eddie!"

"Eddie?" Spanner said, puzzled, and the door
opened. A tall, slim man stood there. He had pale blue
eyes which blinked rapidly several times as he stood
looking at Griffith and Spanner.

"Griff," he said finally. "What are you doing here?"

"I got to talk to you. Can't we come inside? It's important," Griffith said. "Important to both of us."

Spanner was getting nervous. He took a step backwards. Griffith turned and started babbling. "Don't go. This guy knows everything about Hap, everything. It's all right. Come on."

"Sure," the man in the doorway said. "Come on in, it's all right."

Griffith was already twisting past the other man and inside the door. Spanner either had to shoot him, leave him, or follow. He tightened his grip on the gun in his pocket and went through the door.

Several things happened in rapid succession. Griffith and the other man, Eddie, began screaming at each other so loudly that the words of neither could be understood, Spanner saw that there were three other men in the room besides Eddie, and one of them was a black man. Spanner saw that the four walls of the room were covered with aerial maps of the United States and the maps were marked with a series of lines in red crayon, Spanner saw two opened suitcases on the floor bulging with stacks of bills, Spanner heard the door behind him shut with a snap and, finally, Spanner felt what was, unmistakably, the cold, hard end of a gun barrel boring into the back of his neck as the man who must have been standing hidden behind the door when they'd come in, said, "Take your hand out of your pocket empty." Spanner obeyed and the man reached around from behind him and removed his S&W .357 Magnum.

Griffith and the man, Eddie, were still screaming at each other. The black man suddenly moved, crossing the room swiftly and shoving Eddie to one side, at the same time, shouting, "Shut up! Everybody shut up!"

In the silence which followed, Conant looked at Eddie Chilton. "Now what is this all about?" he asked in a deadly quiet voice.

Chilton nodded toward Griffith. "He's Warren Griffith, my half-brother. We had the same mother.

The other guy I don't know. And I swear I don't know how either of them got here, Joe."

"I'll tell you how!" Griffith cut in swiftly, talking now to Conant. "I knew you guys were going to pull a job. Eddie told me that much. But he didn't tell me what the job was or who any of you were. The reason Eddie told me about the job at all is because I was out on a rap, I jumped bail, and he told me if I could see that I wasn't picked up again, he'd take care of me later after the job was pulled. Give me enough dough to get away."

Conant swung around to Eddie Chilton. "You stupid son-of-a-bitch," he said to Chilton, his voice choked with anger, "as carefully as we planned this job, you had to go and blab about it. And to a con!"

"Joe, Joe, listen to me!" Eddie Chilton pleaded desperately. "This guy's my half-brother, family. He took care of me times in the past. I wanted to do something for him, to help him once I got my cut. And I didn't tell him anything! Not about what the job was, not about any of you, as God is my witness! Not even about this house. I don't know how he got here."

"Eddie's telling the truth," Griffith said, nodding his head violently. "Back before you pulled the job, he didn't know it but I followed him one day when he came to this house. It's not his fault. If everything had gone the way me and Eddie had planned I'd never have come here today. But meantime, and Eddie didn't know it, this guy here," he jerked his thumb at Spanner, "he's a private dick, he picked me up on a bail-jumping warrant. The cops were going to send me up again, this time for a long stretch. I had to figure out some way to get out of jail, get to Eddie—"

"Yeah, it ought to be interesting to hear how you arranged that with the cops," Conant said in a cold voice.

A nerve in Griffith's face had started to twitch. "It's not like you think," he answered. "I made up a story. I told the cops some guy had told me about a

robbery, a big robbery, a guy I'd met in a bar. I even
gave him a fake name: Hap. After the Museum was
knocked over, they figured I must have known something." He nodded toward Spanner. "They released
me in his custody and I came here. I knew you'd collected the ransom and I figured you'd come back here
to this house to split it up. Him and me waited in that
bar across the street until I saw you, Eddie, and you,"
he looked at Conant, "drive up in a taxi with those
bags. All the time *he* thought we were looking for a
man named Hap. Then I came over. It's all I could
think to do."

"You mean you led the cops here?" Conant asked,
incredulous.

"No, no, not the cops," Griffith protested. "Just him.
Like I said, he's not a cop, he's a private detective. You
can take care of him. It's going to be all right."

Vince De Angelo, who had been holding the gun
on Spanner, stepped into the room, eyes blazing. After
the tension of the past few days, the responsibility of
keeping Hager and Kroger in line, his worry over possible trouble between Conant and his three friends—and
now this incredibly stupid and dangerous development
—he went quite literally berserk. He had been trying
to keep himself in check for too long and he had
broken.

He waved the gun in the air. "I'll take care of him,"
he raved, and then pointed the gun at Griffith and then
Chilton. "And then I'll take care of you and you." He
swung the gun barrel back toward Spanner and fired
just a split-second after Conant lunged forward, grabbed
his gun arm and twisted it upward. The bullet went
into the ceiling, missing Spanner's head by inches. The
sound of the shot in the small, closed room was ear-
shattering. It had a shocking, sobering effect on all of
them.

De Angelo wrenched free of Conant and took a step
backwards but the terrible, insane fury in his eyes was
gone. He was gasping to catch his breath.

Conant held out his hand, and said softly, "I thought we agreed no guns, Vince. Guns always mean trouble. Give it to me."

De Angelo shook his head and, catching his breath, said in an anguished voice, "It's all right, Joe. I'm sorry, but I'm all right now." He still wouldn't hand the gun over, though, but he shoved it out of sight under his shirt. Conant stood for a moment longer looking at De Angelo and turned away, shrugging his shoulders. "Eddie," Conant said to Chilton, "Check the street. See if there are any signs the shot was heard outside."

Chilton went to the windows, moving from one to the other, scanning the street. It was almost dark outside but he could see there was no activity on the street. "It's all right," he said. "Nothing going on out there."

They were all watching Conant now to see what he would do next. Conant looked at Spanner who stood silent, weak in the knees from his close brush with death. Spanner had pieced it all together with terrible clarity now; there had never been a "Hap." Warren Griffith had made up the name to conceal the whole truth from the police; that his half-brother, Eddie Chilton, had told him the story of the robbery, and that Griffith had used the fictitious "Hap" as a way to lure Spanner to this house where he hoped the gang would kill Spanner and then Griffith, with Chilton's help, would flee from the reach of the police.

"The question," Conant said to Spanner, "is what are we going to do about you?"

Chilton was wrong when he thought the gunshot hadn't been heard outside the house. Two men slumped down in the front seat of a car parked a few yards away from the house had heard the shot. The two men were Detective Sergeants Murray Grebs and Tony Josephson of the 16th Precinct Intelligence Unit, assigned by Max Kauffman since the beginning of the investigation to maintain constant surveillance on Spanner and Griffith any time they left the station house. The two detectives had been right behind Spanner and

Griffith on past nights in Queens and had, today, followed them to Bronxville.

Both had been instantly alert, watching with binoculars, when Spanner and Griffith had come out of the bar and crossed the street to the house. The moment the door to the house was opened by a third, unknown man, Detective Grebs had radioed a report in to the Manhattan 16th Precinct. This dispatcher had called Headquarters to contact Max Kauffman on the beeper signal. When, a little later, the detectives had heard the sound of a shot in the house, Grebs had again called the 16th Precinct. The dispatcher reported that Max Kauffman hadn't yet responded to the earlier beeper signal.

Grebs asked for orders and the dispatcher turned the call over to Captain Ben Sybert since he was in charge of the Intelligence Unit. Grebs had repeated a full report on the developments thus far in Bronxville.

"You sure you heard a shot from inside the house?" Sybert demanded.

"Positive," Grebs answered. "Tony's positive, too. Spanner could be dead by now."

"And you don't know who's in the house? How many?" Sybert asked.

"We think now two other men may have entered the house just prior to the time Spanner and Griffith went over there. We weren't particularly watching the house at that time, but two men did get out of a taxicab just before Spanner and Griffith went over there. We think the men may have entered the same house."

There was a pause over the radio before Sybert said, the suppressed excitement in his voice evident, "Jesus, you know what? I think the whole gang's inside that house."

"So what do we do?" Grebs asked. "Where's the Inspector?"

"We're still trying to reach him," Sybert said hurriedly. "Now listen, here's what you're going to do. Sit tight for the moment. I'll get in touch with the State Police and the local police up there and ask for assistance. We can't take a chance of blowing this one. Soon as you get some help, surround the house and take them."

"Yes, sir," Grebs said. He glanced over at Sergeant Josephson. "How'd you like a promotion, Tony? It looks like our big chance is coming up. But I still wish Kauffman were calling the shots instead of Sybert."

After a while—but sooner than either detective expected—cars began to silently pull into the dark street, running with their lights off, first a couple of unmarked cars, followed by three State Police patrol cars, followed by the County Sheriff's car and another car of deputies, then two more unmarked cars, and four more State Police patrol cars. Men emerged from the cars, shadowy figures, carrying shotguns, rifles, pistols, and huddled with Detectives Grebs and Josephson in the darkness down the street, out of sight of the house.

Inside the house, Spanner had finally found his voice again and he said, very carefully, to Conant, "I think we should have a talk before anybody decides what to do about anything."

"What's to talk about?" Warren Griffith interrupted impatiently. He looked at Conant and the others. "You know what you have to do. You—"

"Shut up!" Conant said. "Keep your mouth shut." Conant looked at Spanner again. "All right, Mr. Private Detective. Like the man asked, what's to talk about?"

Spanner hesitated for a second before he spoke. He was sure he had sized up the situation correctly: the black man, Conant, was obviously the boss, the brains, of the robbery. There was some barely-concealed resentment toward Conant on the part of the others in the room but Conant was still in command. Spanner decided he had to take a big gamble.

"There are some facts about the investigation of the robbery you pulled that you don't know yet," he told Conant. "This is on the level."

"Go on," Conant said in a steady voice.

"The police have already recovered the paintings you stole—"

Everybody in the room started to yell at once. Conant raised his hands in the air. "Keep it down, keep it down!"

Spanner continued: "They found them in that space behind the wall in the Museum where you hid them. They know the identity of two of your men. De Angelo and Hager."

Both De Angelo and Hager became agitated.

"The police have already sent out pickup orders all across the country on De Angelo and Hager," Spanner added, trying to keep his voice matter of fact to prevent the men from exploding into panic. "I don't think either one of them can get far. Or, once they're picked up, any of the rest of you, either."

Conant made a sound like the air escaping from a busted balloon and shook his head.

"Maybe he's lying," Hager said. Conant didn't even look at him.

"He's not lying," was all Conant answered.

"You want me to go on?" Spanner asked.

Conant nodded.

"It could be worse for you," Spanner went on. "So far you haven't killed anyone, the paintings have been recovered and," he made a gesture with his hand toward the open suitcases, "it looks like the money's all still there. You'd get a good deal."

Conant rubbed his face with his hand. "Man, you just don't know how hard I tried on this thing."

"I think I know," Spanner answered. He waited.

Conant lowered his hand. His eyes met Spanner's. "Of course you're right," he said. "We really don't have any choice. We'd have to kill you—" he shook his head.

"Joe—" De Angelo started to say and the words froze on his lips when there was a sudden pounding on the front door and a rough voice ordered, "Open up! Open up in there. This is the police. We have the house surrounded!"

Red Hager began screaming and pulled a pistol from his pocket. Before anybody in the room could move, he aimed and began emptying the gun at the door.

Spanner knew what was going to happen next. Nothing could stop a police shoot-out now. He dropped to the floor and began to crawl over to seek shelter behind the two suitcases. While the others in the room were darting frantically around from one side to the other, Conant headed straight for one of the front windows. He shoved the window up and yelled: "Don't shoot! We give—" Spanner screamed at Conant to get down but Conant never heard him. Spanner's words were lost in the furious crossfire of bullets that crashed in through the walls, windows, and doors from every side of the house.

Spanner saw Conant standing at a front window, his back to the room, at one moment and in the next moment, the whole windowpane exploded in a shower of glass, leaving nothing but an empty wooden frame. Conant turned back to the room. His face was a bloody pulp, and the blood dripped down his neck and soaked his shirt. His body was also bleeding from the chest and the groin. Blind, his hands stretched out in front of him, Conant took two stumbling steps, crashed into a chair, and fell to the floor.

More bullets poured into the room, ripping chunks of wood from the door, blowing holes in the ceiling, walls, the floor, shattering the rest of the windows. The room was a living hell, filled with the blast of gunfire, the sounds of screams, moans, whimpering, and the smell of gunpowder-scorched flesh, and the sweat of fear.

Warren Griffith, panicked, had fled toward the back door and now lay dead, a bullet in his throat, his body blocking the passageway between the dining room and the kitchen. Eddie Chilton was shot in the arm, De Angelo in the left hand, Hager in the stomach, Kroger in the leg. Spanner trying to protect himself behind the suitcases, felt a burning pain in his right shoulder and another pain, like a hornet's sting, in his right thigh.

He put his left hand to his shoulder and then to his thigh. Both places were sticky wet with blood. He wondered if he was going to die.

The gunfire ended and the front door crashed inward. Men poured into the room, waving their shotguns rifles, then stopped and stood silent when they saw the carnage.

One of the State Troopers said, "Somebody call for ambulances. Tell them we need four or five."

In Manhattan, Catherine Devereux lay propped up on one elbow watching Max Kauffman sleeping. He was very quiet in sleep, never moving, his breathing so soft she had to lean her ear close to hear it. She formed the shape of a kiss with her lips and blew it toward his lips while he slept on.

She thought of the secret of Max and herself, a secret she thought of often; they were sensually compatible. The marriage and sex manuals were all wrong. The ones she had read when she was a young girl, the rather chaste manuals, had all emphasized that love had to be based on common, shared interests. Wrong. The later books she had read, all the everything-you-ever-wanted-out-of-sex-and-never-got manuals, emphasized the mechanics of sexual love. Wrong again. Where was the book that could have told her about the sensual compatibility between a Max Kauffman and a Catherine Devereux; the sensual compatibility that was love's true and only aphrodisiac, intoxicating the senses of sight, sound, smell, taste, and touch until one's very being briefly became, outside all dimensions of time and space, the other's and the other's very being became one's own. Maybe, she thought, she'd write the book herself some day. It would give her something to do in her old age on nights when Max went to visit his grandchildren.

She swept her hair back with her hand and leaned over his body lovingly, lovingly. Soon he stirred. "Umm," he murmured drowsily. "What are you doing?" He lifted her face up to his.

"You're crazy, you know that?" he said, smiling.

"I know," she whispered, "but you love it."

"And you," he said, "you love being crazy."

He reached a hand toward her and she arched her body away. "I'm deliciously satiated," she said, smiling and then, "what a lovely word, satiated."

Max Kauffman stretched and shifted higher on the pillow, glancing sleepy-eyed around the room which was dimly lit by a light shining through the open door from the hall. "Where are my clothes?" he asked. "On the chair there?"

"No," she said. "I hung them in the closet while you were asleep."

He swung out of bed and, from habit, went to retrieve the signal beeper from his coat pocket. He opened the closet door and heard the ominous buzz of the beeper. He turned and hurried to the phone in the hall and called Headquarters.

"Jeez, Inspector," the Headquarters Dispatcher said, "I've been trying to reach you for over an hour. There's been a big shoot-out up in Bronxville. At least a couple dead. They caught the perpetrators of the Metropolitan Museum robbery. They're all still up in Bronxville."

"My beeper must have been on the blink," Max Kauffman said coolly. "Get a helicopter ready for me at the heliport. And send a squad car to pick me up." He give the Dispatcher Catherine Devereux's address and hung up the phone. When he turned she was standing in the hall with her hands up to her face.

"I did something wrong, didn't I?" she asked in a small voice.

"No," he said, kissing her lightly. But his thoughts were in a whirl. What the hell had happened? Who gave orders for a shoot-out? He was going to have to watch his step or the PC would have his ass in a sling. And he was going to have to be sure to put that beeper out of order before anybody examined it. He went to the closet and began dressing.

Forty-five minutes later when Max Kauffman strode into the house in Bronxville, the place was swarming

with police, doctors, and nurses, and the street outside
was jammed with police cars and ambulances. The two
16th Precinct detectives, Grebs and Josephson, gave
him a full report on the shoot-out. Max Kauffman asked
only two questions: who gave the orders to surround
the house? And where was the first shot fired from
once the house was surrounded? The answers were:
Captain Sybert gave the orders from the 16th Precinct
and when the police identified themselves at the house,
the first shot had been fired from inside the room.

Max Kauffman went over and looked down at Joe
Conant—he had been told Conant was the ringleader
of the robbery—who, unconscious, was being loaded
onto a stretcher by the ambulance attendants. The Inspector than stood for a long time studying the navigational aerial maps lining the walls of the room. Much
of the maps were in tatters from the bullets that had
penetrated the walls of the room but he still got a
shivery feeling when he saw the big red circle drawn
around one spot on the map, "PINON," and the words
scrawled next to it: "060 Radial, 10 DME—Drop
point."

Max Kauffman walked on across the room to where
one of the police surgeons was working on Spanner
who was slumped up against the wall.

Spanner grabbed him by the arm and pulled him
down toward him. The Inspector could see that Spanner's eyes were glazed.

"Help Conant, Inspector," Spanner babbled urgently.
"The black fellow. Name's Conant. Joe Conant. He
was the one who planned the robbery. But he saved my
life. And he was going to give up, turn himself in when
the police came and the shooting started. Do everything
you can to help him, huh, Inspector?"

"Sure, sure," Max Kauffman said, and then looked
at the doctor. The doctor nodded his head toward
Spanner and whispered. "Shock. Mild shock. But he'll
be okay."

The Inspector gave orders that all the bodies were
to be taken into Manhattan; the wounded, including

Spanner, to Bellevue Hospital, the dead man to the
City Morgue.

The money was closed up into the suitcases again,
and Max Kauffman had Detective Josephson radio
into Headquarters to contact George Shefford, chairman
of the board of the Metropolitan and president of the
National Deposit and Savings Bank, to meet the police
at the bank within the hour and take custody of the
three million, seven hundred and fifty thousand dollars
in ransom money which had now been recovered.

Max Kauffman drove back to the city in the car with
Grebs and Josephson, taking the two suitcases of money
with him. After they'd returned the money to George
Shefford, who was waiting for them at the bank on
Park Avenue, Max Kauffman went on over to Bellevue
Hospital.

The police surgeons had put J. T. Spanner and Joe
Conant in the same hospital room. The Inspector stood
in the doorway. He could see Spanner propped up in
bed, in a cotton gown, bandages on his shoulder and
thigh. A police surgeon was working on him. In the
bed next to Spanner, Max Kauffman could see six or
seven doctors and nurses bent over the unmoving body
of Joe Conant which was connected by tubes to bottles
of plasma and glucose.

One of the surgeons came out of the room and Max
Kauffman asked, "What's going on in there?"

"That fellow Spanner will be okay," the surgeon
said. "He was lucky. He only suffered flesh wounds and
shock. I've tried to sedate him but he's pretty upset
about that other fellow, Conant. I want to keep Spanner here overnight for observation and the way it looks
now he'll be going home tomorrow. The other one,
Conant," the surgeon shrugged, "I don't think he's got a
chance."

"I'd like to talk to Spanner," Max Kauffman said.

"Why don't you wait a while," the surgeon suggested.

The Inspector went on down the corridor to the ward
where the DA and a couple of assistants were taking

statements from De Angelo, Hager, Chilton, and Kroger, who were surrounded by police guards.

J. T. Spanner had seen Max Kauffman standing in the doorway but had purposely ignored him. Spanner was worried about Joe Conant. He could tell from the urgency with which the doctors and nurses were working on the man ever since they'd brought him down from surgery that Conant's condition was critical.

Through the fuzzy haze of his own shock and the medication he'd taken, Spanner could hear the labored, rasping breathing of Joe Conant as the black man's body fought to hold onto life. The sound filled the room and Spanner's head and once in a while in the long hours which followed, Spanner found himself breathing in tortured rhythm with the irregular sounds that came from Conant's lungs. Spanner felt as if he were trying to breathe for Conant.

Sometime a long time later—Spanner had by then lost all sense of the passing of the hours—the room suddenly filled with doctors and nurses and Spanner struggled up in the bed to see what was going on but they had moved a screen into the room and placed it between his bed and Conant's. From behind the screen the sound of Conant's breathing was now like a shrieking, dry rattle and then, without warning, the sound stopped and it was silent in the room.

Spanner wanted to get out of bed and rush over to the screen to see what was going on but before he could move, the doctors and nurses were scurrying past the foot of his bed. They were moving the screen out of the room and he knew that, behind the screen, they were also moving out the other bed with Conant in it.

He watched them move out through the door and then they were gone and Max Kauffman was again standing in the doorway. He came into the room.

"He's dead, isn't he?" Spanner asked. "Conant?"

Max Kauffman nodded. "I'm sorry," he said.

"Sorry?" Spanner said in a caustic voice. "Sorry? Good God Almighty, Inspector! That man should never have been killed. What the hell went on out there in Bronxville tonight? Where were you? Who ordered those trigger-happy Keystone cops to open fire? Didn't anybody give a damn that I was in there when the shooting started? You sent me out there and then you let me get shot all the hell up and a couple of men killed and now you say you're sorry. That's not acceptable to me."

Max Kauffman's face was flushed but his voice was icy as he leaned close and said, "You're entitled to a certain amount of anger for what you went through tonight, Spanner. But you just used it up. So don't push it. You don't like the way my men acted tonight, that's your privilege. Maybe I don't like it, either. But they and I were trying to do the job we're paid to do. Our job was to try to recover the paintings and the ransom money and we did it. You helped, but we did it. The trouble is we don't ever get much thanks for the job we do. We recover the paintings and the Museum's unhappy because they paid the ransom. We recover the ransom and you, and probably a lot of other people, are unhappy because my men opened fire when they were fired upon. You want to shoot off your mouth about how I run my job? There's only one way you're entitled. Get back on the force and become my superior officer."

Max Kauffman shook his head and in a softer voice said, "Get some sleep, Spanner. We'll talk again, maybe tomorrow."

The Inspector went on downstairs. The case was closed. Four of the gang would now be jailed without bail, the fifth, Conant, was now being removed to the morgue.

It was strange, Max Kauffman, thought, how the mind seizes on relatively trivial matters when there were so many more important subjects to ponder. Ben Sybert. He'd already planned to get rid of him. Now he'd have to wait a while—so it wouldn't look like he was putting all the blame on Sybert for the night's shoot-out when some of it was his own—and then transfer Sybert out of the Precinct.

Outside the hospital, he hailed a cab and rode home. The night was full of heat and a dark odor like that of a steaming tropical jungle after a brief rain shower.

CHAPTER TWENTY-FOUR

The following morning Max Kauffman sat at his desk in the 16th Precinct. He knew he should feel pleased about the way things had turned out and he did—except for the unfortunate wounding of J. T. Spanner by the police. The city's newspapers credited Max Kauffman for cracking the case and the Inspector had received in-person congratulations from both the Mayor and the Commissioner. No one seemed concerned about the violence of the shoot-out.

But Spanner was very much on Max Kauffman's conscience that morning, not only because of the way he had been shot up by the police but also because Max Kauffman had some other bad news for Spanner and he hadn't yet figured out how to break it to him. The Inspector had called Bellevue earlier in the morning and talked to the police surgeon who told him Spanner would be released from the hospital that afternoon.

The Inspector was still worrying over the problem when Sergeant O'Dell buzzed him. "Inspector, sir, you have a visitor. Someone wants to talk to you about the man, Joe Conant, who was killed by the police."

"Yes, all right, send them in," Max Kauffman said.

A few seconds later the office door opened and he looked up and was surprised when one of the most beautiful women he'd ever seen came into the room.

"Inspector Kauffman?" she asked and when he

nodded, rising from his chair, she said, "I just came from the City Morgue. I want to claim Joe Conant's body for burial. My name is Holly Broome."

Max Kauffman paid a visit to Bellevue Hospital at 2:15 P.M. that afternoon. He had called the hospital earlier and asked the police surgeon to stall Spanner until he got there. When he walked into the hospital room, Spanner was dressed, his arm in a sling, and sitting on the side of the bed. There were two very attractive women in the room with him. One was a tall, willowy blonde and the other a pert and shapely brunette.

"Inspector," Spanner said, "I thought we finished our business last night. I said all I had to say. I thought you had, too."

"Uh, yeah," Max Kauffman said. "I passed the doctor in the hall. He told me to tell you you could leave any time you're ready now."

"Hell, let's go," Spanner said, standing. He walked with a limp from the wound in his thigh and used a cane.

Both of the women picked up their pocketbooks.

Max Kauffman put a hand out. "There is one thing, Spanner. I'd like to have a talk with you. Alone. Can you do me a big favor? Let me drive you wherever you're going."

Spanner frowned. "The only thing is, the girls were going to take me out, let me buy them a drink, to celebrate getting sprung from here."

"It's kind of important that we talk," Max Kauffman said. He turned to the women. "Can we get you a cab, let me bring him along to wherever you're going to meet?"

The women looked at Spanner. "Yeah, okay," Spanner said to the Inspector and, nodding to the two women, he added, "Look, I'll ride along with the Inspector and meet you at the Palm Court at the Plaza." He turned to the Inspector. "That suit you?"

"Yes, that's fine," Max Kauffman said. The four of

them went out of the hospital and parted at the entrance where Spanner found a taxi for the two women and then he and Max Kauffman got into the Inspector's waiting limousine.

"Have a cigar," Max Kauffman said as the car pulled away and headed uptown.

They rode in silence until Max Kauffman cleared his throat and said, "Spanner, there's something I have to tell you that's going to be, well, kind of disappointing to you, I'm afraid. And I'm sorry. About Griffith, Warren Griffith."

"What about him?" Spanner asked.

Max Kauffman took a draw on his cigar before he answered. "What it is," he said slowly, "is there's been a mixup about Griffith right from the beginning. An official mixup." He paused and shook his head. "You see, to say it straight out: Griffith was innocent of that check-cashing office holdup, all along. The charge he jumped bail on."

Spanner looked puzzled. "What do you mean he was innocent? How do you know that?"

"You remember," Max Kauffman said, "that there were two guys involved in the stickup of the check-cashing office and one was caught and one got away? You also remember that the guy who got caught fingered Griffith later as his partner and witnesses identified him as the second holdup man?"

"Yeah," Spanner said, "that's the way Hymie Rosen, the bail bondsman, told it to me. And later Griffith was indicted and the judge released him on bond, and he skipped, and I went after him. So?"

Max Kauffman grimaced. "The guy who got caught was lying about Griffith. And the witnesses were wrong about their identification. Griffith was never in on the job. It was another guy. This other guy was meanwhile picked up on a completely separate charge and confessed he was the second man on the stickup of the check-cashing office. It seems the guy who fingered Griffith had a grudge against him. They'd been in the pen together and had a fight at one time. When this guy got caught in the holdup, he named Griffith as his partner just out of plain spite. We'd never have known differently if the real second perpetrator hadn't confessed."

"Wait a minute!" Spanner interrupted. "Exactly when did you find all this out, Inspector?"

Max Kauffman gazed out the car window. "The day you brought Griffith into my office and I checked with the judge. The police had already uncovered the truth. The judge told me the fugitive warrant on Griffith had been vacated."

Spanner rubbed his face with his hand. "And Griffith didn't try to convince anybody he was innocent? He never mentioned it to me."

"Oh sure, when he was first arrested he kept claiming he was innocent," Max Kauffman said. "But with his past record nobody believed him. By the time you picked him up, I suppose he'd given up trying to get anybody to believe him."

Spanner was suddenly hit by the full realization of what Max Kauffman was telling him. He jerked upright in the car seat. "Goddamn it, Inspector!" he exclaimed. "The real point of what you're telling me is I don't collect my three Gs from the bail bondsman even though I collared Griffith! Right?"

Max Kauffman didn't answer.

Spanner shook his head wonderingly. "Hell," he said, and then he was struck by another thought. "And all the time I was wet-nursing Griffith out in Queens and up in Bronxville, even getting myself shot up, you knew and didn't tell me there was absolutely nothing in it for me?"

Max Kauffman glanced at Spanner and swallowed uncomfortably. "Yeah, I knew. But Griffith was our only lead, don't you see, and we needed your help—"

"You needed my help, sure," Spanner interrupted heatedly, "and what did I get in return? You didn't even take the precaution to see I was protected when the police shoot-out started." He paused. His face was flushed with anger when he went on again. "Last night in the hospital I asked you what went wrong up there in Bronxville. How come there were only local police and state police in the raid? Where were your men? Where were you, with your beeper signal, your code names, and with the authorization to call in practically the entire NYPD? Last night, I remember you gave me some kind of an answer but I guess I was punchy at the time. I'd like to hear that explanation again."

Max Kauffman stubbed his cigar out. He felt his own anger rising; hell, here he was trying to apologize—in his own way—and Spanner didn't even have the good grace to accept the apology.

"Knock it off, Spanner," Max Kauffman said in a tight voice. "You think you got troubles? Yeah, well, I got troubles, too. You want to know what happened last night? We fucked up, that's what. I didn't know anything about what was happening in Bronxville—the message never reached me—until it was all over. Of course you're right; in my absence the police overreacted and used excessive force. Once the shots were fired from inside that house there was nothing but pure panicked chaos on the part of that cockeyed collection of local and state cops. But I didn't give the orders and I didn't know you were in the middle of it."

Max Kauffman shifted his bulky weight on the car seat and then said, "So far nobody's questioned what happened, except you. If there was a big stink made about how we goofed, it could be my ass. I was in charge. The thing is, we got the paintings back, we got the ransom back, we caught the gang. We did our job. But nobody deserves any medals."

The limousine had reached the Fifth Avenue entrance of the Plaza Hotel. Spanner grunted noncommitally and opened the car door.

"Hold on a minute, Spanner," Max Kauffman added. "There's something else I want to say about all this, too. It's that you can, if you choose to, believe we used you badly. Perhaps we did. But you were a big help and for whatever it's worth I can assure you you've built up a lot of credit with the Department."

"I'd rather have it in cash," Spanner answered, "three Gs worth."

For a moment the two men stared at each other unblinkingly. Then Spanner sighed softly and said, "I guess you kind of stuck it to me, all right, but—" he shrugged.

Max Kauffman pulled two cigars out of his breast pocket and passed one to Spanner. "Have another cigar," he said. "Smoke it in good health."

"Yeah. Well, be seeing you, Inspector," Spanner said and climbed out of the car.

As the limousine pulled away from the hotel, the car phone buzzed and the Inspector answered it. It was the Desk Sergeant at the 16th Precinct calling.

"Inspector," the Desk Sergeant said, "All hell's breaking loose here. Martinelli and Cruz, of Homicide, just radioed in. They went out in answer to a call from the Harbor Police. Turns out the Harbor boys fished a trunk out of the Hudson River at Fiftieth Street containing the severed heads of three young women. No bodies, just heads. Looks like a beaut of a case."

"All right," Max Kauffman said. "Radio them that I'm on the way. And see that the Commissioner's notified."

Max Kauffman hung up the phone and gave his driver instructions to proceed to the West Side Highway and Fiftieth Street. The Inspector leaned back against the seat and searched in his coat pocket for a match. Instead he pulled out the beeper signal which he had carried with him since the beginning of Operation Pandora's Box. For a moment, even though he had earlier purposely broken it, he half-expected to hear a sound from the beeper. But it had done its work and it was silent. Max Kauffman stuffed it back into his pocket, found a match and lit his cigar, his mind already preoccupied with a trunk containing the severed heads of three young women. No bodies, just heads.

ABOUT THE AUTHOR

THOMAS CHASTAIN, born in Sydney, Nova Scotia, grew up in Florida and Georgia. His career as newspaper reporter and editor took him to New York, Baltimore and Hollywood. For the last six years he has devoted himself solely to free-lance writing. During this time he has published several novels, including the bestselling *Judgment Day*. Mr. Chastain lives with his wife in New York City and is currently at work on a new novel.

KENT STATE: WHAT HAPPENED AND WHY
by JAMES MICHENER

Nowhere are the tragic implications of the gulf between young and old more evident than in the terrible events that took place during the first four days of May 1970 at Kent State. Those four days brought America to the brink of a precipice and in the final clash on Monday, left four students dead and nine wounded.

Now in a dramatic day-by-day narrative, James A. Michener vividly re-creates that long weekend, illustrated with startling photographs—some never shown before—of the action, and packed with information gleaned from hundreds of tape-recorded interviews from everyone concerned with the tragedy.

0 552 09186 3—**80p** Illustrated   T99

THE SOURCE *by* JAMES MICHENER

'The Source' is at once a novel and an historical chronicle. Its heroes are Canaanites, Crusaders, Roman emperors, Arabs and today's Israelis. Through the pages, embracing all the dramatic episodes from the annals of Israel, thunder the stories of tribal warfare, revolutions, persecution, crusades, murder, rape and fire-worship. And into this vast canvas, James A. Michener weaves a constant thread, the story of man's spiritual pilgrimage amidst oppression and suffering.

0 552 08790 4—**95p**   Ta100

THE FIRES OF SPRING *by* JAMES A. MICHENER

Tells the story of David Harper . . . from his childhood in
a poorhouse, his first love for a young prostitute, the gang-
ster and great musician who befriended him, the true love
he found in Greenwich Village, to his final emergence as
a novelist who understood himself and thus all men.

0 552 08404 2—**60p**   Ta101

TALES OF THE SOUTH PACIFIC
by JAMES A. MICHENER

Tells of the adventures of a young wartime naval officer,
whose duties take him up and down the South Pacific and
on to the coral specks called islands . . . islands full of
tropical love and violence.

0 552 08501 4—**45p**   Ta102

A SELECTED LIST OF CRIME STORIES
FOR YOUR READING PLEASURE

All these books are available at your bookshop or newsagent: or can be ordered directly from the publisher. Just tick the titles you want and fill in the form below.

CORGI BOOKS, Cash Sales Department, P.O. Box 11, Falmouth, Cornwall.
Please send cheque or postal order, no currency. **U.K. and Eire** send 15p for first book plus 5p per copy for each additional book ordered to a maximum charge of 50p to cover the cost of postage and packing. **Overseas Customers and B.F.P.O.** allow 20p for first book and 10p per copy for each additional book.

NAME (Block Letters) ....

ADDRESS ....

(JULY '75) ....

While every effort is made to keep prices low, it is sometimes necessary to increase prices at short notice. Corgi Books reserve the right to show new retail prices on covers which may differ from those previously advertised in the text or elsewhere.